Love In the Spotlight

HOLLYWOOD REBELS AND ROMEOS
BOOK FOUR

OLIVIA JAYMES

Love in the Spotlight Blurb

Sam Collins would do absolutely anything for his mother. As a single parent, she sacrificed so much when he was growing up. Now that he's made it in Hollywood, he's determined that she's going to live like a queen and have everything she's ever dreamed of.

So when she asks him to pretend to date a pretty kindergarten teacher named Riley, who has been dumped by her boyfriend, he simply cannot say no. He's on vacation after all, and it's only a few nights. He'll make the other guy jealous and then head back home.

There's only one problem...

Unexpectedly, Sam really likes Riley. A whole hell of a lot. She's the kind of woman he could get serious about. If he were the kind of guy who got serious. But he's not. So at the end of the week, he's going to walk away and never look back.

Well...he might look back a little.

CHAPTER

One

"SON, I need you to do me a big favor. Have another piece of garlic bread."

Sam Collins didn't get to see his mother nearly as much as he wanted to. His career took him all over the globe and he loved it, but somehow nowhere ever held a candle to his mom's dinner table. That's where he was tonight, being fussed over and spoiled a little. She'd made him lasagna - his favorite. No one balanced the flavors of tomato and garlic like she could. He shouldn't be eating the carbs but for today, at least, he didn't care. He'd work it off in the gym later.

"Sure, what do you need? Some lightbulbs changed that you can't reach? The lawn mowed? Some boxes moved up to the attic?"

Paula Collins always had a few tiny chores whenever he came to Florida and he was happy to do them for her. The last time he'd visited he'd helped her shop and carry home a new artificial Christmas tree with LED lighting so she didn't have to worry about light strands any longer. The damn thing was about eleven feet tall. He'd also boxed up all the decorations after New Year's and stowed them in a spare bedroom of the house. He'd purchased the home for her when she'd retired from school teaching in Ohio, not long after he'd made it big in Hollywood.

There wasn't anything he wouldn't do for this woman. She'd sacrificed so much for him when he was growing up. He adored indulging her now that he had the money to do it.

"How about some more lasagna? Or maybe some wine?"

Chuckling, he shook his head. He still had a full plate and she was already pushing a second helping on him. She loved to feed him up when he was home, teasing him that he was too thin.

"I'm good, Mom. So what can I do for you?"

"I have chocolate cake for dessert."

"I'll save room, I promise. Now what do you need done?"

Maybe it was something unpleasant like killing a nest of wasps. Or telling a neighbor they were too loud.

Sitting back in her chair, Paula folded her hands together on the table. She was sixty-two to his forty-five, so they'd practically grown up together. She still looked young though and could easily pass for fifty. Her light brown hair didn't have a strand of silver in it, but then she might dye if for all he knew. Her skin was amazingly unlined except for the smile lines that fanned around her eyes. He wondered not for the first time why she'd never remarried. He'd never asked out loud though because he had a bad feeling that it might be because of her dedication to him.

"I want you to hear me out completely before you say yes or no."

Sweet baby Jesus, did she want him to wrestle an alligator or something? Wait...did she need money? Had she gambled it away at the casino in the next county?

He reached across the table and patted her hand. "Mom, if you need money just tell me how much. There's no shame in making a few bad decisions."

Her brows flew up in surprise and then she began to laugh, softly at first and then more loudly. "Son, you are a treasure. You'll always be my baby, you know that?"

He'd hit the jackpot in the mother department. His dad might have been a total loss, but Paula Collins was solid gold.

"I do, although now that I'm over forty it feels a little weird to hear you say that. So I guess it's not money." He decided to tease her a little. "Do you want a new fancy sports car or maybe a world cruise? How about a date with Sean Connery? You name it, you got it."

Huffing, Paula gave him a look that would have had his teenage self shaking in his shoes.

"Sean Connery is far too old for me, young man. Now that Idris Elba, he's a looker. Can you get me his phone number?"

"Is that the favor you want because I probably could get his number for you."

"No, that's the not the favor." She dabbed at the corners of her mouth with her napkin. "First, answer me a question. That girl you were dating a few months ago...that was just a setup, right? It wasn't real. What do you call it?"

Yes, Tiffany Lawson. She was a nice girl, up and coming in Hollywood. She'd helped him keep his name in the press while he recovered from a torn meniscus in his knee.

"A showmance," he replied. "Just a PR relationship. It wasn't real but she was a nice kid. I would say that we were friends, and we had some fun."

"So it doesn't bother you?" Paula frowned as if trying to understand. "Pretending to care about someone, that is. You're fine with it?"

"It's what I do for a living, Mom. A showmance is just another form of acting. Besides, no one was getting hurt or anything. Tiffany and I both knew it was a business arrangement."

"But other people thought you were a real couple," she pointed out. "You don't think that's kind of misleading?"

Sam honestly didn't know where this line of questioning was heading. He loved his fans and he owed them big for the wonderful career, but he'd learned early that he had to play the Hollywood games.

"You think I'm not being ethical?" he asked. "I guess I just look at it as feeding the beast. If I didn't give the press something to talk about they'd just make it up themselves. At least this way I have a modicum of control."

"Good, I'm glad you feel that way." She clasped her hands together and her smile widened. "I want you to have a showmance with a woman that I know from the elementary school. It wouldn't take much of your time. Just a few days but it would really help her out. You'll do it, right?"

Paula may have finally found the one thing he wouldn't do for her.

A showmance? Who was she? And why?

CHAPTER
Two

SAM HAD LISTENED to his mother's explanation, but he needed a few clarifications. This wasn't a run of the mill request like fishing out the Tupperware container from the back of the fridge where it had sat for the last six months growing fuzzy and disgusting. This was far different.

"Let me get this straight," Sam said, watching Paula's expression closely. He was still in some sort of shock. "You want me to pretend to be some woman's boyfriend because some guy dumped her for her best friend and they're getting married? Does that sum this situation up?"

She nodded eagerly. "That's right. Riley is such a sweet young woman and that man is such a douche bag. She needs to get a little revenge and you're perfect to help her deliver it."

"Mom, do you even know what a douche bag is?"

He'd had his mouth rinsed out with soap in his youth and now his own mother was dropping insults like a foul-mouthed comedienne?

"Do you?" she shot back with a sigh of exasperation. "Because if you did you wouldn't be asking that question of a female. Really, son, I thought I taught you better than that."

He felt his cheeks go warm as he realized what he'd asked. Of course, she would know what one was *in reality*, but did she know what one was in the insulting sense?

"Okay, okay." He held up his hands in surrender. "It's just that you normally are careful not to insult people, but suddenly this guy is a douchebag."

"Fine, he's an asshole. Is that better? And I most certainly do have things to say about people but you're rarely here to hear them. Maybe if you visited more often..."

Cue the guilt. He should have known it was coming. He'd had a busy year and hadn't seen her as much as he'd hoped.

"You're right, I'm a terrible son and you have a mouth like a sailor on a three-day pass. Happy now?"

Paula smiled sweetly. "Ecstatic. Now are you going to do it?"

Sam could deny his mother very little so he was probably going to eventually say yes, although he thought it was a terrible idea. But that didn't mean he couldn't make Paula work for it a little bit more, especially after the guilt trip she'd just packed his bags for.

"Let me ask you a question. Is this her idea or yours?"

His mother was already shaking her head. "Completely mine. Riley has no idea at all. In fact, she'd be mortified if she knew I was asking you. We might have to convince her to go along with it. She has her pride, after all."

That was good. This wasn't some harebrained scheme put into his mother's head by a woman that wanted to get closer to him. Point in this Riley person's favor.

"She was dating the douchebag, I assume?"

"She was, and although I didn't think much of him I never said anything to her because she seemed happy. But between you and me I never thought he was good enough for her. Too smug and a little too arrogant. Born into money and thought he was a big wheel, yet I don't think he ever worked an honest day in his life."

That was a major issue with Paula Collins. When Sam had gained some notoriety as an actor he'd had to bring her out to the set so she could see that he actually worked and worked hard. She had thought that it was all champagne and caviar.

"And he cheated on her with her best friend?"

Not much of a best friend, though. She needed to up her standards in friendship. Way up.

"Yes, and now they're engaged. Riley has been invited to the engagement party this weekend. I'm sure it's just so they can rub her nose in it, that Monica is a real bitch now that she's caught a man that can handle her expensive tastes. I think she was just using Riley to get to Chad."

Rubbing his chin, Sam had to concede that the story was messy and gossip-worthy. Just the way his mother liked them.

"And you know Riley from school?"

Paula had been an elementary school teacher before she retired and even now she volunteered, helping kids learn to read when they were struggling.

"She teaches kindergarten and she's the sweetest thing.

Please say you'll help her, Sam. She didn't deserve this to happen to her." His mother wasn't going to give up. "It's just a week or so out of your life. You'll take her on a few dates and go to the party, act like she's the most beautiful woman on the planet, and then she can tell people that it just didn't work out because of the long distance. Please? You said that fake relationships don't bother you."

Of course Paula had caught him with his own words. He had said that and he did believe it. It wasn't a big deal. He'd kissed actresses that he barely knew. It was all part of the job and it wasn't personal. This would be fine too, but what if Riley forgot the rules? What if she tried to make it personal? That would be a mess.

Paula also hadn't mentioned what Riley looked like, which was a huge hint that perhaps the young woman in question might be a little...plain. When described as *the sweetest thing*, that didn't bode well for the beauty department. Not that a woman had to be gorgeous for him to be interested. She didn't. He liked brains and a sense of humor more than anything, but somehow he usually ended up with a looker, too. Beauty was all too common in Hollywood. Brains and a good sense of humor were in short supply, sadly. Common sense was practically an endangered species.

His mother was waiting for him to respond, a hopeful and knowing smile on her face. He was fooling himself if he thought for one moment that he wasn't going to say yes. When was the last time he'd done that? He couldn't remember it had been so long. If ever. But he didn't have to make it an unconditional surrender.

"Have you really thought this through, Mom? If she's

seen with me, her picture is probably going to go up on social media. She won't have much privacy."

"She doesn't now," Paula shot back. "This is a small town, remember? Everyone knows everyone else's business. They all know what happened with Captain Douchebag and of course they'll see you two together. That's the whole plan."

His mother wasn't seeing the bigger picture.

"Is part of the plan for her face to be plastered all over Twitter and Instagram? Because it will be. I can't control if other people take our picture and post it. I also can't control what the press writes about me."

That last part wasn't completely true. His publicist had some power but getting photos or stories pulled down always had a price and it usually consisted of Sam giving the media outlet some sort of exclusive content.

"I'll warn her, but I doubt she'd be worried about that. A few pictures and then everything will blow over in time. If it were more than a week I might be more concerned."

No one cared about publicity until it was their face splashed across a tabloid with a lurid headline. If this woman had a lick of sense she'd run far away from one of Paula Collins's outlandish ideas.

Clearly, he was dumb as a bag of hammers.

"I'll talk to this Riley," he conceded. "If she's amenable to the plan and understands that it is strictly business then I'll do it."

Paula's face lit up and she clapped her hands together with glee.

"But," he warned, holding up a finger of caution. "If she thinks that this is anything more than a charade I won't do it. I won't play with her emotions that way, Mom. It wouldn't be fair to her."

Paula rolled her eyes. "Samuel Christopher, you're starting to read your own press. You think every woman in the world wants you. Riley's far too level-headed and down to earth to have her head turned by a little charm and romance from you."

Level-headed and down to earth? She didn't sound all that exciting. But that was honestly for the best.

He could only hope that Riley hated his guts and found him physically repellant.

CHAPTER

Three

"DON'T FORGET YOUR BACKPACK, ALEX," Riley called out to her scampering six-year old charge. This particular child had a habit of forgetting things. Lunch, books, shoes, backpacks. Thankfully they lived in Florida, so he didn't need to remember cold weather items like mittens, hats, and scarves.

The little blond-haired boy came to a screeching halt and turned around, a grin on his slightly dirty face - a mixture of juice and grime from the playground. He grabbed the tiny Captain America backpack and slung it over his shoulder. "Oops. Thanks, Miss Bridges."

"You're welcome, Alex. See you Monday."

Finally the weekend. Riley couldn't wait to put her feet up and have a glass of wine. She loved being a teacher, but some weeks were exhausting and this had been one of them. She began straightening up the room, pushing in chairs and retrieving stray pencils that had rolled under desks. Her usual Friday routine.

"Riley, do have a minute?"

Having crawled under a table to pick up some loose crayons, she didn't have to turn around to know who that was. She'd know Paula Collins's voice anywhere. She spent every Tuesday in Riley's class helping the children who were struggling with their reading and writing skills. A former teacher herself, Paula was invaluable and had become a good friend to Riley.

"Just a second," Riley called out. "I just need to grab...this...crayon."

"Can I help? I have longer arms."

Freezing at the sound of another, unfamiliar voice, Riley slowly twisted her head around but she could only see a set of masculine legs. Well-muscled, strong thighs. The skin revealed by a pair of cargo shorts was tanned with a sprinkling of golden brown hair.

That was when she realized that the view he was seeing was far worse than her own. Her rather ample bottom was sticking out from under the table, and the denim skirt she was wearing didn't do much to make it look smaller.

Stretching her arm out as far as possible, her fingers were able to wrap around the offending red crayon. "Thank you, but I've got it. I'll be out in a sec."

It turned out that there was no graceful way to back up on your hands and knees while two other people watched so Riley didn't even try. She managed to get to her feet without tripping over herself and that was a victory as far as she was concerned, especially as she wasn't the most graceful person on the planet. Her dignity would just have to take the dent because there wasn't anything she could do about it. Tossing the crayon into a storage bin, she finally took a good look at the man attached to the nice legs and almost had a coronary. Or a stroke. Or a coronary and a stroke. Either way it felt like her heart was racing and stopped dead all at the same time while her brain exploded into a million little pieces.

Holy smokes. Paula had brought her son. The movie star. The extremely famous and sexy Sam Collins.

Paula was extremely proud of her son and rightly so. She talked about him all the time and had pictures all over her house, but Riley had never met the man. Until today. She'd never expected to either, so this was a shock to her system.

He certainly looked good with his dark hair, light blue eyes, and tanned skin. Just as good as in the movies and on magazine covers, maybe better. But then Paula was a beautiful woman, looking far younger than her actual age. It must be in the Collins genes.

"Riley, I wanted you to meet my son, Sam. Sam, this is Riley Bridges."

Rubbing her suddenly sweaty palms on the denim of her skirt, she held out her hand for Sam to shake. He accepted it, enfolding it in his much larger one, the skin warm and slightly callused. It was a firm handshake, not too hard and not too wimpy. Some men didn't seem to know how to shake hands with a woman or were uncomfortable with the entire business.

"It's nice to meet you, Sam. Are you here to visit your mother?"

"I am," he replied easily. "Hoping to get a little rest and relaxation."

"Our little town is a good place to do that."

In fact, the tiny Gulf coast community of New Hope Beach hadn't had anything exciting happen in it since the last time a few Weather Channel guys had hung out here waiting on a hurricane that had turned more east and went elsewhere.

The conversation lagged and Riley glanced back and forth between Paula and Sam. It was sweet of her friend to introduce her son, but they hadn't turned to go yet. Did they need something else?

"We'd like to talk to you if you have a moment," Paula finally said. "Can we sit down for a minute?"

"Sure, we can sit here." Except that a large man like Sam would look ridiculous in one of these miniature chairs. "Let me get my desk chair for you, Sam."

Apparently he'd been thinking the same thing because he smiled gratefully. "Thank you. I might be able to sit down but I might never be able to get back up again."

Sam settled into her chair and she and Paula sat down in the small chairs around the art center table. "So what did you want to talk to me about?"

Riley had a sinking feeling that Paula was about to tell her that she was moving to be closer to her son and wouldn't be able to volunteer anymore. As much as she hated to lose the best reading tutor she'd ever had, she was determined to be happy for her friend.

Patting her son's hand, Paula gave Riley a smile. "I've talked to Sam and we want to help you if you'll let us."

Huh? Did Sam want to volunteer as well? Did he need to research the role of a teacher?

"You want to help in the classroom?"

Paula laughed and shook her head. "No, dear. We want to help you with your problem. You know...that asshole Chad and our ex-skank friend Monica."

Those were the exact same words Riley had used to describe her ex and former best friend. She had several other names to call them as well, but they weren't nearly as polite and as an educator of young minds she tried to keep her vocabulary as clean as possible.

Sneaking a glance at Sam, she couldn't quite make out his expression. He wasn't smiling but he didn't look unhappy, either. He looked...neutral. As if he didn't have an opinion about what Paula was talking about. She kind of hoped he didn't have a clue as to what his mother was talking about. The details were mortifying enough without him knowing her humiliation too.

"And how do you want to help me?"

I ask with true fear in my heart. What are you up to?

What did Paula think she could do?

Now Paula was beaming, her hand on Sam's shoulder. "Isn't it obvious? Sam will pretend to be your boyfriend. You can show those two cheaters that you're not heart-broken at all."

Whoa. Just...whoa. Had Paula had an early Happy Hour? Riley snuck another glance at her son and this time she was caught red-handed. Sam was watching her as well and their gazes collided, causing her to flinch and look away. He saw way too much. She'd never been good at hiding her emotions.

"I don't think it is obvious. I think it's really sweet that you both want to help me but that sounds like an outrageous plan that no one would ever believe."

Never in a million years would anyone believe that a movie star and sex symbol was dating a boring plain Jane such as herself. Riley didn't have an exciting, seductive bone in her body and Chad leaving her for Monica was Exhibit A of that fact. She was many things - practical, hardworking, well read, organized, and notoriously punctual - but she simply wasn't Hollywood girlfriend material.

Paula waved away her concerns. "Of course they'll believe it. We'll just say that you and Sam met through me and hit it off. You'll make a cute couple."

Sam would make one half of a cute couple if he were dating Quasimodo.

So far he hadn't said much and Riley was getting the horrible feeling that he'd been dragged here kicking and screaming, holding on by his fingernails. She turned her attention to him.

"Listen, I'm sure this is the last thing you want to do. I've been dealing with Chad and Monica and I'll continue to do so. On my own. I really do appreciate your offer, though. This is certainly going above and beyond for your mother."

From the look of things, Sam was an amazing son. Riley loved her parents, but she wasn't sure she was prepared to date a stranger for them. They'd offered a few times over the years to set her up with a son of a friend, but she'd turned them down in no uncertain terms. She'd choose her own man, thank you. The problem though, according to her mother, was that she was far too picky.

Of all the problems in the world to have that didn't seem like a bad one.

Sam was looking at her again, that appraising gaze that

seemed so discerning, and she squirmed underneath its weight.

"Mom, can you give me and Riley a minute?"

No! Don't leave me here alone with him.

Paula smiled and slipped out of the room despite Riley wanting to run after her and beg her to stay. This conversation was going to be nothing but embarrassing and she didn't want to talk about it. Living through it had been bad enough.

When the door swung shut, Riley took the bull by the horns. "Listen, your mother is such a wonderful person and friend. I know she's worried about me these days but honestly, I'm fine. There's really no need for you to help me. I'm sure you have better things to do."

Give an interview. Date a groupie.

Sam didn't answer her right away, instead standing and walking around her room looking at the finger-painted pictures on the walls along with the clay works of art on the shelves. Finally, he stepped back and seemed ready to reply.

"I know this has to be a delicate situation for you. My mother told me what happened."

Riley couldn't help but wince. He did know the worst. Dammit.

"You must think I'm completely pathetic."

Her words tumbled out before she could stop them. What the hell? It was what she really thought.

"I don't." Sam shook his head, but his expression hadn't changed since he arrived. He still looked rather...bland. She couldn't read him at all. "I do think this Chad fellow sounds like a real jerk and your so-called friend needs a visit from karma."

Where was the karma bus when you really needed it?

"People like Monica never get a visit from karma. They just skate through life unscathed."

A brow quirked up in question. "Do you really believe that? I think karma always pays them a visit. It may not be today or tomorrow, but eventually. It's just that we're not always around when it does. She must be a thoroughly miserable human being to have taken up with your boyfriend. It might have made her feel better for a little while but if he'll cheat on you, he'll cheat on her. Trust me on this. I come from a town that's known for its cheaters."

"Hollywood," Riley murmured. "They do seem to have a reputation."

Do you cheat? Don't go there, Riley. Don't even think about it.

"But it always bites them in the ass," Sam replied. "And it will with Chad and Monica. Jesus, even their names sound pretentious and snotty. It sounds like they deserve each other."

"I don't want him back and I wasn't in love with him," she declared. She didn't want him to think she was still in love with her ex. She wasn't. "I was actually thinking about ending things when it all happened. It's just that it was so public. Monica is a teacher here at the school. That's how we met and became friends."

They'd been best friends. Monica the beautiful one that always had men buzzing around her and Riley the quiet one that always volunteered to be the designated driver.

That was her role in life. The responsible one. No wonder Chad had jumped ship the minute he laid eyes on Monica.

"It's their shame, not yours." He spun the globe next to her desk. "Mom says they invited you to their engagement party. To make you feel even crappier, I assume."

They'd succeeded, too. Just when she'd thought she was moving on they'd sucked her back in.

"Yes," she sighed. "And if I don't go then I'll look like the petty one that can't move past all of this. But if I go, I'll look pathetic. I can't win."

"I don't think anyone would blame you for not going, but you're right when you say that they might try and spin it that you're still bitter and hurt. If you go they can't say that, but you can't stop people from comparing the happy couple to you."

Sam seemed to have a firm grasp on her predicament but that still didn't explain why he cared.

"Can I ask you a question? Why would you agree to help me? You don't know me at all. The entire time I've lived in this town and been friends with your mother we've never had an occasion to meet, so that would probably continue to be the case except for this. You don't have any skin in this game. I just don't get it."

"Because I'm a movie star?"

The way he said the last two words, with such amusement, made her smile.

"Well...yeah. Shouldn't you be off on a yacht partying with Bono or something?"

"Bono doesn't own a yacht. He sold it a few years ago." Sam came back and sat down. "As for why I'm doing it? My mother asked, and you may not know this, but I'm a sucker for anything she wants. I don't remember the last time I said no to her. She sacrificed when she was bringing me up and now I can't help but spoil her."

Paula had one good son. She must be a hell of a mom to inspire such devotion in a child. Riley should be so lucky someday.

"But this isn't about her. This is about me."

For the first time, Sam smiled. Really smiled, and it was breathtaking. No wonder he'd been slapped on hundreds of magazine covers. He was one gorgeous man. It was a good thing she was sitting down because her knees would have given out.

"She's pissed off at Chad and Monica, and wants you to have one good week that will get them off of your back." He shrugged as if the whole thing was no big deal. "She thinks seeing me with you will do that."

It might just do that, but still...it was far too much to ask of another human being.

"I would imagine spending time with some girl you're not interested in would be a terrible way to spend your vacation."

He never would have asked her out of his own volition.

"It's not the first time." He leaned forward as if to whisper to her. "Don't tell anyone because it's a not very well-kept secret in Hollywood, but not every relationship you see in the magazines is real. Sometimes it's simply business. That's what this would be, Riley. A business arrangement between two people."

Business? Just business. An interesting concept. But...

"Make believe?"

"That's it exactly. A little smoke and mirrors. And this

part is really important because I don't want there to be any confusion. We'll pretend to be romantic for the good people of New Hope Beach, but behind the scenes we're just friends. I don't want to lead you into thinking that there's more here."

Message received and noted. He wasn't interested. At all.

She'd never thought he would be but it kind of stung when he said it out loud.

"Got it," she replied, a trifle annoyed that he felt the need to voice his disinterest. She wouldn't have assumed anything different. "Just business and only friends. No romance, no sex. That's fine and all but I just don't think I should do this. Who would believe it, anyway? No one is going to buy you dating a regular-looking kindergarten teacher."

She didn't buy the gossip magazines or follow the blogs but even she couldn't avoid seeing photos of him with a beautiful woman on his arm. They were all glamorous, sexy, and much skinnier than she could ever hope to be even if she starved herself for weeks on end. An image of herself standing next to Sam made her inwardly cringe. He was out of her league.

"I think you're underestimating my acting ability."

"I think you're overestimating mine," she replied back quickly. "I'm a terrible liar. I just suck at it. I couldn't pull this off and then we'd both be mortified. Really, I'm doing you a favor here. Thank you...but no. The offer was sweet but I'm going to have to pass on it."

Sam looked like he was going to argue with her but

then he simply nodded and stood, shoving his hands in the pockets of his cargo shorts.

"I appreciate your candor. Please know that if you change your mind I'll be staying with my mom for the week. Just give her a call."

"Thank you again," Riley also stood as he turned and walked toward the door. "And thank Paula for me. It really was a lovely gesture."

She could breathe much easier when Sam left the room. His mere presence, so large and masculine, in this room set up for tiny humans had made it feel far too small for both of them.

She'd made the right decision. The calm, rational, practical decision that made sense.

As enticing as it had been to say yes and show up with Sam on her arm at the engagement party, it wasn't really real. She wouldn't be able to play off like he was her boyfriend and no one would believe that he was interested in her romantically.

The entire idea was ridiculous. But oh so tempting.

CHAPTER
Four

SAM WASN'T a man that was surprised often. Jaded
from his years in Hollywood, he'd seen all kinds of people
from saints to sinners, so he'd ceased long ago to be
shocked or horrified when someone thought only of themselves, caring little for the well-being of others. Greed and
self-interest were part and parcel of the movie business
and he'd learned quickly that he had to be just as ruthless.
Even more, sometimes.

With that, he was still a little surprised that Riley
Bridges had turned down their offer to help her out. From
where he was standing, he could only see an upside for
her. She'd get a moment to rub her ex's face in it, plus a
one-up on her former best friend. But she'd said no, that
she'd deal with it herself.

Which he was actually kind of sad about because the
more he'd talked to her the more he'd liked her. She
seemed to be just as his mother had described - a
genuinely nice person who had been royally screwed by

two not so nice people. He'd wanted to help her and had even found himself sort of looking forward to it. Playing this part would have been a pleasure. He already didn't like Chad and Monica and he hadn't even met the couple. But he knew dozens of people just like them.

It wouldn't have been any hardship to squire Riley around for a few days. If Paula liked her that meant that she was pleasant to be around. She had to be smart as well because his mother didn't suffer fools gladly.

The pretty teacher wasn't exactly hard to look at, either. Dark blonde, almost caramel colored hair had been pulled up into a ponytail, showing off her graceful neck and delicate features. Her figure was one that he favored but rarely saw in the movie business, not fat in the least but not skinny either, generous curves that a man could hold on to. Riley was one very attractive package. Not that he would have done anything about that. He'd learned long ago never to mix business with pleasure.

And this was business. Plus, she was friends with his *mother*. Riley was officially off-limits.

But he did wish her well. She was a brave woman to have dealt with all this bullshit and he hoped that she was around to see when the karma bus pulled up in front of her ex's house. Right into the driveway, horn blaring and lights blinking.

———

Riley slid down into the hot bathwater up to her neck and gave a huge sigh of relief that the long week was over. She had two days to do whatever she wanted. Well...that wasn't exactly true. She needed to clean her little condo and do some grocery shopping, but after that she was in the clear. Teaching kindergarten, she didn't have much homework to grade, although she spent a great deal of time putting together projects for her kids. Last weekend she'd spent most of her Sunday putting together a huge diorama of the ocean ecosystem.

Closing her eyes, she let all her muscles relax one by one until she was a limp noodle in the water, her head lolled back against the rim. Her mind drifted back to earlier today in her classroom and meeting Sam Collins. He'd been taller than she'd envisioned and much more handsome in person. What had surprised her - and it shouldn't have after knowing his mother - was how kind he was. For some reason she'd expected a spoiled movie star but instead she'd found him genuinely nice.

And yes, really sexy.

She'd certainly been tempted to take him and Paula up on their offer. She could picture herself now walking into that engagement party - new dress, makeup on, hair done - with her on Sam's arm. It would make a stir in this sleepy little beachfront town and would certainly be talked about for a long time to come. But doing it would be tantamount to a lie.

Wasn't she always lecturing her students about telling the truth? How a lie will come back and bite you in the ass? Okay, she didn't tell her kids about the biting of asses but she told them that a person couldn't keep track of their lies forever.

Then Emma Drake had raised her hand and suggested that perhaps liars should write them down.

That's how her mother kept track of things she needed to remember.

Out of the mouths of babes, as they say.

Riley didn't know how long she lay there in the rapidly cooling water but the jangle of her ringtone had her climbing out of the tub. Wrapping a towel around herself, she grabbed the phone from the bathroom vanity.

"Hey, Tara. What's going on? I thought you had a date night with your husband planned."

Tara was also a teacher at Riley's school along with Monica, her ex-friend. The three of them had at one time been inseparable. It felt like a long time ago.

"I had to call you the minute I heard the news." Tara voice was unnaturally squeaky, a dead giveaway that she was excited. "There's a rumor that Monica's pregnant."

So much for relaxation. That was out the window.

And yet... Riley wasn't all that shocked. Monica would do everything in her power to solidify her place in Chad's life. She'd made that crystal clear, throwing aside her close friends without a second thought. Riley wasn't the only person Monica had hurt on her way to a wealthy husband and financial security.

"Monica is going to be even more obnoxious at that damn engagement party. You have to go, you know. If you don't, Monica will go on and on about how fucking heartbroken you are. She doesn't care if it isn't true."

Riley hated that she cared what other people thought about her. If she were a better person she'd shrug the entire situation off and just go live her life.

It was petty and she admitted it. She didn't want people feeling sorry for her or thinking she was too pathetic to hold onto a man. And the idea of Chad and Monica smiling smugly while they whispered half-truths to their guests pissed her off to no end. Bad people shouldn't win. It wasn't fair, although she'd long ago stopped expecting life to be that way. Every now and then, though, she wanted it to be. It was the little girl still inside of her. The one that believed the best of people and had her whole life in front of her.

So incredibly stupid. This is why I'm home most Saturday nights.

"My friends will know what's true and what's not."

Jesus, that sounded lame and more than a little goodie-two-shoes. She wasn't talking to her kindergarten charges, this was her best friend. A friend who had been there when Riley had been dumped.

"You need to go to that party with a total stud muffin on your arm," Tara declared. "That would show them. They couldn't say anything then."

Tara had no idea what she'd just said. That had been an actual option earlier today.

Not really, though. No one in their right minds would have ever thought that Sam Collins was interested in Riley. The entire idea was laughable. She was far too...normal.

"Stud muffins are in short supply in New Hope," Riley said. "I just think I won't go to the party."

And it would be a relief to stay home.

"You have to go. You can't let that bitch win."

At this point, Riley wasn't even sure what winning would look like. She sighed as she padded into her bedroom on bare feet to retrieve her robe. "Even if it's a game I don't want to play? They're going to twist this any way they want to no matter what I do. Why bother?"

Someone had to be the adult around here and it always seemed to fall to her to do it. Just once she'd like to throw away all the rules and just have fun.

That's never going to happen.

Riley was far too boring for that. Too...staid.

"I'd just as soon skip the party and pretend Chad and Monica don't exist on this planet. It's better for my blood pressure and overall general mood."

"You're a better person than I am. They should make you a saint."

That had Riley laughing. If her friend knew all the things she'd been thinking...

"A secure woman wouldn't care what other people say about her."

Except that Riley wasn't all that secure. She had to live and work in this town.

On the other hand, it doesn't pay to be a doormat.

It was tempting. All over again, Riley found herself contemplating what it would be like to walk into that party with a man like Sam on her arm. The satisfaction she'd feel knowing that Chad and Monica wouldn't be making her the fool in their little play.

"Just think it through," Tara urged. "Hank and I can be your date. We won't leave you alone all night, I promise."

Even Riley's own best friend thought she was pathetic, and she knew good and well that Riley had never loved Chad. Not even for a second. What the hell did other people think?

"I'll think about it. I'm going to have a cup of

chamomile tea and read a good book. How about lunch tomorrow at the cafe?"

"You're on. Noon?"

Riley agreed and hung up the phone, placing it on the bedside table, her mind far away. She'd love to see Monica's eyes widen with shock and envy if Riley showed up on the arm of Sam Collins.

I am the pettiest person on the face of the planet.

Nothing good could possibly come from such a charade. She'd been right not to give in to her shallow side and say yes. Be strong. Be independent.

Don't give a furry rat's ass what others were saying behind her back. Those people didn't matter in the long run. In a few months - or a few years - no one would even remember that Riley dated Chad at all.

Probably. Hopefully. Maybe.

CHAPTER
Five

"THAT'S THEM," Paula hissed to Sam over their up-to-now serene lunch the next day. They were eating in a small cafe off of Main Street in the funky art and antique district. He'd been telling his mother about a possible upcoming movie project and enjoying a chicken and avocado wrap. "Don't turn around!"

Placing his sandwich back on his plate, he wiped his hands on the paper napkin. "How can I know who you're talking about if I don't turn around?"

His mother leaned farther over the table, her gaze darting around the restaurant like she was a spy for MI-6. "I will tell you who it is. It's Chad and Monica. Look at them acting like they don't have a care in the world."

Paula practically spat out the last sentence, the color high in her cheeks. Sam hadn't realized until this very moment just how much his mother didn't like these two people.

"I can't look because you won't let me turn around."

Rolling her eyes, Paula gave him a look that he recognized from his youth. Part exasperation and part love.

"Fine. You can turn around but don't be obvious about it."

"I'm an actor. I think I can pull this off."

If he couldn't, the Golden Globe committee was going to want their statue back.

With his elbow, he knocked his spoon off the table and onto the floor so he had to reach down to retrieve it. It gave him the perfect opportunity to take a quick look.

The couple wasn't difficult to identify. Their expressions were a little too smug and their clothes were a little too fancy for this casual establishment.

"So that's Riley's ex."

The guy was good-looking enough if you liked the boyishly handsome type. Blond hair and blue eyes, tanned skin. Sort of the lifeguard type if you didn't look too closely at his physique. He was probably charming too - when he wanted to be - and had good table manners honed in some expensive school where he'd met all the right people from all the right families.

Sam had seen the type in Hollywood, wanting to bankroll indie flicks with daddy's money while rubbing elbows with A-listers. They liked the parties and the glamour and the lunches at The Ivy. The work? Not so much.

"He's a little prick, cheating on Riley," Paula muttered, her lips so tightly pressed together they'd almost disappeared into her face. "Is there any way I could convince you to kick his ass?"

Sadly, no. As much as this Chad guy probably needed it, Sam didn't want the bad publicity.

"Mother, your language is shocking. You would have washed my mouth out with soap."

"Maybe I've seen too many of your movies. You don't hold back in those."

No, he didn't and that's why they were usually rated R. At least the *Thunder* movies were.

Paula's eyes went wide and she quickly schooled her features into a neutral mask. "Don't look now but they're coming over here. Because of you, I'm sure."

Now his mother was simply exaggerating. She was quite popular in town and had tons of friends. Anyone would want to cultivate a relationship with her.

"Paula," the young woman exclaimed, a big smile on her face. "What a surprise seeing you here today. Is this your son?"

No, he was her new boy-toy boyfriend. Who else would he be?

But Sam knew the drill and he was too well-trained by his PR people to show even a smidgen of his real emotions or thoughts.

Holding out his hand, he gave them his best "I'm just happy to be part of this amazing ensemble cast" smile. It had a touch of charm and a smattering of humble, all wrapped up in friendliness and approachability.

"Nice to meet you," Sam said, shaking first Chad's hand and then Monica's. "I am Paula's son, Sam."

"We've seen your movies," Chad said, his arm wrapped around the woman's waist. She was about Riley's age, somewhere in her early thirties, with pale blonde hair and dark brown eyes. Quite slim, she was a tall woman, probably five-ten or eleven even without the heels she was wearing. "We're big fans and it's such a thrill meeting you."

Sam murmured the appropriate words of thanks while Monica dug her cell phone out of her handbag. "Would you mind if I took a picture of the two of us? My friends will never believe this really happened."

Of course he would take a few selfies with them. This was standard operating procedure.

The photos were taken. One with only Monica. One with Monica and Chad. And finally, one with all four of them, smiling like they were old friends.

Her hand flying to her mouth, Monica's smile grew even wider. "I just had the most wonderful, amazing, and completely fabulous idea. Are you going to still be here this weekend? Chad and I are having our engagement party on Saturday night at his family's home. You absolutely must come. Please say you will. Having you there would just make everything perfect."

Because everyone needed a movie star to round out their guest list and to make others jealous.

Chad seemed to think well of the idea, slapping Sam on the back like they'd known each other for years. "We just won't take no for an answer, will we, honey? It's the social event of the season. Everyone will be there."

Not everyone. Riley wasn't planning on attending.

Sam was still formulating a polite way to say no when his mother piped up. "He'll be there because he's escorting Riley."

Sam had to stop himself from slapping his own face.

Jesus, Mary, Joseph, and the camel. What was Paula thinking? She'd been there yesterday when Riley had turned down their offer and now she was saying that he was Riley's date? This was fast becoming a cluster that would certainly come back and bite them on the ass. Multiple times.

His mother was now smiling happily but her statement had wiped off the smug grins worn by the town's power couple. Chad's mouth had fallen open and Monica's forehead had furrowed as if Paula was speaking in a language she didn't understand. Swahili perhaps.

Chad was the first to find his voice, albeit slightly squeaky. "You're taking Riley?"

There was silence for a moment as everyone waited for Sam to reply. Riley had been quite clear with her wishes last night. She didn't want any part of their playacting, preferring to deal with this on her own.

But his mother...shit. Paula had inserted herself into this bitch of a situation and now he had to do something. He had to say no. He wasn't escorting Riley.

Except that he couldn't throw his mom under the bus like that. Not ever. So he tried to play it off as best as he could. He was a professional, after all.

"I'm not sure Riley plans on attending," Sam hedged. "There's so much going on this weekend."

To his chagrin, Paula wasn't backing down. Apparently, her motto today was go big or go home. "If she decides she wants to go, you're taking her, though."

She'd thrown down the gauntlet. He'd have to pick it up. Sort of. He gave the wishy-washiest answer he could.

"Whatever Riley wants is what I'll do."

Riley was going to be pissed the hell off when she found out what Paula had just done.

"Wow," Monica said, twisting the strap of her purse with her fingers. "I didn't even realize you two were seeing each other. How long has that been going on?"

Yeah, Mom, how long? You got an answer for everything?

Waving the question away, Paula acted like it was no big deal. "They met a while ago. I'm surprised Riley never told you."

Although she made it sound as if she wasn't surprised at all.

"I haven't seen her much lately," Monica said, a flush creeping up her cheeks. "But this is...great news. Just fantastic."

Monica sounded and looked like they'd just told her that she had a terminal disease. The young woman was not happy in the least.

To Chad's credit, he appeared to have recovered more quickly and seemed to be genuinely happy about the news. "Riley's a great girl. You're a lucky man."

Now Monica was unhappy and pissed off, too. From where Sam sat it didn't look like she'd expected her Prince Charming to have anything nice to say about his ex-girlfriend.

"I am a lucky man."

He could say that with utter truthfulness and confidence. He'd been incredibly fortunate in his life.

"We hope you can come," Chad said. "Paula, you're going to be there, aren't you?"

"Wouldn't miss this for the world," Sam's mother assured them. "It should be quite an evening."

Paula had pretty much ensured it would be.

The hovering hostess finally wrangled the couple to their table, leaving Sam and Paula alone. He didn't often find himself angry with his mother, but she'd just put him and Riley in a really shit-sandwich situation.

And she'd known it when she did it.

Luckily, Monica and Chad were far enough across the crowded cafe that they couldn't hear the conversation.

"I cannot believe you did that, Mom. Riley specifically said no."

His mother dabbed at the corners of her mouth with her napkin, acting far too calm for the circumstances. "You're angry with me."

It was a simple sentence but so very true.

"I'm livid," he said between gritted teeth. He hated being mad at Paula, but this little stunt was beyond the pale. "Riley has enough problems in her life without you adding to them. That poor girl just wants to be left alone. She was planning to skip the party and hold her head up around town, dealing with this like an adult. Now you've thrown her into the lion's den and she doesn't deserve any of this."

"You're right," she nodded in agreement. "Riley deserves much better than she's gotten in the past. She's too sweet to demand it for herself. That's why I want to help her. You can do that for her."

Sam had a feeling that when backed into a corner the lovely and kind kindergarten teacher could come out swinging if she needed to.

"She doesn't want us to do this."

"She doesn't know what she needs. She's making decisions based on emotions, not logic."

From what he'd seen it had been the exact opposite.

Rubbing his now throbbing temples, Sam shook his head. "Are you sure you didn't just describe yourself? Because Riley made a well-thought out argument yesterday and so far, all I've heard from you is that you don't like these people. That sounds emotional to me."

Paula's eye sparkled with unshed tears. "Okay, fine. You win, son. Are you happy now? I'm a sentimental fool of an old woman and I want Riley to be happy. You didn't see her like I did. It wasn't so much that she was heartbroken over that cad, it was that she was so hurt that one of her best friends could betray her like that. She trusted Monica. Frankly, we all did. I know that Riley had her doubts about her relationship with Chad so I think she felt it was all for the best, but I know that she was deeply hurt by what her friend did. I think she finds it hard to trust now and I don't blame her. I'm having a tough time, too."

Clearly this was as much about his mother's hurt as Riley's.

"You're not a sentimental old fool, Mom. You're just incredibly softhearted. But you didn't think this all the way through. Riley doesn't want any part of this. Ultimately, it's her decision."

"Leave her to me. I'll talk to her."

Heaven help Riley Bridges. When his mother was determined to do something it almost always happened. The poor kindergarten teacher didn't stand a chance.

He might as well capitulate gracefully.

"Then I'm going to need a tux."

Paula patted his hand and smiled. "Son, I already called your assistant. I'm way ahead of you."

That wasn't anything new.

CHAPTER

Six

RILEY COULDN'T POSSIBLY BE HEARING what she thought she was hearing. It sounded like Paula had said that she'd told Chad and Monica that Sam was taking her to the engagement party. That they were *dating*. Like a real couple. The words still rang in her ears like a song she couldn't get out of her head.

"I don't think I heard you correctly."

Sam was leaning against her kitchen counter, a long-suffering look on his face. "You heard her. My mother decided that you were wrong and she was right. Welcome to the not-very-exclusive club."

Paula shot him a nasty look over her shoulder. "I can do this on my own. In fact, I'm not sure why you're even here."

"I'm here for the show. And since I'm involved in this up to my neck I figured I'd better be here in case you make any more unilateral decisions on Riley's or my behalf."

Riley didn't want to get between mother and son, but she had questions. So many questions.

"Let me get this straight... You saw Monica and Chad in a cafe and things sort of snowballed from there. Is that about right?"

Paula slapped her palms down on her thighs and then hopped up from the chair she'd been sitting in having a cup of tea just a few moments ago. "It just makes me so mad the way they've treated us...I mean you, of course. They've treated you terribly and they need to learn a lesson they won't forget in a hurry. The words just seemed to tumble out of my mouth but once I said them I knew it was the right thing to do."

Heaven help us all, this was really happening.

"So she doubled down," Sam said with a grim smile. "The only way I could have denied it was to say that she hadn't taken her medication yet that day."

Riley was a cautious person but even she'd had times in her life that her mouth worked faster than her brain. Words had spilled out that couldn't be taken back.

Then there was Paula's little Freudian slip. It hadn't just been Riley that had been hurt by Monica's betrayal. They all had in their own ways. They'd all been close, a little group of friends that liked to spend time together whenever they could.

Then Monica had blown up their cozy little bunch. Riley couldn't really say that Monica had stolen Chad because he was a human being and belonged to himself. It had been his fault, too. If he hadn't wanted to be "stolen", he wouldn't have been. Full stop. But that didn't change the fact that the friendship was torn beyond repair and everyone had been shocked by what had happened. People had picked sides and the whole situation had been ugly.

"I do understand," Riley finally said, realizing that both Paula and Sam were waiting for her to reply. "I know that emotions are still running high about this even four months later and that you were angry. But I do have to say that you've put me in a really precarious position here. If I don't go to the party with Sam, you're going to look like a liar. If I do go, I have to pretend that he and I are in some kind of a relationship when we barely know one another. And then he leaves and I have to make up some story about a long-distance relationship gone wrong. That's a lot of lies to pile one on top of the other. I'm not sure I'm capable of it."

Paula looked like she was going to cry, and Sam looked like he wanted to yell. Loudly.

"Are you mad at me? I just..."

Now Paula really was crying, and Sam strode over to his mother and wrapped her in his arms. "Now Mom, calm down. It's all going to be okay. We'll figure this out. Three smart people can find an answer to this."

Helpless and not knowing what to do, Riley wanted to throw up her hands and walk away. Try and forget this ever happened, but she couldn't. Paula was her friend even if she had done something kind of dumb. Sam was right. They could figure out a solution somehow.

"I'm not mad." Was that the truth? Yes, it was. Paula hadn't done this with any malice. But... "I am frustrated because I don't know what to do. And I'm sorry you've been dragged into this, Sam. You came home for a vacation."

He patted Paula on the back as she buried her face in his shirt. "I have to admit it's been a long time since I had to work this hard to get a date with a woman."

He'd injected some much-needed levity into the room and Riley found herself smiling and laughing. "Well, I'm picky when it comes to my social life, especially after Chad."

"I'll have to dig out my resume," he teased right back. "I think I have some fairly recent head shots, too."

Paula had lifted her head, her gaze darting back and forth between her son and Riley.

"This is no laughing matter. We have to make a decision here."

"No, Mom." Sam eased back a few steps so he was looking down at her tearstained face. "Riley and I have to make a decision. You need to go into the living room with your tea and watch some television."

"But–"

Shaking his head, Sam interrupted. "No, this involves the two of us. You've done enough for one day. We'll take it from here."

Riley thought Paula might argue but she seemed to sense her son's resolve and did as he asked, taking her tea and disappearing into the living room.

"I'm shocked," Riley said, still staring at the door that separated the two rooms. She could hear the sounds from the television. "How did you do that?"

Sam came to sit down at her kitchen table, the chair legs scraping against the tile and grating on her already raw nerves. This was not what she'd had planned for her Saturday afternoon.

"You mean get Mom to actually listen? She knows when she's screwed up. Now it's up to you and me to fix it, and I'm afraid we don't have too many options."

Leaning forward, her elbows on the table, Riley let her head fall into her hands. He was right, of course. They'd only been pretending that there were multiple resolutions to this messed-up situation.

"What do you think we should do, Sam?"

Rubbing his chin, he gave her a rueful smile. "Let's just say I already have a tux being sent here from my home in New York."

The stiffness went out of her shoulders along with her pent-up breath. It's what she'd known all along. They'd been pretending otherwise. "That's what I figured. We can't really get out of this without making Paula look bad and I don't want to do that."

"I think—" He hesitated a moment before continuing. "I think that my mother was more hurt by Monica than she lets on. She says this is about helping you. I hate to say it, but I also think a good chunk of this is about her as well. She keeps saying that she wants them to learn a lesson and I guess you and I are going to deliver it."

She couldn't help but feel sorry for the man. He'd been dragged into this by Paula and he was being gracious and nice about it. So much for the stereotype of an arrogant Hollywood star.

"I'll be honest with you, Sam, because you're being honest with me. I should actually be thanking Monica. I had a lot of doubts about Chad and her actions showed that they were well-founded. As I think I said yesterday, I'm not upset that they're together. I'm upset that they can't seem to leave me out of their relationship. Personally, I'm happy to forget they even exist on the planet but they keep dragging me back in, so the last thing I want to do is get involved enough to teach them anything. But it looks like that's exactly what I'm going to be doing."

His lips twisted, and she noticed that he had a small scar near the corner of his mouth. She had to resist the urge to reach over and trace it with her fingers or ask him where it came from. It wasn't any of her business.

"Listen, how about we forget about teaching any lessons and just have some fun. You were right when you said that I'm here for a little vacation. I just want to relax and enjoy myself. How about we ignore everyone else and do as we please?"

She could do that. She *would* do that. Being squired around town by a kind, handsome man wasn't the worst thing that could happen to her.

Although I'm sure there's something wrong with him, too. There always is.

"That sounds like something I can handle."

Smiling, he held out his hand for her to shake. "Then it's a deal? We spend a little time together. Just as friends. I'll escort you to the party and we'll be a happy, loving couple for the masses."

Extending her arm to shake his hand, she paused for a moment. "Are you sure about this? There's still time to back out."

"I'm not backing out. We can do this. Just friends. No monkey business."

She moved the rest of the distance and they clasped hands, hers cold and clammy, his warm and reassuring. He was a hell of a lot more confident about this than she was, but then he acted for a living.

"So what do we do first?"

His brows shot up and his chuckle was pure glee. "That's easy, my dear Riley. We go out and be seen. We can't teach them a lesson if we're not the hottest couple in town."

She was going to be one half of the hottest couple in town. That would be...new.

She was going to regret agreeing to this. She just had that feeling she couldn't shake off. Somehow, some way she was going to wish she'd said no. Anything built on a lie was like constructing a house on shifting sand.

"Then I'll follow your lead."

But not too closely. They were only going to be friends, and she better remember that.

CHAPTER

Seven

TO BE SEEN TOGETHER by the town, they had to hang out in public. It was Saturday night and they were both hungry, so it was only natural to head to a local restaurant for dinner. They were both dressed casually, having decided to hit a popular place on the beach that Riley assured him served great food. He was wearing khaki slacks and a cotton button-down, the sleeves rolled up and out of the way. She was wearing a light blue sundress that showed off the tanned golden skin of her arms and legs. Tonight she'd left her hair down around her shoulders and the light behind her seemed to create a halo around her head, the strands like spun gold. If she was wearing makeup, it was undetectable to his expert eye. She had a natural, fresh beauty that would capture any male attention easily.

Whoa there, tiger. This is only business. The last thing you need is an emotional entanglement. Leave the poor girl alone.

The restaurant was open to the water, and if you

stepped out of the back door you'd be walking in the sugar white sand of the Gulf beaches. Sam could smell the salt in the air and the slight tang of rum and coconut from the bar where tropical drinks were whirring in the blenders. The aroma mixed with the wafting fragrance of charred meat and fried fish, drawing a growl from his empty stomach.

The building was weathered with graying planks on the floors and walls, along with beaten-up metal tables and chairs that looked like they'd seen their best days back in the 1950s. This wasn't a place that tourists hung out. This was a place for locals.

They were shown to a table by a wide-eyed waitress that quickly took their drink orders before disappearing back behind the bar. Sangria for Riley and a beer for him.

"This is very...authentic," Sam said, taking in the decor around them. They'd only been inside for a few minutes, but he already liked it. It had a good vibe and kind of reminded him of some of his favorite places in New York City where no one bothered him. He could just go and be himself. "Very Florida. Do you come here a lot?"

Riley smiled and for the first time he noticed that she had dimples in her cheeks. Was this the first true smile he was getting from her? Her blue eyes even sparkled when she was really happy.

"Believe it or not, this is your mother's favorite restaurant. She loves their homemade Sangria. We come here on Sundays as often as we can. They make a great brunch."

"I should have known. Mom loves a good Sangria, almost as much as her Cabernet." He opened the menu and perused its contents. "Looks like they specialize in burgers and seafood. I haven't had a good cheeseburger in awhile."

Because he was always getting ready for a role. It was a luxury right now that he didn't have to worry about his weight. The next movie he was going to work on wasn't action-packed. A few pounds would be acceptable.

"They do make a great burger," Riley agreed with a nod, closing her own menu. "But you might want to try the smothered chicken, if you like cheese and mushrooms. I highly recommend it."

The description of the dish sounded right up his alley. Anything that was smothered in melted cheese just had to be delicious.

"I think I will."

The waitress, much calmer the second time, came with their drinks and took their order before disappearing into the crowd. The tinkling of plates and silverware along with the din of conversation made the room rather loud and boisterous. There was a television on over the bar in the far corner and a group of young men were watching a basketball game and cheering every now and then. Was it the NBA playoffs? Or maybe the NCAA? He never had much time to follow teams anymore, so he couldn't be sure.

He was aware however that they were being watched. Closely. The other diners often turned their heads and stared for a few moments and then looked quickly away as if not to get caught. Passersby headed for the bathroom or the exit weren't that sly, slowing down and gawking before eventually walking away. Sam was used to it, but he was also hyper-aware of the attention and he noticed it before Riley did. Eventually, however, she was shifting uncomfortably in her chair, her gaze darting around the restaurant and then back to him.

"I kind of feel like we're on display."

"That's an excellent way of describing this particular phenomenon. We do seem to be capturing the interest of the citizens of this town. The news should get back to Chad and Monica by morning."

Being seen was the whole point, though. This wasn't a real date.

"Does this happen to you all the time?"

"It depends." He shrugged casually, pushing the basket of rolls the waitress had dropped off closer to Riley. Cheese was one thing, but bread was a bridge too far. He'd already had garlic bread since he'd arrived, and he needed to use some common sense while on vacation. "In places like Los Angeles and New York they are far too cool - or at least think they are - to notice a celebrity, but yes, sometimes it's like this. I just try not to dribble the soup all over my chin. Otherwise I just ignore them and live my life."

Her glass paused halfway to her mouth, her gaze following a couple who weren't making much effort to disguise the fact that he and Riley were the topic of their conversation. They'd stopped in the middle of the restaurant and were huddled together whispering. They even went as far as taking out their phones and snapping a few photos.

Those were going to end up on social media. No doubt about it.

This. This right here was what his mother hadn't thought through. He could squire Riley around town for a few days, take her to the party, and then exit at the end of the week with a story about long distance relationships. But that didn't mean that she would be insulated from what it meant to be in his orbit. Luckily there were no paparazzi here, but there were people with camera phones. That usually meant Twitter or Facebook or Instagram or some other media platform. He didn't comment on his relationships and he wasn't going to start now, but her picture was going to end up on the internet.

He should have warned her, but dammit, sometimes he just forgot about it. He'd been doing this so long half the time he didn't even register the attention. He'd long ago learned to tune most of it out.

"I'm sorry about this. When I said we should be seen I meant by the people in town, not the world on Twitter. Do you want to leave?"

Her eyes widened and she took a gulp of her drink. "We're going to be on Twitter?"

"I don't know that for sure, but when people take a photo they often post it online. I'm serious, we can leave if you want to."

She paused for a moment but then shook her head. "No, it's not a big deal, I guess. If strangers see it they won't know who I am, will they? So it doesn't really matter." She frowned and signaled the waitress for a drink refill. "We're not going to end up on the cover of a tabloid, are we?"

Sam chuckled at her naïveté. "Doubtful. I hate to burst your bubble on Hollywood hype, but most of the people you see on the covers of magazines and supermarket tabloids are on there because their publicist made a deal with the editors. They tipped off the paparazzi that they were going to be coming out of such and such restaurant at a certain time with a certain person. Sure, there have been occasions when I've been hounded by the press, but you'd be shocked at how much is all staged to look spontaneous."

"Do you do that?"

"Yes," he replied honestly. "I have in the past, although I don't have to do it as much anymore, thank goodness. It's harmless stuff, really. My publicist would tell *TMZ* that I'm getting off a plane at LAX so they'd be there to take pictures and ask me questions about an upcoming movie. Or maybe I'd be coming out of a nightclub and the paparazzi would be there. It keeps my name in the press, especially if I have a film coming out. Otherwise, all those tabloids wouldn't have much to put in their pages. Most actors and actresses are boring as hell. I know I sure am."

"You say that with such pride."

"Damn straight. I've seen too many people get caught up in the partying and the money. They end up burnt out in rehab or dead. That's not going to be me."

Her head tilted as she studied him, and he wanted to ask what she was seeing. She smiled a little, so it must have been good. "No, that wouldn't be you. You're far too down to earth for that. Were you always that way? Even when you first went to Hollywood?"

"I like to think so." He leaned forward so he could whisper. "Courtesy of one Paula Collins. She never let my head get too big. Her mission in life was to keep me humble and hardworking."

"It appears to have worked."

Chuckling, he nodded in agreement as the waitress slid

their smothered chicken in front of them. It smelled heavenly and his stomach gurgled with expectation. This was going to be way better than a humble cheeseburger. The butterflied chicken breast was covered with cheese, mushrooms, bacon, chives, and a few other items thrown in for good measure. The first bite was delicious and practically melted on his happy tongue.

"Damn, this is good. You know your food."

Laughing, she cut into her own chicken. "I know my cheese, anyway. I'm glad you like it."

"Do you come from a long line of cheese lovers?"

"How did you know? My parents were originally from Wisconsin, but they moved here when all of us kids were small so that they could be closer to my aging grandparents. I was about four and I thought that living next to Mickey Mouse would be the coolest thing ever."

"I think you were right," he teased. "Although I can't remember the last time I went to Disney World. Did you go a lot when you were little?"

Snorting delicately, she shook her head. "I think we went once when I was growing up. I was one of five children, and even though both my parents worked there never seemed to be enough money for a vacation like that. Mostly they'd pack up the car and come to the beach for a week, which of course we adored."

Sam tried to picture Riley as a little girl, maybe with long braids and freckles on her nose. She'd probably been a real cutie.

"Five kids? That sounds like a houseful."

"Two parents, two girls, three boys, four bedrooms, and two bathrooms. Add in two Labrador retrievers and a rabbit named Fluffy and you'd describe our household. It was always busy and always loud. Sometimes I'll just sit in my living room and enjoy the silence."

It sounded like a wonderful, idyllic childhood. The kind he'd only seen on television.

"Are you still close to your family?"

She nodded, taking another bite of her chicken. "I talk to my mom about once a week and I see them several times a year. My brothers and sisters are sort of scattered all over and only one still lives in the Orlando area. Mom and Dad are talking about retiring in five or six years and they want to move back up to Wisconsin to be near my mom's brother and his wife."

That was different. Most people retired *to* Florida.

"What are they retiring from?"

"My mom is a high school history teacher and my dad works in the legal department at an insurance company. They say they're ready to play golf and drive slow in the left lane."

Sam couldn't imagine retiring from acting, but maybe he'd feel differently in twenty or thirty years. Riley seemed to relax after that, ignoring the stares and whispers that came their way. While they ate their food, he found out a little more about her family and he talked about his own childhood, including a few funny stories with his mother. With her own mother being an educator, it wasn't difficult to see why they'd hit it off and become friends.

She was easy to talk to even when they discussed what might have been controversial subjects. Luckily, she was polite even when disagreeing with him, presenting a well-thought out rebuttal. He was going to have to rethink his position on school funding after listening to her arguments. Usually the women he dated were in the business and that's what he ended up talking about all night. This was a refreshing change.

He was having fun. Too much of it. She was the best date he'd had in ages and this was not a date. This was a favor because her ex was a jerk and her best friend a gold digger. He was already anticipating a good night kiss and there wouldn't be any of that. No touching, no kissing, and absolutely no sex. He'd hold her hand in public, maybe even put an arm around her but that was as far as the evening was going to go. He needed to get his libido under control.

Placing her fork down on her now empty plate, Riley clasped her hands together. "That was wonderful. If Paula talks you into coming here tomorrow for brunch, I recommend the chocolate chip pancakes."

That sounded like carb-heaven. Much tastier than an egg white omelet and a single slice of turkey bacon. He was glad he'd passed on the bread because pancakes were far superior.

"You must know that from experience. Do you come here a lot?"

"At least once a month," Riley confirmed. "Me, Paula, and Tara."

She didn't have to add that Monica was part of that group at one time.

"I don't think I've met Tara."

"You'd know if you did. My friend Tara is one of your biggest fans. I should probably warn you that when you do meet her she is definitely going to want a selfie and an autograph. And if you give her half a chance, she's going to want to know all the Hollywood gossip on her favorite stars. She especially loves Nate Mason."

Sam chuckled at the mention of one of his best friends and co-stars. "I can truthfully say that Nate and his wife are living on very little sleep since the birth of their twins, and I can also say that I think they're terrific parents. Nate took to the whole father thing right off the bat and of course Paige was already a mother. Annabelle and Andrew have him wrapped around their finger and they're only a few months old."

Nate and Paige had it all. True love, parenthood, and great careers. At one point he'd thought that maybe he'd have that too, but now he knew better. He wasn't cut out for that kind of life.

"With parents that good-looking, I bet they're really cute."

The check came and he made a grab for it before she could. Wrinkling her nose at him, she tried to retrieve it from his fingers but he held it out of her reach.

"I'm getting the check. This is a date, remember?"

Her mouth was set in a mutinous line. She wasn't going to give up too easily. It was actually kind of nice to have a woman that didn't think of him as her personal ATM machine.

But he still wasn't going to let her pay.

"Not really," she said, keeping her voice low. "Let me at least pay for my half. It's only fair."

He placed his credit card down on the check and kept his hand there until the waitress took them both away as she breezed by.

"I am not letting a kindergarten schoolteacher who probably has to buy supplies for half of the kids in her class pay the dinner check. I'd lose my man card. I'm happy to get it, so I'm asking you to please allow me to do this."

She nodded but there wasn't much surrender in her eyes.

"Okay, but you have to let me cook you dinner one night while you're here."

"Deal," he instantly agreed. "I don't get much home-cooked food, although Mom made me lasagna when I got here. Are you ready to go?"

The waitress had returned his credit card and the slip, so he scrawled his name on the dotted line.

Riley nodded toward the beach. "How about we walk off some of this dinner?"

A sandy beach, a moonlit sky, a beautiful woman. What could go wrong?

Say no, you idiot. You'll try to kiss her for sure.

"That sounds like a great idea."

CHAPTER
Eight

THIS WASN'T the best idea Riley had ever had. In fact, it was downright lousy.

She'd simply wanted to work off some of her heavy meal, but the entire activity had taken on a different feel as she and Sam walked down the beach, their toes digging into the wet sand. The stars twinkled in the inky night sky and a warm breeze caressed her skin. Even in early April, Florida had left the cold weather far behind. There was silvery moonlight and the scent of salt and hibiscus in the air, along with the faint sounds of laughter from somewhere off in the distance.

It was romantic. The last thing she needed right now.

After she'd found out about Chad and Monica, Riley had decided to take a break from men for awhile. Not because she'd been deathly heartbroken, but because she wanted to be on her own. She needed to think about what had led her to stay with Chad for as long as she did. She'd known deep down that he was wrong for her, but she hadn't taken the final step of breaking up.

She'd chickened out every time she thought about it. Rationalizing that all relationships had ups and downs. No one was perfect. Was she afraid to be alone? Or was she afraid that maybe it was *her* that was the issue?

She wasn't the most exciting woman on the planet, nor the prettiest. She wasn't model-slim and her wardrobe was decidedly utilitarian. She was intelligent but no genius, funny but not hilarious. She couldn't remember the last time she'd cut loose and had a wild night. In fact, she was pretty sure that had never happened in all of her thirty-one years. She was organized, practical, and the level-headed grownup in any situation. She was good in a crisis, too, which was helpful in her line of work.

In other words, she was run of the mill, ordinary, forgettable. And what man had said to his best friend over a couple of beers, *"I'm looking for a female that's pretty much just mediocre. I don't want her to have any special qualities."*

Or perhaps it was something she didn't even have a clue about. Either way, she wasn't happy with her actions, so she'd decided to take a hiatus from dating. There weren't any men around that she was interested in anyway, so it wasn't much of a sacrifice. Until now.

She liked Sam Collins. A whole bunch. And it wasn't just because he looked like a sex god, although he certainly did. It was because he made her laugh and he made her think. He listened too, not acting like he knew it all. He was kind and dammit, he loved his mother. How was Riley supposed to ignore a guy like that when she was walking in the moonlight with him?

He was nice, which was why he was here with her at all. This wasn't about him being attracted to her. She had a vague memory of the last woman he'd dated. She'd seen a picture of the two of them in a magazine when she was waiting her turn at the salon to get her hair cut. That female had been tall and slender with high cheekbones, full lips, and hair down her back. Perfectly coifed and made up, that actress probably didn't ever have to dig clay out from under her nails or get paint out of her hair.

They lived two completely different lives. Her a routine existence - not that she was complaining in the least - and Sam a jetsetting life filled with champagne, parties, and the kind of people she only saw on television. She needed to keep her head on straight and her feet on the ground. He wasn't going to be interested in a girl like her. He was way out of her league and to get any different ideas was to set herself up for disappointment.

But she couldn't help but enjoy walking quietly next to him. Neither of them felt the need to fill the silence with chatter, content to listen to the tide roll gently in and out, almost like a whisper in their ear. He smelled amazing, a mixture of citrus and spice and it mixed with the salt in the air, creating a heady fragrance. His large figure made her feel safe and protected even though there wasn't even a hint of danger around. She did, after all, live in the most boring little town in Florida. Possibly all of America as well. She didn't need a bodyguard, but it didn't hurt either.

"Should we turn around and head back to the car?"

His deep voice jolted her out of her drifting thoughts and pulled her firmly back to the present. They'd come to a stop and he was looking down at her, waiting for her response. There was only one answer. The madness needed to end.

"That's a good idea. It's probably getting late."

It was already far too late for Riley. As much as she wanted to be, she simply wasn't immune to a good person like Sam. She could fall for him...if she let herself.

So she'd keep her distance as much as possible and not let herself get too close. She wouldn't embarrass him or herself by letting him know how attracted she was to him. It was only for a week. One single week. Then her life could go back to normal, and Sam would go back to Hollywood.

This was only make-believe and she'd be a fool to think otherwise.

———

Sam was easily the dumbest man on the planet. Bar none. Sure, there were other dumb people, but he'd cornered the market on stupidity and raised it to an art form.

It was a safe bet that he'd been dropped on his head as a baby, but his mother had never admitted it. If he'd had two brain cells to rub together, he would have known that a walk along a moonlit beach with a beautiful woman was an idiotic idea.

Correction. A beautiful woman who was off limits. This was no romantic date where he might expect things to move toward the bedroom at the end of the evening. He was doing a friendly favor and he'd be wise not to get *too* friendly.

Neither one of them said much as they walked back to

his rental car in the parking lot, nor did they speak much as he drove her home. They kept to safe topics such as the weather and the best place to get lobster but the tension he felt continued to build with every second they sat next to each other.

Sam could smell the fragrance of her skin and feel the warmth from her body, sitting only inches away. She was only riding alongside him, but his entire being was attuned to her every movement and breath. There was an anticipation building that was destined to be unfulfilled. There would be no goodnight kiss, no inviting him in for coffee and then later leading him into her private sleeping sanctum where they would finish the evening with plea-surable orgasms. Preferably several.

By the time he pulled up in front of her home, the tension was almost a palpable thing that he could see and touch. He found himself clearing his throat and sweating like a teenager on his first date. Thankfully, Riley seemed oblivious to his inner turmoil.

He hoped.

I'm supposed to be a sex symbol. I'm supposed to be legendary with the ladies.

"I'll walk you to your door."

"No!" Her hand had flown to her throat and even in the half-light he could see her panic. "I mean...you don't need to. It's only a few feet to the front door. I'll be fine."

He'd laugh at the situation, but it wasn't in the least funny. Maybe in a few years he might get a chuckle out of it. Make that a few decades.

Riley wasn't as oblivious as he'd thought. She knew what was up and she didn't want him near her. Smart girl.

He wouldn't press the issue. "If that's what you want. I'll make sure you get inside, though."

That tension was still shimmering between them as Riley placed her purse on her lap and one hand on the door handle, ready to make a quick escape from his company. "Thank you for dinner. I had a good time."

"You're welcome. I enjoyed myself, too."

He reminded himself that he'd never make a decent screenwriter because he sucked at dialogue. His tongue felt like it had swelled to twice its normal size, so words were more difficult than usual.

"Well...goodnight."

"Goodnight. I'll call you tomorrow."

Pushing the car door open, Riley exited the vehicle and climbed the stairs to her front porch. She quickly unlocked her door and stepped inside the house, flipping on a lamp by the entrance. Turning back, she gave him a smile and a wave.

He could leave now. His brain was telling him to put the car in reverse and drive away.

Every other part of his body - the parts he was determined to ignore - was telling him to follow her and see if her lips felt as soft and pillowy as they looked.

The brain won. This time. After waving back, he drove away and only then did his breathing and heart rate return to normal. It was a potent sexual attraction, but Sam wouldn't be drawn in. It was one week. He'd be charming but keep his distance, and then after the party he'd leave. No getting involved.

They'd both be better off.

CHAPTER
Nine

"THAT DRESS IS PERFECT. ABSOLUTELY PERFECT," Paula gushed when Riley stepped out of the opulent dressing room.

They'd driven into the larger city about fifty miles away so she would have more selection. Paula had dragged her to an upscale dress shop downtown that Riley would never have entered on her own, but it made sense in a cruel way. Sam Collins wouldn't be seen with a woman on his arm that wore cheap clothes. She had savings and she could wear the dress again. When? She had no idea, but theoretically she could wear it over and over.

If I ever had any place to go.

Frowning at her reflection while the saleslady hovered in the background, Riley wasn't as sure as Paula was. This dress was...fussy. The hem and neckline had shiny silver rhinestones sewn on and Riley wasn't someone who enjoyed bling on her garments. It also had far too many tiers of fabric and she felt swamped in the outfit. It fit perfectly and the dark purple was lovely, but it didn't look like something she would wear. Maybe that was the point?

"I was hoping for something simpler," she finally said, turning to face the saleswoman named Jaclyn. Paula had taken charge when they first arrived so the changing room had been filled with beautiful dresses, but none of them felt quite right. "I look like a visual representation of Las Vegas. I was hoping for something far simpler. These dresses are gorgeous but they're wearing me, not the other way around."

Jaclyn didn't get a chance to respond, however, because Tara joined them, a huge smile on her face and her cheeks pink with excitement. She was carrying a dress over her arm and she presented it with a flourish.

"Ta da! Well...what do you think?"

It looked like a white shapeless blob on the hanger, but Riley didn't want to say that out loud. Clearly Tara was excited about her find.

"I think you'll look beautiful in it. But I thought you already had a dress for the party."

Rolling her eyes, Tara pressed the garment into Riley's hands. "It's not for me, it's for you. I think this is what you've been looking for."

Paula frowned at the dress. "You don't like the one she has on?"

"She looks like a fancy cake."

Paula frowned harder and then burst into laughter. "Oh dear, I think you might be right. I just wanted something... Special, I guess."

"That's special, alright," Tara giggled, giving Riley a push toward the changing room. "Go try it on. You're looking at me like I'm crazy but that doesn't mean I don't know how to pick out a dress."

She had a point. Besides, it wouldn't hurt to take a few minutes and try it on, if only for her best friend.

Closing the changing room door behind her, Riley took off the fancy cake dress and then removed the new dress from its hanger. Up close the silky white fabric looked completely different, shot with threads of gold that caught the light whenever it moved.

It slipped over her body easily, the fabric cool against her skin. Stepping back from the mirror to get a better look, her eyes widened in surprise. What had looked like a shapeless bag on the hanger was actually a gorgeous dress that lovingly hugged every curve of her figure without being obscene. The delicate spaghetti straps held up a bodice that draped over her cleavage in a vee, ending in the valley between her breasts. The back of the dress was cut low with crisscross straps, and the skirt ended in a soft puddle of fabric around her feet. It was simple yet sophisticated and she looked like a million bucks in it.

If I do say so myself.

"Are you going to show us or not?"

Tara's voice could be heard through the flimsy door and Riley didn't take any more time to admire herself in the mirror. She stepped out and twirled around a few times for their inspection. She didn't need their approval, but it would be nice if they liked it too. There was only one question left in her mind.

Just how much does this cost? Will I have to take out a mortgage for it?

Tara clapped her hands together and practically

jumped up and down. "That's it. That's the one. It's perfect and you look amazing in it."

Paula had stood and was inspecting the dress closely, but she was smiling, too. "I stand corrected. This is what you should be wearing to the party Saturday night. It is perfect."

Even the saleslady was beaming and nodding her head, and she hadn't cracked a smile in almost an hour.

"How did you know?" Riley asked Tara, who was snapping photos with her cell phone.

"You cannot judge a dress by how it looks on a hanger, but even I didn't know it was going to look this good. I just liked the fabric."

Riley ducked into the changing room and slipped off the dress and back into her own clothes. When she was done, she held her breath and closed her eyes for a moment before opening them again to search for the price tag. She only hoped it would be less than the monthly payment on her condo. She still had to find shoes that would go with the outfit. She didn't have anything that would look right with this. Luckily, she had jewelry that would be fine.

She found the tag pinned discreetly inside the dress and swallowed hard as she forced herself to read it.

She exhaled slowly, partly from shock and partly from relief. The price was more than she'd intended to spend today, but it wasn't the king's ransom that she had been imagining. She did some quick mental arithmetic and decided that she could swing it. Normally she liked to pay off her credit card every month but that wasn't going to be possible this time. Maybe next time, too. She'd have to tighten her belt and put off replacing her aging refrigerator, but the dress was simply too beautiful to pass up. If she didn't go crazy in the shoe department she'd be okay.

This one time she could be frivolous and unpractical. Let someone else be the adult today.

An image of Sam's face when he saw her all dressed up popped into her mind, but she ruthlessly pushed it away.

He wasn't her boyfriend. He was a nice, attractive man and he was becoming a good friend these last few days, but he wasn't anyone she should be having romantic thoughts about. That simply wasn't going to happen.

It didn't help that she'd spent three evenings with Sam this week, talking and having dinner. He had a way of making a person feel like they were the only human being in the world at that moment and his focus was solely on you. She was sure it was an affectation he'd perfected in Hollywood, but it sure as heck worked. She found herself thinking about him far more than she should, daydreaming when she should be concentrating on something else. Last night as she'd watched him drive away she'd given herself a stern talking to about the futility of falling for movie stars. It was just that...

Sam seemed to enjoy her company as much as she liked his. He laughed, joked, and in general appeared to be having a good time. She gave him all sorts of excuses and outs but he continued to try and see her every day, even it was only for a few minutes. Part of her kept saying that he was just being polite, but there was a small part of her that thought that maybe...just maybe...he was attracted to her too.

But that might just be even worse.

They led completely different lives. He traveled the world and made movies, she lived in a tiny beach town and taught kindergarten. He made millions. She made thousands. Her car was a nice, sensible Honda Accord that she'd paid cash for used. She didn't know what he normally drove when he was at home, but she'd bet it wasn't an Accord. It was probably a sports car, racy and red, worth more than she made in a year. Or five years. They didn't have enough in common to make it work. It was better that they were simply friends.

Tomorrow night she'd attend the engagement party with Sam and then the next day he'd catch a plane - first class, of course - and fly back to his real life. Getting any more involved with him than she already was wouldn't be prudent. She didn't run around and chase rainbows and unicorns. Reality was where she lived, not the make-believe of Hollywood.

"Are you ready to go yet?"

Tara's voice once again drifted through the door, sounding impatient to go. They still had more shopping to do and it was already past dinnertime. Riley wasn't seeing Sam tonight, but he probably wanted to spend some time with his mother. Paula was, after all, the real reason he was here.

A fact that Riley simply couldn't allow herself to forget. Not for one single second.

CHAPTER
Ten

"DO you even want to do another *Thunder* movie?"

Sam couldn't believe he was having this conversation with one of his best friends Nate Mason. He'd assumed that they were all done with the *Thunder* franchise. They'd fulfilled their contracts and even the last film had felt a little tired, the premise having run its course. The studio had more movies planned but with a younger, fresher cast, including the hot new actor on the block Kirby Glenn. Now, however, based on some focus group from hell, the studio wanted to bring back some of the original cast including Sam, Nate, Max, and Tyler.

"Not particularly," Nate replied, his voice soft. His wife Paige had just put their twin babies Andrew and Annabelle down for the night and he didn't want to wake them up. They'd been cranky because of the time change between London and New York where the couple was filming the adaptation of one of Paige's novels. "I don't even know how they would write my character since he died in the last movie, for chrissake."

Sam had forgotten about that. Nate's character had been killed and his death had spurred the entire team to go and get the bad guys.

"That would be a problem unless they want you to show up as the voice of a ghost or our conscience. Did they indicate how they would bring you back?"

"My agent thinks they're thinking a prequel. A movie that wouldn't be with the newer cast but one with just us old farts. Jesus, I'm too old to be jumping off buildings on a motorcycle. What about you?"

If Nate was too old, then Sam was ancient.

"I'm definitely too old."

Nate chuckled on the other end. "That's not what I was asking. Are you interested in doing another *Thunder* movie? Whether it's a prequel or a continuing part of a series?"

"No."

That was the short answer.

"My agent says they're going to throw a truckload of money at us."

That's what Sam's agent had said as well. Money up front and points on the back end too, plus producer credits.

"How much money do you need? Those kids already running up bills?" Sam teased his friend. "If I remember correctly, you're so frugal you should squeak when you walk. You must have saved a mint these last ten years."

"It's not the babies, they're great. But you know how expensive it is to produce your own movies? I'd rather be able to finance them myself than have to go begging for cash from investors. I think you would, too."

And that was the longer answer. Sam had all the money he would ever need. Personally.

Professionally was a whole other kettle of fish. More money equaled the ability to get projects green-lighted that right now were only a pipe dream. He could even have it written into his contract that if he did the *Thunder* movie the studio would finance his next indie project.

"It would have to be a pretty big money truck," Sam finally replied. "I'm kind of over my character and I think I've done all I can with him, frankly."

"The studio execs don't care about art. They only see dollar signs."

"I know and that explains the last two pictures, but another one? Are they planning to turn back the hands of time and make all of us look younger, too? We started making these films thirteen years ago and now they want to do a prequel. We're going to need a plastic surgeon on the set."

"No one with a knife is coming near me," Nate growled. "I'm with you about the movie but I'm not sure I can pass up the money, to be honest, although I hate to say it. That kind of payday would go a long way toward a second film for Paige's book series."

"What does Max and Tyler say?"

"You know Tyler," Nate laughed. "He said he was booked for the next two years but if they wanted to wait he'd think about it, which is basically his way of saying no. Max would rather have oral surgery with no anesthetic, or at least that's how he put it. You know he's getting ready to start rehearsals for a play in the West End, so his mind isn't on Hollywood."

"Well, I told my agent that I wasn't committing to anything until I saw a contract, a finished script, and the director attached to the project."

Actually, he'd said that he wanted directorial approval but Nate didn't need to know that. Hell, Nate may have said the same.

"With any luck this will all go away like so many ideas do," Nate said. "So when are we going to see you again? Don't you start filming in New York in a few weeks?"

"I do," Sam confirmed, stretching out on the sofa of his mother's living room. It was unnaturally quiet when Paula wasn't there. She'd gone shopping with Riley and Tara. "Looking forward to it. The script is good, the cast is good, and the director isn't an egotistical asshole. It might even be fun."

"Are ready to get back to work? It must be boring sitting on the beach all day long working on your tan."

Sam hadn't been to the beach since the night he and Riley had taken a walk after dinner. He'd made double-sure that they didn't share any more moonlit strolls together after that first one. She'd been far too beautiful and tempting for a mere mortal man such as himself. The sooner he exited town the better. He was enjoying her company far too much for comfort.

He didn't have what she needed. A woman like Riley needed a husband and a family. The kind of man that sat down to dinner every night and went to the hardware store on the weekends so he could tinker with some home improvement project. The kind of man that was there when the chips were down and the shit hit the fan. He wasn't that guy.

"I'm ready. Let's meet up when I get to New York."

Tomorrow night he'd escort Riley to the party and make sure that Chad and Monica knew that she wasn't heartbroken or sad. Then Sunday morning he'd pack his bags and hightail it out of town. He'd enjoyed every single second that he'd spent with her this week, but that was all he was going to get. If he was smart, he'd keep his distance tomorrow night, play it cool and not get too close.

But then no one had ever accused him of being all that intelligent.

CHAPTER
Eleven

RILEY LOOKED INCREDIBLY GORGEOUS. Sam had seen a multitude of beautiful women in his lifetime but not one could hold a candle to the woman standing in front of him in her living room. He'd been nervous tonight as he'd dressed in his tuxedo and tried to tame his hair that had grown a tad too long in the last few weeks, but when she'd opened the door he'd almost swallowed his own spit.

Her dark blonde hair was coiled up off of her neck and face, showing off creamy skin that didn't need all the layers of cosmetics he was so used to seeing. Her dress was white, cut high on her leg and low in the back, showing off every mouthwatering curve of her body and highlighting her golden Florida tan. Good old Chad was going to kick himself repeatedly in the ass for leaving this woman.

"Are you ready to go?"

Surprisingly, his voice sounded completely normal despite his body vibrating from the inside out. His reaction wasn't only to her physical beauty; it was also that he knew what lay beyond it. The intelligence, the kindness, even the silly sense of humor. She was fun, sweet, and the most normal woman he'd met in ages.

This is not real. You're just doing a favor.

Riley turned and checked her reflection in the foyer mirror. "I think so. This is about as good as it's going to get."

"You look beautiful," he assured her. "You're a knockout and every man at that party tonight is going to wish he was me."

Laughing, she gathered up her purse and dropped her house keys inside. "Of course, they're going to wish they were you. You're Sam Collins, movie star. It won't have anything to do with me."

"You don't give yourself enough credit."

"And you give yourself too little."

The drive to the party was short and Riley kept him entertained with stories of his mother with the children at school. When he pulled into the long driveway in front of the beachside mansion, he had a quick moment of doubt that he felt deep in the pit of his stomach. It felt all wrong to be pretending this way with Riley. She wasn't one of the actresses he usually worked with that knew the movie business rules inside and out. If he'd learned anything about her this week it was that she was an honest person and what they were about to do was far from those ideals.

"There's still time for me to turn around and go back," he heard himself say. "I know Paula pretty much cornered you into this."

"She cornered you, too," Riley reminded him. "We're here now so we might as well go in, but I doubt I'll want to stay long. I can't imagine that we're going to have much fun tonight."

Sam was determined that Riley was going to enjoy herself despite everything they had going against them. He just needed to know one more thing...

"How do you want to do this? Do you want to make sure that Chad and Monica see us together? Seek them out? Or just go in and have fun and if they see us, then fine?"

"The latter." Riley's tone was firm. "I'm not sure it's even all that smart to be here so I don't want to make a production of it. Other people can do that for us if they want to. Let's find your mother and Tara, have a few cocktails, and maybe even dance. Everyone will know that we're having a good time and then we can leave. How does that sound?"

"It sounds perfect to me, but I would have been good either way, although I have to tell you that my mom might have other ideas. She's the one that's pushing this, remember?"

As if they could forget that Paula had thrown Riley under the bus. And Sam along with her. Those tires hurt like a bitch.

"I think she knows she overstepped," Riley replied as they pulled up in front of the home, a large modern monstrosity that tonight was all lit up with people bustling around the entrance. "I don't think she'll be pushy tonight."

Riley's prediction turned out to be true. Paula was on her best behavior at the party, gushing about how they were the most handsome couple there and pulling them both in for big hugs. Riley nudged his elbow and nodded toward Paula who was flirting harmlessly with a young waiter bearing champagne flutes.

"You should ask your mother to dance. She'd love that."

"I haven't even danced with you yet."

Smiling, Riley's gaze settled on Paula. "I can wait. She's your mother and the real reason you've spent your vacation here. I think she's earned the first dance. I'll be fine here with Tara."

Tara had come as Paula's date since her husband, the firefighter, was on duty at the last minute.

"Mother, would you care to dance?"

Paula's face lit up and she clasped her hands together in delight. "Trip the light fantastic with my favorite son? I believe I will." But then her smile fell and she glanced nervously at Riley. "But shouldn't you dance with your date first?"

Riley nodded toward her best friend. "Tara and I want to catch up a little, so please go on with Sam."

The smile was back and Sam couldn't help the rush of love that ran through him when his mother looked this happy. She'd done so much for him, sacrificed so much, and he'd do anything to make sure that her golden years were as happy and peaceful as possible.

Which brought him around to what he and Riley were doing tonight. It wasn't real. Or was it? Truthfully, if he'd been invited to this party the one woman he might have asked to be his date was Riley. So maybe it wasn't so fake.

Forget it, man. Riley is off limits.

Paula was a hell of a dancer and Sam was only okay, but they managed to find an equilibrium that seemed to suit them both. In other words, she allowed him to lead. Up to a point.

"Riley looks lovely tonight, doesn't she?"

"She does. So do you, though. Is that a new dress?"

Chuckling, Paula shook her head. "I wore this to the premiere of one of your movies, but I can't remember which one. You bought it for me in Milan when we vacationed there."

He truly didn't remember, but then women's fashions weren't something he noticed often, or at all.

"You look beautiful in it."

"Don't look at me." His mother nudged his shoulder. "Look at Riley. She's the one you should be paying attention to. She's the perfect woman for you."

The idea of any one female being perfect for Sam amused him to no end. He didn't believe in soulmates, although a few of his friends might have come close.

"Are you playing matchmaker, Mom? Because you're wasting your time. I'm a lost cause and you of all people should know that."

Paula had been there when Sam's marriage had fallen apart and she knew that it was his fault. He'd failed as a husband.

"That was a long time ago, and you deserve happiness and love just as much as anyone does. You'd be a wonderful husband and fa-"

"Don't," Sam interrupted, his entire body stiffening. "I'd be a lousy husband. When I'm working on a movie the hours are terrible and we'd never see each other. When I'm not working on a film I'm traveling all over the world to promote the last one I made. None of this is conducive to making a marriage work and there are hundreds, if not thousands of broken Hollywood marriages as evidence."

"I just think–"

"Leave it, Mother," he said, his tone harsh. "Your baby boy is fine. The last thing I want to do is drag a nice girl like Riley into my life. She'd hate it there and she's already had enough heartache, don't you think?"

Paula was silent for a long time as they finished their dance, the notes of the song drifting away. He placed his hand on her shoulder as they walked back to the others, but at the edge of the dance floor she stopped, so he had to as well.

"I will leave it, but I want to say one thing first and you, young man, are going to shut up and listen to me. Do you understand?"

Paula had that tone that he knew so well from his youth. He'd better pipe down and let her have her say or he'd be scrubbing garbage cans as punishment.

"I'm listening."

Her eyes narrowed and her finger stabbed him right in the chest. "Don't take that tone with me. I changed your diapers. You might be a big movie star to everyone else but you're still Samuel Christopher to me."

And she'd never let him forget it.

Thank goodness.

"I know, Mom. I really am listening."

"That's better." Paula visibly relaxed but she still had a determined glint in her eye. "I'm worried about you, son. I'm not going to live forever–"

Panic and blind fear clutched at his chest, making it hard to breathe. "Wait, are you sick?"

Paula's gaze ran around the room and then she grabbed his arm, dragging him out to the patio that overlooked the intercoastal waterway. "I am not sick, but I am getting older."

He could finally inhale and exhale.

"So am I. We all are. Stop talking like you have one foot in the grave and another on a banana peel. You're in great health."

"And I intend to stay that way as long as I possibly can, but you're not getting any younger, either. You need someone to share your life with." She held up her hand when he would have spoken. "Don't tell me about all the friends you have or about all the women you date. It's not the same. You need a partner to share your life with."

His mother meant well. She truly did.

"You think Riley is the woman for me?"

"I think she could be if you gave her a chance."

The key phrase there was...*if he gave her a chance.* He wasn't planning to do that.

"Is that what this charade was all about? Not the engaged couple, but about fixing me up with a wife?"

Paula shook her head but she wasn't looking him in the eye, instead staring out over the water. "It was about how they hurt Riley."

"And you."

"And me," she conceded. "To be honest, in the beginning I wasn't thinking of you and Riley as a couple, but after what I've seen this week I think you would be a fool to let her go. You two are perfect for one another."

This week. It had been wonderful. Riley was an amazing woman and if he were a different person with a different life he might have stayed and tried to make their relationship have a future. But he was who he was.

"Riley is terrific but it's just not going to happen, Mom."

His mother finally turned to him, her gaze seeing far too much. As always. She'd never bought any of his bullshit when he was younger, and he was a terrible actor when it came to lying to her.

I'm not really lying. I like Riley. I'm attracted to Riley. But I'm leaving tomorrow.

"You'll miss her when you're gone."

He couldn't deny that he would, but he intended to stay so busy he wouldn't have much of a chance.

"You might be right, but it still isn't going to happen. I'm leaving tomorrow and going back to my life. Believe me when I say it, you'll thank me later when Riley finds a nice man and settles down with him. You can still have brunch with her on Sundays and go shopping, and of course see her at school."

Sam didn't much like thinking about that though. He couldn't think of one person who was good enough for her. He sure as hell wasn't.

Paula's eyes glittered with unshed tears. "I'm sad when I think about your life. I want so much for you but then I see you taking opportunities and just throwing them away. You act as if women like Riley will come into your life every day or whenever you want them to. And even more frustrating is that you act like you have everything you could ever want to make you happy. You have fame and fortune but frankly, son, I've never once seen that make anyone truly happy. This is your second chance and you're going to turn and walk away from it. Stay a little while longer. Spend some time with Riley and see what might happen. No pretending, for real this time."

His second chance. Did men like him get second chances? Certainly they did, but the real question was did he deserve it? His ex-wife had been very clear as to who was at fault when she'd left him and filed for divorce.

"I can't stay," he replied, wanting to put an end to this uncomfortable conversation. Paula only wanted what she thought would make him happy, and if he were brutally honest with himself, Riley was the kind of woman that could do that. But he wasn't the type of man who could settle down. "I know what I am, Mom. I'd hurt her and that's something I don't want to do. We should go back inside. They're probably wondering what happened to us."

Just tonight. That's all that was left. He'd give Riley a wonderful evening and then he'd go. No looking back. No regrets.

CHAPTER
Twelve

THE CHAMPAGNE BUBBLES tickled Riley's nose but the cool golden liquid slid smoothly down her parched throat. She'd danced a few songs with Sam but it wasn't the tempo that had her out of breath. He'd had her laughing so hard with his silly stories about some of the movie sets he'd been on in his career. Although the hours sounded brutal, it appeared that the actors and crew could get goofy from time to time to break the monotony and liven things up.

"I'm not sure I believe you," Riley said, holding her side where it ached from laughing. He'd told a particularly funny story about Tyler Gaylord and Nate Mason dressing up for Halloween. "That's pretty out there."

And nothing that she'd ever read in *People* magazine.

Sam held up his right hand. "I swear it happened. There are pictures somewhere, although I don't have them. Max does, though. I can call him and he can send them to me." Glancing at his watch, he winced and shook his head.

"On the other hand, it's around two in the morning in London. He might not appreciate that."

"I'll try to believe you without the evidence, but let's just say that I'm on the fence about it."

A waiter stopped with a tray of champagne flutes.

Sam reached for a glass. "Another?"

Riley was half done with her drink, but she'd already had a couple before. She'd spaced them out, drank some water in between, and eaten from the buffet so another wouldn't make her tipsy, but she definitely wanted to pace herself. Getting drunk at her ex's engagement party wasn't a smart thing to do.

"Not right now." She nodded towards the staircase. "I think I'll go powder my nose if you don't mind."

"I'll try to find Tara and my mother. Last time I saw them they were debating fiscal policy with some poor bastard. When my mother gets going on politics everybody needs to look out."

"Tara knows to change the subject when it gets too heated. How about we meet by the patio doors in about ten minutes?"

"Perfect, but take your time."

Riley climbed the large, curving staircase to the second floor and slipped into the hall bathroom to freshen up. She'd been in this house a few times when she was dating Chad and had never quite felt at home. The furnishings, while opulent, seemed cold and uninviting. There only appeared to be one rule when they had decorated this house - if it didn't have a shine then it had to be covered in expensive fabric. Mostly velvet but there was some brocade as well. It gave the home a stuffy, formal feeling, the kind that made a person afraid to touch anything.

Before exiting the bathroom, she swiped on a fresh layer of lipstick and pushed a few stray strands of hair out of her face. She didn't look too bad tonight. There had been appreciation in Sam's eyes when he'd picked her up and it had sent tingles all the way down to her toes as if she was a giddy teenage girl going to the prom. Tonight was a fantasy and she'd decided to let herself relax and enjoy it.

The blatant jealous stares from other women, the more surreptitious glances from envious men. Women wanted Sam and men wanted to be him. Certainly not because he was with her tonight but because of what he was. Or maybe what he represented.

Financial success and freedom. Glamour. The pinnacle of one's chosen career. Public adoration. Rubbing elbows with the beautiful people, especially women. Lots and lots of women. Sam had dated his share too over the years. She'd seen his picture on tabloids and in the magazines at the supermarket checkout stand. All of them tall, slender, gorgeous, and not anything like her at all.

But he was hers tonight. In front of all of these people, she didn't have to pretend that she wasn't attracted to him. They expected her to be. It was only in private that she had to act as if he wasn't funny, smart, and gorgeous. Tonight was - in a way - a relief.

She could pretend that when he took her hand it was because he wanted to. Or that when he danced a little too close it was because he wanted more, much more, later. Sam Collins was a great actor, so she'd be a fool to believe that he was enamored with her.

But a girl could play make believe. Just for one night.

She was so lost in her daydreams that she wasn't looking where she was going. Before she could move out of the way, she'd run headlong into a man in a tuxedo. She started to apologize but the words died on her tongue when she looked up into the male's face.

Chad.

"Are you okay?" he asked, his forehead furrowed. "You looked completely lost in thought."

I was thinking about Sam. And the moonlight.

"I guess I was. You know how busy school gets after Spring Break is over."

As excuses go it was lame, but Chad seemed to buy it.

"Your dedication is how all teachers should be."

Most of them were, although she had to remind herself that he had Monica as his main example.

Time to get out of here.

"That's very nice of you to say. Congratulations on your engagement, Chad. I hope that you and Monica will have a long happy life together."

Moving to the right so she could walk around him, she was once again blocked when he did the same, blocking her escape–

No, make that blocking my path. I'm not escaping.

"Can we talk for just a minute?" There was a pleading tone in Chad's voice that she hadn't heard before. "There's something I need to say to you."

There was nothing that he had to say that she wanted to hear. That champagne she'd drank earlier suddenly didn't feel all that terrific in her tummy. Of all the things she'd hoped for, she'd wanted to keep her distance from Chad.

"I don't think that's a good idea. Sam is waiting for me downstairs."

There. Throw her new man in Chad's face. Her *fake* new man but the details weren't important at the moment.

"Just a minute. I won't keep you long, I promise. It's important, Riley."

All that meant was that it was important to *him*, but she'd been brought up to be polite no matter what. Especially in a public venue like this one.

"Fine. What did you want to say?"

His gaze darted around at the few people who were upstairs to use the facilities. Apparently this conversation wasn't one that could be had with an audience.

"Let's step in here," he said, wrapping a hand around her upper arm. She quickly shook him off but did follow him into what appeared to be a television room with a large screen at one end and comfortable brown leather recliners in two rows.

"Talk," she said, a trifle impatiently, her fingers clutching the tiny purse as if it was a lifeline. This had *bad idea* written all over it. "People are waiting for me."

Shoving his hands in his trouser pockets, Chad's gaze fell to the tips of his shoes. "I guess I just wanted to say that I'm sorry for what I did. I realized the other day that I never had apologized and I owed you that. I should have been up front about Monica but I took the coward's way out and just pretended nothing was going on."

Riley's irritation turned to surprise. She hadn't expected an apology. He was correct in saying he never had before so she hadn't thought to receive one at this late date. Still, it was an apology. Better late than never.

"Thank you, I appreciate your apology." But she couldn't resist a small dig. She was only human, after all. "I deserved better from you."

His head jerked up and his cheeks had turned bright red. "You did and I'm sorry. It was just..."

His voice trailed away and that impatience and irritation were back. He was the one that had wanted to talk.

"It was just what?" she prompted, her toe tapping on the lush carpet. "You were just a douchebag?"

His eyes widened and then he smiled, chuckling a little. "You've changed. You wouldn't have said that before."

She shook her head sadly. "You never knew me at all, did you? You only saw what you wanted to see."

He was doing the same with Monica.

"It was just...Monica was so...sensual. So sexy and adventurous. She made me feel like...well...in a way I'd never felt before."

Riley rubbed at her temple and turned toward the door. "I don't think this is anything I want to discuss."

"Wait," Chad pleaded, throwing his hands up. "I'm just trying to explain."

She shot him a look that had him taking a step back. "By telling me how I'm lacking? Why on earth would you think that's a good idea? You need to take a close look at your people skills."

"You weren't lacking," he quickly denied. "But I think we both know that you weren't all that into me...not like Monica is. She let me know from day one that she wanted me and only me. I never got that feeling from you."

She'd never had that feeling either from him, but she hadn't cared. She'd never been convinced that Chad was the man for her.

Pot, this is kettle...

But she'd been nice for too long. She wasn't going to let him act like what he did was okay.

"I'm sorry your delicate ego was so bruised. That's still a pathetic excuse for cheating on me."

Looking at Chad now, Riley couldn't see one quality that had attracted her all those months ago. If she'd met him tonight she would have been less than interested.

He nodded in agreement. "No argument there. I shouldn't have done it and I am sorry. But I guess I under-stand now. I mean...you sure as hell never looked at me the way you do Sam Collins. And he looks at you the same way. I wasn't the one and he is. He's a lucky guy to have a woman like you."

Except that she wasn't acting and Sam was.

"I don't know if he's...the one. It's early yet."

She couldn't tell him that she and Sam were breaking up in the morning.

"From what I can see, you two have what it takes. I'm really happy for you, Riley. Seriously. Sam seems like a good guy. I just hope he treats you right."

Somehow she managed to speak despite the lump that clogged her throat.

"Thank you. I need to get downstairs before they start looking for me."

This time Chad didn't stop her when she turned on her heel to leave. Her footsteps made no sound on the thick carpet as she descended the stairs, her gaze scanning the room for Sam. She found him exactly where he'd said he would be, smiling and waiting for her, Tara and Paula with him.

He'd done what he'd said he would do. So many men didn't. It only made this harder. Her attraction for him had grown to such proportions she didn't know how she was supposed to pretend that she didn't want to kiss him.

Just a kiss. She'd studied his lips when he wasn't watching, fascinated with their shape when he spoke. She'd never found a man's mouth as captivating as she did his but surely that couldn't survive an actual kiss.

It was the unknown that was alluring.

CHAPTER
Thirteen

THERE WAS a determined glint in Riley's eye when she returned from the ladies' room. Their gazes met and held as she weaved through the crush of bodies in the large living room that opened on to the circular patio. Stopping right in front of him, she gave Tara and his mother a quick smile before speaking.

"I think I'm ready to go now. How about you?"

"So soon," Paula protested. "You and Sam have only had a few dances together."

They'd had five, actually. Five slow dances - Sam didn't do fast - where their bodies had been way too close for comfort.

"I think we've done what we set out to do," Riley replied, glancing over her shoulder to the staircase she'd just descended. "Chad caught me when I was upstairs and he wanted to talk. I think I'm done with this party."

A muscle worked in Sam's jaw at the thought of Chad trying to make a move on his—no, Riley wasn't Sam's - on his date. This might not be a real romance, but she was his real date.

"What did he say?"

The question came out more harshly than Sam had intended but no one seemed to notice his agitation, which was a testament to his acting skills.

To that movie critic in the Times, *screw you.*

"He wanted to apologize."

Tara's laughter turned into an awkward cough. "Took him long enough. I hope it was a good one."

Riley shrugged. "It was okay, but I think I've had enough of this party. I did call him a douchebag, though."

"Good for you," Paula cheered. "But you don't have to leave. He'll probably stay away from you the rest of the evening."

Maybe, unless the asshole thought all was forgiven and they were good friends now.

Sam still wanted to punch Chad. A whole bunch.

"True, but what if Monica doesn't? I don't think I could take the Chad and Monica Apology Tour. As I told her the last time I talked to her, I don't care that they're together. I just don't want to be dragged into their relationship if at all possible."

"Sure, we can leave." Sam leaned down and placed a kiss on Paula's cheek. "I'll see you in the morning. Are you staying much longer?"

Tara and Paula exchanged a glance and then his mother shook her head. "I wanted to talk to Betty about the summer programs for the kids, but then after that I think we'll go."

Riley hugged her friends and said something to his

mother, but she spoke too softly to be heard. The valet didn't take long to retrieve Sam's rental and they were driving away from the mansion within fifteen minutes.

"Do you mind if I roll down the window? It's such a nice evening," Riley asked as the lights of the house faded in the rearview mirror.

"Sure, go ahead."

It was warm but not too humid. The spring night air smelled of lilacs and hibiscus mixed with salt, so different from Beverly Hills, New York City, or London. This sleepy little town, however, had a charm all its own. He'd be back to visit his mother, but he didn't know when. Riley was here and that complicated the matter. He'd want to see her, but it wouldn't be a good idea. By the time he returned she would have another man and be happily in a relationship, shopping at Ikea and picking up muffins for Sunday brunch.

Sam didn't even like muffins and he'd never been inside an Ikea. His assistant making the trip and picking up a shelving unit didn't count.

The drive was much too short and before he knew it they were pulling up in front of her condo. The evening had come to an end, and tomorrow he would board an airplane and go back to his life.

"It's still early. Do you want to come in for a little while?"

CHAPTER
Fourteen

RILEY SHOULDN'T HAVE ASKED Sam to come in, but the words had popped out of her mouth before her brain had engaged fully. This was a dangerous move. There had been a fleeting thought about kissing Sam but now that he was actually inside of her home, looking sexy and gorgeous, her mind had drifted to far more carnal pursuits than a simple kiss.

I'm only human.

It was probably a good thing that Sam was leaving in the morning because if he stayed around much longer she was going to fall head over heels in love with him. He had so much going for him other than his incredible good looks. He was funny, intelligent, kind, and humble.

He was the kind of man she'd always wanted.

Too bad, so sad. You can't have him.

Yes, I can. Just for tonight, though.

You won't be satisfied with one night.

I can be. I can do this and let him walk away in the morning.

You're deluding yourself. Don't cry to me later.

It was like having an angel on one shoulder and a devil on the other. Who was she going to listen to?

"Riley?"

Sam's voice brought her out of her mini-trance and back to her kitchen where she was pouring two glasses of wine. She whirled around, a glass in each hand and a big smile on her face. Everything was fine. She was completely okay and normal.

"Sorry, I just have a lot on my mind. So much going on next week at school. We're studying the American Revolution and I was thinking about ways to make it more exciting for the children."

And...she was babbling. She had a tendency to over explain when she was nervous.

Shut up.

"Maybe you could do a play?" Sam suggested, accepting the wine glass. "Or is that the actor in me talking?"

Wrangling twenty-four five-year-olds for a production starring the Founding Fathers sounded like a slice of hell. Add in interfering parents and it was a recipe for disaster. She'd learned her first year of teaching that a play was a bad idea.

"That's something to think about."

Riley took a gulp of her wine, hoping it would calm her nerves. Her pulse was racing and sweat was beginning to pool on the back of her neck. She wasn't playing it off well, though, because Sam was giving her a strange look.

"Riley? Are you okay?"

No, I feel like I could jump out of my skin. I don't think that's normal.

"I'm nervous."

Blurt.

"Nervous," Sam repeated, his expression neutral. "How come?"

Don't speak. Don't speak.

"Because you're here."

I am so screwed.

He set his glass down on the kitchen counter and managed not to look offended.

"Do you want me to leave?"

"No."

His smiled widened, showing off those amazing dimples in his cheeks. "Do you want me to stay then?"

More than I'm willing to admit out loud.

She nodded and took another drink of her wine. It wasn't helping.

Sam's gaze ran over the room, seeking something. "Do you have a radio or a stereo?"

Was there a ballgame on? Was she so boring he needed some entertainment? When he was invited into a woman's house he probably didn't spend time chatting and drinking wine.

"In the living room. Why?"

He turned and walked out of the kitchen with her trailing behind him. "You were really relaxed tonight at the party and there was music and dancing. How about we try that again?"

Dancing. With Sam. It had been nice and an activity she wouldn't mind repeating. She handed him her phone and let him scroll through her eclectic music collection. She liked a little rock, a little country, some oldies, and when she was in just the right mood, some classical.

Billy Vera and the Beaters came over the small but surprisingly loud speakers. *At This Moment* was one of her favorite songs and it was perfect to slow dance to. A romantic slow dance, that is. There was no mistaking the sultry sway of the music or the mournful lyrics of a love lost. His arms reached for her and she moved unresistingly close to him, their bodies brushing with each beat of the song.

It was the perfect storm of seduction. Dim lights. Soft music. A glass of wine. Riley closed her eyes and let her other senses come alive. The way his hard body felt under her touch. The smell of his skin when she buried her face into his chest. The thud of his heart under her ear, strong and steady. Just like Sam.

His hands burned through the silky material of her dress all the way to the sensitive flesh underneath. His lips were nestled against her temple, his breath soft and warm against her cheek. For this one moment, there was only the two of them. The outside world and all of its demands didn't exist. Sam didn't have to leave in the morning and there was no good reason for them not to take this to its inevitable conclusion.

They floated like that on a cloud of delusion, letting the song wash over them like the tide against the sand. Reasons. All the reasons she shouldn't do this dissolved away leaving her with one plain truth. She wanted Sam, and she hadn't wanted any man like this. Ever.

Would it be so terrible if he stayed? She'd have this

night to always remember. She could tuck it away and look back on it in the years to come. It would be just for her and no one could take it away.

The song couldn't last forever, though, and the final notes hung in the air as they separated slightly. Cool air couldn't soothe her fevered skin, however. On fire from the inside out at Sam's mere touch, her body blotted out all of the objections that whirled though her head. For once, she was going to take something just for herself. She wasn't going to be the designated adult.

She gazed up at him, taking in every detail of his face and committing it to memory. The slightly stubbled jaw. The blue of his eyes. The lines that fanned out when he smiled.

I'm not in love. But I could be.

It was a scary thought. He wasn't for her and never would be. She might be heading for heartbreak but right now her brain simply wasn't working. Or maybe it didn't care.

"Sam, will you stay the night?"

———

Sam couldn't have heard Riley correctly. It was clearly wishful thinking that made him hear her ask if he wanted to spend the night.

Because he did. So fucking much. He'd been thinking about it for far too long and holding himself in check was becoming increasingly difficult with every passing hour and day.

The look on her face, however, told a different story.

She was nervous but hopeful. Shy but expectant. In other words, she'd really said it. All he had to do was say yes.

Hold on a minute.

His better angels kept him on a firm rein. He liked Riley, cared about her, and he didn't want there to be any confusion come tomorrow morning. He still had to leave even if he didn't want to. He'd signed contracts, made commitments, and people's livelihoods depended on him. He couldn't suddenly flake out and decide to take a beach vacation because of a beautiful woman.

And he couldn't take advantage of Riley.

"I want to," he said and her eyes lit up. "But we need to talk first."

That light dimmed slightly but she nodded and stepped back, making him want to pull her into his arms. He didn't, though, taking a step backward himself. It would be easier to be practical with a little distance between them.

"Okay..."

Her brows were pinched together in worry as if she truly thought he might say no. Had she missed all the signs of his desire? To be fair, he'd missed hers. He'd never thought she'd come right out and invite him to stay. It was sexy, her courage in going after what she wanted, and it only made her even more attractive.

"I want to make love to you, Riley. More than I have words to express. Way more." He groaned as a small smile began to bloom on her face. "I just want to make sure that we're on the same page here."

Her smile wobbled slightly but she nodded in affirmation. "I know it's just for this one night. I know that you're leaving tomorrow."

His body was screaming to take her at her word, but his brain was still in charge. Barely.

"Do you?" He needed to make sure she understood. He would be on a plane tomorrow morning no matter what. "I'm not in a position to make any commitments, honey. Tonight is all there is. Can you be okay with that? I don't want you to regret this later."

"I won't regret it."

He should walk away. Turn and run out of the front door. Staying would complicate his life. Riley was friends with his mother and he'd be down to visit from time to time. They might run into each other, although they hadn't until this trip. Still...it made things more complex. Any time he involved his body and emotions he usually regretted it. One or the other was fine, but this was both. Not a good combination.

But damned if he could leave. He wanted her and by God he was going to have her. If they only had one night, then he'd make sure it was one they'd both remember for the rest of their lives.

"Then yes, I want to stay."

CHAPTER
Fifteen

HIS HANDS and mouth were everywhere all at once. Somehow they'd moved into the bedroom, their anxious hands pulling and tugging at their clothes until they were just pools on the floor. Sinful scenarios ran through Riley's mind and she wanted to enact them all with this man but there would only be tonight. She had to pick and choose. The choices were mind-boggling, but the first thing she wanted to do was explore the fine male form she'd been admiring for a week.

Pushing him back onto the mattress, Riley straddled his waist as she pressed her lips to every inch of exposed flesh that she could reach. Every groan and moan she managed to elicit only made her own arousal climb higher. She ran her tongue down his torso and over his ridged abs, leaving a wet trail in her wake. His grip on her hair tightened, but unlike most men he didn't push her head lower or try to take control, seemingly content to let her explore. A task she was happy to continue.

Riley swirled her tongue in his bellybutton, drawing a growl of frustration from his throat but she ignored it, feeling heady with her success so far. She placed open-mouthed kisses on his chest and neck before finally giving his earlobe a gentle tug with her teeth.

It was as if she'd flipped a switch. One minute she was on top and then next he'd rolled her over onto her back, his large powerful frame hovering above her. He was smiling, a sort of evil smile, as his gaze raked her naked form from head to toe. She felt a blush crawl of her skin at the smoldering desire he didn't bother to hide. He looked a little like a tiger and she was a tasty snack. But this prey had no intention of running.

"Did you think I was going to let you stay up there and play all night?" he asked with a chuckle, his voice deep and gravelly. It sent shivers from her toes all the way to her head. "Looks like I'm in control now."

He was, and she didn't mind a bit because if being in charge meant that he used his fingers to play with her already hard nipples or his tongue to draw a playful path on the sensitive part of her neck she certainly wasn't going to complain.

The bedroom temperature soared and a fine sheen of sweat covered their bodies as his mouth nipped and kissed his way down her belly, but he didn't stop there. Her heart stuttered in her chest and she sucked oxygen into her aching lungs as his tongue meandered over to her hip before brushing against her inner thigh. His breath was warm against her drenched slit and she cried out when his finger ran up and down, parting her folds before pressing slowly inside of her, his thumb lightly skittering over her clit. She mewled, wanting more but not able to form the words to ask for it.

"Easy, honey. We've got all night."

Her body bowed off the mattress and white-hot flames licked at her flesh, but Sam appeared determined to take his time. A second finger was eased inside of her and those clever digits easily found her sweet spot, rubbing until she thought she might go mad with pleasure. Tossing her head back and forth, she chanted his name over and over, her arousal building with every caress and stroke of his fingers.

Panting, her hands scrambled for purchase, crumpling the sheets in her tight fists as he played her body perfectly. Blood roared in her ears when he bent his head and swiped his tongue against the swollen button before taking it in his mouth and sucking gently. That was all it took to send her into the heavens. Fireworks exploded behind her eyes and she twirled among the stars until it was time to come back to earth.

Riley slowly opened her eyes to find Sam rummaging through his pants pocket and pulling out his wallet. Confused at first, it made sense when he pulled out a condom and held it up triumphantly, a silly grin on his face.

"Someone was optimistic this evening," she couldn't help but observe, although she was glad one of them had thought of it. She had condoms somewhere in the bathroom, but she wasn't sure where they'd migrated. "Did you bring just the one?"

She'd dig for those condoms if she had to. There were only a few places they could be.

"I've got one more in there," he said, placing the package between his teeth to rip it open. If he wasn't careful he'd put a tear in the condom. "I'm not as young as I used to be."

Giggling, she reached out to help him roll the condom over his impressive erection, probably making it more difficult than it should have been. But it had been fun and if it was possible he was even harder and larger than before. Her fingers traced a vein on the base of his cock and then caressed his balls, drawing a moan and a shudder from him. They were already drawn tight to his body, a testament to how aroused he was.

"I promise you can play as much as you want afterward," he vowed, tossing the outer package away and bracing his hands on either side of her body. "But I've waited so long for this I can't delay anymore. Are you ready for me, babe?"

A million times yes. He pressed her thighs wider and the hard tip of his cock nudged against her entrance. Her fingers curled into his biceps as he pushed relentlessly forward. He wasn't small and it had been awhile, but she was so wet he glided in to the hilt without much fuss.

This feels amazing. So good. So incredible.

Her walls gripped him tightly as he began to move, stoking the simmering fire in her abdomen and sending shock waves of pleasure all the way to her toes with every stroke. To her surprise, she was climbing toward release again, another explosion shimmering just out of her reach.

Wrapping her legs around his lean waist, she canted her hips just as Sam changed the angle of his thrusts. Heaven. Perfect.

Her hiss of pleasure must have told him he'd struck gold because he buried his face in her neck and didn't so much as pause, thrusting hard and aiming at that spot deep inside of her that was threatening to send her into outer space like a rocket. Her breathing ragged, she tried to hold off and make the pleasure last longer, but it was simply too strong. It turned her inside out and sideways, spinning out of control into the beckoning clouds.

His release came right after and she watched fascinated as he threw his head back, his male beauty never more potent than at this moment. He was a fierce conquering warrior, but he was also supremely exposed, his emotions laid bare for her perusal. She wanted to lock onto this moment and freeze time there, hold it for a little longer to enjoy, but that's not how life worked. Soon enough, he was groaning her name and slumping on top of her, their hearts pounding in perfect tempo. His weight was delicious and she savored the feeling, running her hands up and down his damp spine and delighting in the afterglow of their lovemaking.

Eventually he rolled onto his back, taking her with him so she was tucked into his side but sort of sprawled on top of him as well. Her fingernail traced whirly patterns on his chest as their breathing returned to somewhat of a more normal pattern. She was afraid to speak in case she broke the spell. If she said something would he think it was time to leave? She wasn't ready for that. Not yet.

"Do you want some water or something?"

Little Miss Awkward. She never knew what to say after the first time with a man. Not that there had been tons of them but there'd been enough to know that she wasn't good at this.

"I don't ever want to move from this place."

He was teasing but she liked the sound of it.

"You don't have to move. I can go get it for you."

His arm tightened around her waist.

"I don't want you to move either."

Frankly, neither did she.

"Then what do you want to do?"

Somehow, he'd insinuated himself between her legs and turned her onto her back. He was wearing that evil grin again. She was beginning to really like that smile. A lot.

"I want to do it again."

What a fantastic and amazing coincidence. So did she.

———

The sun wasn't even up the next morning when Sam opened his eyes. For a few seconds he wasn't sure where he was but then all the memories of last night came flooding back to him, bringing a smile to his face. He'd slept with many women in his lifetime, but he'd surely remember Riley on his deathbed. For someone outwardly appeared to be quite conservative - a kindergarten teacher, after all - she'd been rather wild and wanton between the sheets. Vocal too, just how he liked it.

The focus of his thoughts was sleeping peacefully next to him, her head pillowed on his shoulder and her leg casually tossed over him. His fingers trailed lightly over her soft skin and delved into the silken strands of her hair that smelled a little like vanilla. She stirred but didn't waken, luckily. He needed a few minutes more to simply lie here and enjoy the warm closeness. The feel of her skin touching his and the weight of a sexy and beautiful woman against his body. Even after their lovemaking last night, he hungered for her again this morning, his body hard and ready. That part of his anatomy was destined to be disappointed.

He also needed the time to figure out how to make a graceful exit. He didn't have anything planned as to what to say or do, but sneaking out while she was still asleep was out of the question. They'd been honest and upfront with each other last night. He wouldn't be disrespectful in the light of day.

They'd both known that he couldn't stay.

A sigh escaped from Riley's lips, the puff of warm air sliding over his chest, and his arms tightened instinctively, pulling her a few centimeters closer.

He was leaving in a few hours but that didn't mean that he could never talk to her again. They could stay in touch. Between texts, email, and Skype they could keep up with each other's lives without too much hassle. She would have time off this summer, too. She could fly out to where he was on location and visit him. Then maybe in the fall he could come here for a few days.

Stop. Right now.

Riley was a good woman who had generously allowed him into her life. She didn't do it so he could fuck it up with some half-assed relationship that when he played it back in his head sounded more like a booty call than dating. It sure as hell wasn't in the least romantic. It might start out sounding that way - making space for each other in their hectic lives - but Sam had a nasty feeling that the result wouldn't be nearly as poetic. A "sometimes" relationship where his career drove all the decisions. It wasn't a good deal for Riley and he wasn't going to be the asshole that offered it to her.

Riley would move on and forget about him soon enough. If he was a decent human being he'd want her to find a nice guy, settle down, and have a passel of kids. Hell, maybe they'd name the first one Samuel. Or not.

Next to him Riley stretched and fidgeted, softly groaning as her lids fluttered open. Levering up from the mattress, she lifted her arms over her head, the sheet pooling around her waist, baring her gorgeous body. It was all for the best though that the room was only dimly lit with the weak sunlight just beginning to filter through the curtains. He didn't need the temptation this morning.

Finally she leaned over him and flicked on the bedside lamp. "Hi."

"Hi."

There was a pink tinge to her cheeks and she seemed to be a little shy despite all the debauched things they'd done to each other last night. Or maybe she was embarrassed because of it.

"Did you sleep okay?"

He nodded, his fingers strumming the silky skin of her lower back. "I did. How about you?"

"Good." She nodded toward the bedroom door. "Why don't I make you some breakfast so you don't get on the plane hungry?"

Surprisingly he wasn't in the mood for food, his appetite only for her. But that wasn't going to happen. He didn't have much time and if he made love to her again he'd do something stupid like promise to call.

When he knew good and well that he wasn't going to do any such thing.

CHAPTER
Sixteen

RILEY WAITED for Sam's answer, kind of hoping he'd say yes so she'd get to spend more time with him but also hoping that he'd say no and he'd go. His very nearness was disturbing her equilibrium and it might be better for her if he simply left.

It wasn't a surprise that he had a flight out this morning. She'd known it all week and they'd talked about it last night. She was fine with it...really. She'd get over him eventually, but she hadn't realized it was going to feel this rotten. That she hadn't expected.

It was probably just the sex, anyway. There weren't enough superlatives to describe last night, so of course she was going to be a little sad when he left. No more great sex, right? It didn't have anything to do with him as a person. She barely knew him.

Except that she had spent a great deal of time with him and he seemed like a good person. Not movie star-ish at all. Really down to earth and normal. She'd expected an arrogant asshole and had instead found a hard-working man trying to do the best he could.

But then he was one of the most famous actors on earth so maybe it was all make-believe. It would make it easier if she could convince herself that the whole thing was simply Sam's acting skills. Like he didn't really care about her as a person and he'd just used her for sex.

Although he could get sex from many willing women, several of whom had been at the party last night.

"I'm afraid I can't," he replied, swinging his legs off the bed and grabbing his tuxedo trousers. "I still need to go back to Mom's to shower and pack. The car picks me up in a few hours."

She was relieved and disappointed.

"Don't you have to take your rental back?"

"The company will have someone pick it up."

That didn't make any sense. Why not drop it at the airport since that's where he was going anyway?

Movie star stuff. He didn't have to return his own rental, make sure the tank was filled and so on.

His phone chimed and he fumbled in the pocket of his jacket to answer it while Riley shrugged into her robe and tightly belted it around her waist. She suddenly felt very naked. Too naked. He must have felt it too because he was dressing quickly, while moving the cell phone from hand to hand while he talked.

"Sure, Bobby. I'm flying into New York today." He zipped up his trousers and began working on the shirt studs. "Don't worry, unless the flight is late I'll meet you at three at Le Cirque."

Riley had a vague notion what Le Cirque was. She was

pretty sure she'd heard it mentioned on television. It sounded expensive and exclusive. A place that kindergarten teachers rarely hung out unless they were waitressing as a second job.

Sam didn't put on the tuxedo jacket, simply draping it over his left arm while he held the phone in his right. "I know how to handle his type. Make a fuss over his last film and admire his trophy wife. We'll have the financing for the project by the time the waiter delivers the check."

Already Sam was in his regular world, barely even aware that he was standing in her bedroom in some podunk beach town in Florida. She could almost feel him pushing toward the front door, anxious to get back to work and to his life.

So different from her own. Last night had been a fun fantasy but she'd be foolish to think it was anything more. He wasn't going to miss her when he left or think about her when he was supposed to be doing other things. He wasn't going to call her in the middle of the night because he forgot what time zone he was in. He definitely wasn't going to show up at her school with flowers and sweep her off her feet because he couldn't get her off of his mind.

She couldn't say he hadn't been honest, though. He'd warned her and she'd said she didn't care. She wasn't in love with him, either. And she wasn't. But she did like him and if he was anyone else...

He seemed to realize she was standing there because he straightened and gave her a crooked smile, holding up one finger.

"Listen, I need to get off the phone so I can get ready for

the limo. I'll call you from JFK when we touch down. Yeah, thanks, Bobby. I'll see you soon."

Sam hung up and tucked the phone in his pocket. "Sorry about that. I guess my vacation is officially over."

"They didn't give you much respite." She glanced at the clock. "The sun is just coming up now. Your friend Bobby must be an early riser."

"He's my publicist and I swear he never sleeps. No matter what time of the day or night I've talked to him he sounds like he's had his coffee and eggs. He might be immortal or a vampire."

Sam was trying to make a joke to lighten the atmosphere, so she laughed even though it wasn't all that funny.

"He sounds like an interesting person."

"He is," Sam assured her, his gaze coming to rest where she stood across the room. He seemed stiff and not nearly as relaxed as he'd been all week. "I guess I need to be going."

This was awkward. So incredibly awkward. Last night she hadn't been thinking about the inevitable goodbye. Should they kiss? Hug? Riley had never had a one-night stand so she wasn't sure what the rules were.

Not sure what to say, she led the way out of her bedroom and to the front door. He slipped into his shoes and palmed his car keys as they stood there, each one waiting - or hoping - for the other to say something and break this painful tension.

"I hope you have a safe flight and there aren't any delays."

A neutral statement.

"I hope so, too."

It was like a slow torture. Neither of them knew what to say, but there was one thing she needed to do.

"Riley–"

"Sam–"

They'd both spoken at the same time, which was funny as neither one of them had been too keen on speaking only moments ago.

"Ladies first," Sam said with a smile.

Taking a deep breath, Riley could only smile back. The tension had lessened enough that it was easier to breathe.

"I just wanted to say thank you for what you–"

"No, you don't have to do that." Sam was shaking his head and waving away her words. "I don't need a thank you for doing the right thing. I'm just glad I could help. It was my pleasure, Riley. You made this vaca-tion...special."

Those blue eyes were dark with emotion and that last word had come out reluctantly, as if he hadn't wanted to admit it. He was probably thinking that she might push for more. He could relax because she wasn't going to do that and embarrass them both.

"Not everyone would have done it," she pointed out. "But I am grateful."

Reaching for the phone in his pocket, Sam checked the display, probably watching the time. There was a ticking clock on their relationship, after all.

"Actually, I have a favor to ask of you, Riley. Will you look after my mom? Just keep an eye on her, that's all I ask. I worry about her when I'm halfway around the world working and don't get to talk to her much."

That was an easy promise to make, and one she did happily.

"I will," she promised. "Paula is one of my best friends and I love her very much. We'll keep her busy, how does that sound?"

"Fantastic. I appreciate it more than you know. Having met you and Tara, I can sleep a little easier knowing that Mom has a group of loyal friends around her when I can't be."

Silence again. They'd run out of things to say so it must be time for Sam to go. She reached for the doorknob but his hand was there first, his touch shocking her as a bolt of lightning ran up her arm.

Physical attraction still there? Check.

"Riley." Her name came out softly, almost like a sigh. "I have to go."

"I know. We talked about this last night and it's okay. I'm not going to cry or beg you to stay. We both knew it was a one-time thing."

"It doesn't mean it's easy to leave this morning." His fingers came up under her chin so that she had to look into his eyes. "If I were a different kind of guy...fuck...I never wanted to hurt you–"

She pressed her fingers to his lips to stop his flood of words. "You haven't hurt me. I'm not in love with you, Sam, and you're not in love with me. There's lust and friendship and maybe a few other things but we're not in love." She smiled then because the memories from the week were flitting through her mind. She'd had fun - real fun - for the first time in a long time. "But I will miss the dancing to the oldies."

His answering grin was dazzling, good enough to be in the movies.

"I will, too."

Leaning down, he brushed his lips over hers once, twice, and then a third time before deepening the kiss until she had to grab onto his shoulders to keep the room from spinning. He stepped back and she felt the loss of his touch immediately. Twisting her fingers together to keep from reaching out to him, she mustered up another what she hoped looked like a carefree smile.

"What is it they say in the acting business? Break a leg?"

"Thanks," he chuckled. "I could use the luck. I start a new picture in a few weeks. Goodbye, Riley."

It was time. No more putting it off.

"Goodbye, Sam."

He stomped down her front porch steps, the light from the rising sun making a halo around his retreating figure. What a crock. Sam Collins was no angel. Devil, maybe. But he'd also been, for one week only, a good friend. And for one night, a wonderful lover. It would have to be enough and it was more than many people ever got.

Goodbye, Sam. Have a nice life. I'll be fine.

And she would be. In a few weeks, he would be a lovely memory that she would cherish for years to come. But right now she was going to eat lots of ice cream.

———

The limo driver loaded the bags into the trunk of the vehicle while Sam said goodbye to his mother. He'd showered, dressed, and packed and was now ready to head to the airport. He had a business meeting this afternoon and a new movie that was scheduled to start filming in a few weeks. Vacation was over.

"I can't believe you're going to just leave like this," Paula said, clearly agitated by his departure. Normally she was sad to see him go but she didn't get this upset. "Have you lost your mind?"

Pulling his mother into a hug, he pressed a kiss onto her forehead. "I'll come back and you can come visit me in New York if you want. You can go shopping and see some shows. It'll be fun."

Throwing up her hands, she rolled her eyes. "That's not what I'm talking about. Of course I'll see you again. I was already thinking I might join you in New York for a few days. I'm talking about you and Riley."

Stiffening, he simply shrugged. "What about Riley? We went to the party last night just like you wanted us to."

Paula's brows rose. "And then you spent the night with her."

Busted.

He should have known his mother had a bullshit detector that had been working overtime since Sam was old enough to tell a fib about who had spilled his juice. Or maybe it was that she'd been wide awake when he walked into the house this morning still wearing his tuxedo from last night.

"About that–"

Holding up her hands, Paula shook her head. "I don't need the details. You're my son and Riley is my friend. That would be creepy. But I do love you both and want the best for you and frankly, my darling baby boy, there is no woman in the world that would be better for you than Riley. You're a fool to walk away. She'd be the perfect wife for you."

His mother knew all the reasons that wasn't going to happen, but she kept beating this particular dead horse.

"I think it's a bit quick to be talking about marriage. But let's just say that Riley and I did keep dating and that we fell in love. Let's just say that happened and we got married. You say Riley would be the perfect wife for me, but would I be the perfect husband for her, Mother? Can you honestly say that I'd be a good husband for one of your best friends in the entire world? Think about it before you answer."

Riley had been correct - brutal but correct. They weren't in love. Not yet. There was a ton of lust and passion, along with a healthy dose of friendship and respect. Perhaps if they'd had more time they might have fallen in love but he didn't stay in one place very long, and Riley wasn't the type to allow herself to be dragged around the globe, living in the shadow of her famous beau and at the whims of the paparazzi and press corps.

Riley was far too sweet for Hollywood. It would chew her up and spit her out. He was doing her a favor by leaving.

"You're letting your past dictate your future," Paula scolded, her finger wagging under his nose like it had when he was thirteen. "It takes two to make or destroy a marriage."

"It didn't take two to not be there when Trish needed me. It only took me."

Sighing, Paula shifted on her feet, looking older than

she had a few minutes ago. "How long are you going to punish yourself for that? It wasn't your fault. If you'd been there—"

"There might have been something I could have done. It doesn't matter, Mom. I have to go. Riley and I talked about this. We'll both be fine."

"I still think you're being foolish. Riley is a wonderful—"

"Mom," Sam cut in, unwilling to keep arguing about this. The decision had been made. "It's already over."

And that was that. He hugged his mother again and promised to call from New York City when he landed. She waved goodbye to him as the limo drove away but she had that look on her face. The one that said that he might be done arguing but she wasn't.

He hadn't heard the last of this.

CHAPTER
Seventeen

IT SEEMED like everywhere Riley went there was a memory of Sam there, too. Like a ghost, he haunted the sidewalks and cafes, even the soft white sand of the local beach. She couldn't find a respite from the thoughts of him no matter what she did.

Frankly, she was damn tired of it. Sam was gone and the sooner she forgot him the better. She'd made it a priority to keep busy so she wouldn't have too much time to think about him.

Today she was meeting Tara and Paula for brunch at that local place on the beach where she and Sam had dined that first night. Despite the harsh light of day, she could still see the two of them strolling along the moonlit beach, the water lapping at their bare toes.

"Sorry I'm late. I overslept."

Again. She'd been spending too much of her free time sleeping lately but that was the perk of being between men...plenty of time to loll in bed.

"It's fine," Tara assured Riley. "We ordered you an iced tea but if you want something different I'll call over the waitress."

Caffeine sounded heavenly and just what she needed.

"That's perfect, thank you."

The windows of the restaurant were open today and the weather was sunny and warm. The squawk of seagulls could be heard in the distance along with the muted sounds of laughter every now and then. Summer came early to Florida and the temperature would rise into the high eighties today despite the calendar only reading May.

"I was just about to ask Paula what she's going to do this summer," Tara said as they perused the menu. The action was by habit rather than actual need. They knew it by heart and usually ordered the same thing. "Hubby and I are planning a trip up to visit my in-laws in Chicago as soon as school ends and I get the classroom packed up."

Paula gave Riley a sidelong glance. "I'm not sure what I'm going to do. Sam is in New York right now so I might go visit him for a few days."

It had been a little over four weeks since Riley had heard his name spoken out loud. Tara and Paula had been tiptoeing around the subject since the day after the engagement party.

Riley wasn't going to allow one man to affect her life like this. Sure, she missed him but she was fine. Her friends needed to know that she wasn't going to fall apart every time a *Thunder* movie came on television.

"That sounds wonderful," Riley said. "I've always wanted to visit. So many things to do. Chicago's the same way and I love their pizza."

"You should go visit." Paula closed her menu and gave all her attention to Riley. "Have you heard from Sam since he left?"

As casually as possible, Riley followed suit, shutting her menu and setting it on the table before answering. "No, but then I didn't expect to. I would imagine he's busy shooting his new film."

She'd successfully sounded like it wasn't a big deal. Which it wasn't. Riley had expected nothing from Sam, so she could hardly complain when that's exactly what she'd received.

"He is," Paula confirmed. "I've only heard from him twice since he started ten days ago. He sounds good, though."

The waitress interrupted them and they all ordered. The same as the last time they were there. Nothing much ever changed around here.

Sitting back in her chair, Paula took a sip of her orange juice. "You should call him."

Riley's gaze darted back and forth between Tara and Paula. To whom was Paula speaking? To Tara, urging her to call her husband? Or to Riley, urging her to call...?

Sam? No. Not going to happen.

Since Tara didn't respond it appeared that Paula's statement was directed at Riley. No time like the present to nip this in the bud.

"Why?"

She didn't wrap it up in a bow or try to soft-ball the question. Better to get it all out and then they could move on with their lives.

If Paula was thrown off by her directness, however, she

didn't appear fazed. "You and he really seemed to hit it off when he was here. It looked like you became good friends and I thought you might like to keep in touch."

Tara was watching the verbal by-play with great interest and her brows were raised waiting for Riley's response.

"We did get along great and enjoyed ourselves, but there was never any question of us staying in touch later. We have separate and very different lives."

Paula's fingers rubbed the edge of the table. "Sam has few people in his life that he can trust."

Riley had no doubt of the truth in Paula's statement, but Sam had specifically structured his life that way. It wasn't up to her to change or fix it.

"I'm sure Sam has things under control," she replied, hoping for a no-nonsense tone. "We had some fun and we've parted ways. I like Sam, I think he's a great guy, but there's nothing between us, Paula."

That shrewd gaze saw way too much. The older woman probably knew too well that Sam had spent that last night someplace other than Paula's own home, but she was too polite to bring it up.

"That's a pity. I thought you made a lovely couple."

"A fake couple," Riley corrected her friend. "It wasn't real, remember?"

After a month apart even their night together no longer seemed real. She was sure she'd simply conjured it out of her fertile imagination.

"If you say so." Paula shrugged and surrendered far too easily. It wasn't like her to give up without at least a little fight. "Now Riley, what are you going to do this summer?"

Keep moving on. Have some fun. Forget about Sam Collins.

The one thing she wasn't going to do? Sit around and wish things had gone differently. Everything was exactly as it was meant to be.

———

Sam twisted the cap off of a bottle of water and settled down into the cushions of the couch. He was trying to relax in his trailer between takes but his publicist was determined to check a few things off his to-do list whether Sam liked it or not.

"She seems like a nice girl," Bobby remarked, holding up his phone so that Sam could see the photo of the young actress and the subject of the discussion. "I'm thinking a ninety-day PR contract with an option to extend if you two get along. It will be just in time for the promotion of both of your new projects and also the summer season. We can have you and Mandi out at the beach, maybe a vacation in Cancun or Hawaii. I can see you two walking hand in hand in Cannes as well. Sound good?"

Scowling, Sam took the cell phone from his publicist's hand. "How old is she?"

"I dunno. She says she's twenty-four but who really knows?"

True. It was Hollywood, after all.

"And you don't think that my dating a girl under thirty is just a little creepy? I'm forty-five, for fuck's sake. I could be her daddy."

Bobby frowned and plucked the phone out of Sam's hand. "What's going on here? Your last showmance was with a girl that young and you didn't say a word. It's totally normal for an older man to date a younger woman."

Sam had been doing some thinking and he'd made a few decisions.

"I'm too damn old for this."

"This?"

"All of this," Sam replied grimly. He was about to make Bobby's job harder. Or maybe easier, depending on how one looked at things. "I'm too old to be dating girls that don't remember who shot J.R. Hell, the last one couldn't even do basic math because she asked me where I was when Kennedy was shot. Shit, I wasn't even born yet. But to anyone under thirty I'm just an old fart, which I probably am, but I don't need to be reminded several times a day. No more showmances, Bobby. No more tipping off *TMZ* that I'm flying into LAX. No more posting paps outside restaurants and nightclubs. I don't want to be on the cover of *People Magazine* and I sure as shit don't want to be named the Sexiest Man Alive. I'm a serious actor and I want to act that way. Is that too much to ask?"

His longtime publicist didn't say a word, his eyes round and his mouth fallen open.

Great, I've rendered him speechless. First time for everything.

Shaking himself out of whatever shock he'd been feeling, Bobby appeared to recover.

"No, of course it's not too much to ask. I get what you're saying. It's a change to your image but I support it. In fact, I wish I'd suggested it. I think it's a...classy transition for you."

"Good. Let's make it happen then. No more contract relationships, no more thinking about what kind of ink I can get."

Bobby shoved the phone in his pocket. "You've changed."

If his publicist meant that Sam was grouchy and humorless lately then yes, he'd changed.

"Everybody changes."

"Some more than others. There was a time that you would have killed to get on the cover of a magazine. Now you don't give a shit. You even turned down that new *Thunder* movie."

Bobby didn't get it at all but then that wasn't surprising. Only someone in Sam's unique position would understand.

"First of all, I didn't turn it down. We couldn't come to an agreement. They're trying to play hardball with actors who have other options. Not smart. Tyler, Nate, and Max will tell you the same story. As for killing another human being to get on a magazine, I certainly was a lot hungrier early in my career, but I can truthfully say that murder was never an option for me."

Now that Sam was directing and producing his own indie films, he didn't want to be pigeonholed as *that guy from the Thunder movies*. He had more to offer than that.

"So what happens now?"

"I'm not sure I understand the question. What do you mean? The whole idea is that nothing happens now. I work, I make movies, I promote them and in between I disappear."

Bobby stood, tucking his many folders back into his briefcase. "I guess what I mean is what are you going to do now?"

That was an easy question.

"Anything I want to."

Chuckling, Bobby sidled towards the door. "Good for you, man. Good for you. I need to head back to the office but call me if you need me. Although it sounds like you're not going to need me too often in the future. Did I ever mention that I don't give discounts?"

It was Sam's turn to laugh. "Believe me, it never occurred to me that you would."

Bobby exited the trailer leaving Sam all alone with his thoughts. It felt good to put his foot down and take control of his career. He'd been allowing others to call the shots for far too long. Honestly, he'd been moving in this direction for awhile as his agent and business manager knew well. Today was the final shot in the battle and Bobby hadn't put up any fight. Sam had expected his longtime publicist to protest that the industry expected certain things, but he was glad that they didn't have to argue about it. Maybe Bobby recognized that Sam wasn't going to change his mind.

I could even become a mysterious recluse.

If he had more time he could visit Paula more often.

Which would of course lead to him seeing Riley.

It hadn't been only his publicity that had been weighing on his mind these last few weeks. Riley had been there too, and he couldn't seem to shake her no matter how busy he kept himself. It had been all he could do when he talked to his mother not to ask her about Riley.

But he hadn't.

Thinking about Riley was one thing, but doing anything about it was something far different. He had to keep his head in the game and forget about her.

Easier said than done.

CHAPTER
Eighteen

WITH SHAKING, sweating hands and a pounding heart, Riley set the timer on her cell phone for ten minutes.

Ten - freaking - minutes.

In that short amount of time, everything could change and nothing would ever be the same. Or perhaps she'd only imagined the slight morning nausea and the fatigue. And maybe her math skills had completely deserted her when she'd looked at her calendar this morning and realized that she hadn't had a period since Sam left six and a half weeks ago.

After the last day of school today she'd driven to the next town over and bought several pregnancy tests, all different brands, because she needed to be sure. Obviously, she couldn't go into her local pharmacy and purchase a test because that would get out and before she knew it she'd have Paula on her doorstep.

Whether Paula would be happy about being a grandparent when Riley was the mother, she had no idea.

So she'd dragged the test boxes into the bathroom and peed on all of the sticks, which wasn't as easy at it sounded. They were now lined up on the edge of her vanity like a row of tiny soldiers guarding her hand soap. If even one of these tests came out positive, she was going to have to see her doctor.

And tell Sam.

Maybe. Probably. Shit, she had no clue what she was supposed to do in a situation like this. She'd always been so careful and cautious, never taking any chances. And the one time she did?

Bam! Right in the ovaries.

Riley checked the countdown on her phone. Still five minutes to go. The longest test took ten minutes, so she'd decided to wait and see them all at the same time. But now she was sweating through her nicest white blouse as she waited for the verdict.

Pushing her hair off of her neck where sweat was currently pooling and then trickling down her back, she dragged in a lungful of oxygen trying to slow down her galloping heart.

A baby. There might be a baby from her one night with Sam.

She'd have to tell him. She couldn't keep something like this a secret. If she was pregnant that meant that he was the father and he deserved to know. Whether he wanted to be in the baby's life was a whole different question, but then she needed to take them one at a time.

Of course, there was Paula in this equation too. Unless Riley planned to quit her job, sell her condo, and move before she started showing there was no way to keep this from Sam's mother. And if Paula knew...well...Sam was going to know.

But she might not even be pregnant. It could be just a weird convergence of symptoms that had nothing to do with gestation. She could be tired because it was the end of the school year, and she could be nauseous because she was tired. As for being late, periods could get messed up all the time, right? She'd always been fairly regular, but she'd heard some horror stories from other females. It could all just be a fluke because of stress. She wasn't pregnant and that night with Sam had never really happened.

Her clammy fingers tightened on the phone as the timer chimed that ten minutes was up. It had felt like two seconds and two weeks all at the same time and Riley was sure that couldn't be the case. Taking a deep breath, she steeled herself to walk back into the bathroom and check the test sticks. Standing, she had to grab onto the dresser for a moment as her knees seemed made of jelly, but she finally pushed her legs into moving across the room until she was standing in front of the vanity.

All four tests stared back up at her, taunting her, seemingly innocent but she knew better. They appeared innocuous enough with their white plastic and their results windows, but they had so much power to change a woman's life. She reached for the first test on the left.

A plus sign.

The second test?

Two blue bars.

The third?

Another plus sign.

The fourth?

The word *pregnant* all typed out neatly. Just in case she didn't believe the first three.

She was pregnant. There was no denying the results. She couldn't pretend anymore, although she'd been doing exactly that for the last few weeks, making excuses for not feeling quite right.

Pregnant. With Sam's baby.

Would he even care?

Did it matter? His emotions didn't change anything.

Her hand pressed against her still flat - for now - belly. It didn't matter if Sam Collins wanted to be a father. She was going to be a mother and she'd be the very best one she could be. If he wanted to be a part of this miracle, that was fine. If he didn't that was okay, too.

She was going to have a baby either way.

CHAPTER
Nineteen

IT WAS good to sit down for lunch with friends like Nate and Paige. They were in New York City, along with their twin babies who were back at the hotel being minded by Nate's mother and a nanny, working on the movie adaptation of Paige's book. Nate had teased that the children were going to become intrepid travelers by their fifth birthday. The three of them spent the time while waiting for their dinner looking at pictures of the babies on Nate's cell phone.

Off in a quiet corner, no one bothered them but then this was New York City. People didn't get starry-eyed about a couple of actors eating antipasto at a small out-of-the-way restaurant in Little Italy.

Nate took a sip of his water. "You probably heard that I turned down the new *Thunder* movie. They had no idea how they were going to write me in since my character died. Honestly, it sounded like they hadn't really thought about anything. They just wanted us all together again."

That was the understatement of the year. The studio seemed to have the belief that the script didn't matter as long as the four men were on the theatre marquee.

"I turned it down as well and I have to agree with you. If there had been a decent script...or any script at all, well, I might have made a different decision."

"Were they willing to finance your next project?"

Sam chuckled as he remembered that conversation with his agent. "Yes and no. They were willing to finance a project, but they wanted to be far too involved in it for my liking. When I produce and direct a film I like to have control over it. I'm funny that way."

Paige nodded in understanding. "I'm learning that about myself, as well. I think you both did the right thing." She glanced at her husband and then at Sam. "But that doesn't mean that you can't work together again. If the project was right."

Interest piqued, Sam leaned forward. "Do you have any ideas? I'm listening if you do."

Nate was already shaking his head. "Don't encourage her. I didn't realize what being married to a writer was going to be like. She gets ideas for stories all the time. Anywhere and everywhere and at all times of the day or night. She has a notebook filled with them and one whole section is devoted to stories that I could star in. Now she's thinking about movies that all of us could do together."

Sam couldn't think of men he'd rather work with than his *Thunder* castmates. They'd made some hellishly awful shoots much more bearable.

"Send some of those ideas over. I'd be open to all of us doing another picture together, just not another *Thunder* movie. That franchise needs to go out while it's still on top."

Paige gave her husband a smug smile. "See? I told you he'd be open to it."

"Don't say I didn't warn you," Nate laughed. "You're about to be bombarded with texts twenty-four hours a day."

"I look forward to it."

"You're always such a gentleman," Paige sighed. "Now enough about us and the babies, tell us how your vacation was. Did you get some well-deserved rest?"

Poor Paige had no clue how loaded her seemingly innocent question was.

"Some. It was nice to see my mother. She might come visit me here in the city in a few weeks."

"What did you do?" Paige pressed, taking a bite of her lasagna. "I love the beach."

Paige was originally from another part of Florida, but she'd made her home in London with Nate. She was still getting used to the rain and cold.

"Really not much." Sam didn't like being evasive with his best friends, but he wasn't sure he wanted to get into this with them. Lately he wasn't sure of anything at all.

Blissfully eating his chicken piccata, Nate didn't appear to have a clue the inner turmoil that Sam had inside, but Paige was a different matter altogether. Like so many women, she seemed to have a sixth sense about things. Right now, she was looking at him with the same shrewd gaze his mother had.

Shit.

"Did something happen while you were on vacation, Sam?"

He took a big bite of his pasta. "No."

Paige wasn't buying what he was selling. She set her fork on her plate and cleared her throat delicately.

"I hope you know that we're your friends and you can tell us anything. We'd never disclose what was said in confidence."

"I do."

"So if something happened and you're upset about it, it might help to talk it out."

"Maybe."

Another sigh, but this one wasn't nearly as happy as the last one. "Let me stop beating around the bush and get right to it. Do you realize that you've been answering me in one or two-word replies?"

"So?"

"It rather suggests that there's something you don't want to talk about."

Nate placed a hand on his wife's arm. "Then maybe we should take the hint, sweetheart. If Sam doesn't want to discuss it..."

She was looking him up and down or as well as one could when he was sitting. That sharp gaze was appraising, probing, seeing right through his bullshit. Heaven help poor Nate. He'd never get away with even a tiny fib, but then Paige had a teenage son so she'd had to have finely tuned mother radar.

"It's a woman."

The pronouncement was calm and sure, like Paige herself.

Nate winced and shook his head. "Then we really need to mind our own business. Let the man eat in peace."

"We just want to help," Paige said gently. "But I'll drop it if it bothers you."

These were his friends and friends wanted to help. They simply didn't understand that there was nothing they could do to make this better. It was far too late.

"I appreciate that but there really isn't anything you can do. You're right, I met a woman, but I doubt I'll be seeing her again."

This time it was Nate who spoke. "Why not? Did you argue?"

"Not at all. She's a lovely woman and we got along very well. She's a kindergarten teacher and a friend of my mother."

Paige smiled with excitement. "She sounds perfect. Why aren't you going to see her again?"

"Because she's the type of woman who wants a real relationship," he explained patiently. "Commitment, children, an actual home life. Not a man that gallivants all over the world for work and is never home. We're too different."

Nate frowned, his gaze narrowing. "And you don't want any of that? Not even a little bit?"

"I had it," Sam reminded his friend. "I had it and I blew it. I'm not cut out for happily ever after."

"One mistake doesn't mean you can't try again." Paige reached for her husband's hand. "The second time around can be pretty great. As for your marriage, it takes a lot of work *from two people*, not just one. You can't take it all on your own shoulders."

He could because they didn't know the whole story. A situation he wasn't anxious to rectify.

"Let's just say that Trish had a good reason for divorcing me." He realized how that sounded, though. They'd think he cheated on her.

"You were young," Paige argued. "I doubt you'd make the same mistakes."

He wouldn't want to but he might, and he couldn't take that chance. Not again.

"Trish was pretty clear when we split up that I was the worst husband on earth. She hated me and said she never wanted to look at my face again and she hasn't. The divorce settlement was very generous. It's the least I can do for ruining her life."

Nate frowned, his brows pinched together. "Is that what she said? That you'd ruined her life? That's harsh."

She'd said that and a few other things that day. The last day he'd seen her. Even during the divorce he hadn't seen her again; they'd conversed completely through attorneys.

He hoped she'd found some sort of happiness in her life. He'd loved her once and he wanted the best for her.

"I don't really want to talk about my ex, if you don't mind. Let's just say that I'm not looking to get married again and leave it there."

Paige looked like she might cry. Damn, she was soft-hearted. "I think it's sad, though. I don't want you to live your life alone, Sam. You're a good person and you don't deserve that."

"I'm living my life...on my terms. It's all good."

Tilting her head, Paige seemed to consider his words. "But she made you think about it? Just a little bit."

More than he should have. Riley wasn't for him. Obsessing about what could be wasn't good for his mental health.

The buzzing of his phone mercifully interrupted their conversation. The phone displayed a photo of his mother that he'd taken when he was home.

"Excuse me, it's my mom. I need to take this."

Nate and Paige nodded in understanding, turning toward each other to give him a little privacy.

"Hey, Mom. What's going on?"

"Um, Sam? This is Tara, your mother's friend."

Why was Tara using Paula's phone?

"Hi, Tara. Where's Mom?"

A cold feeling was beginning to crawl through his veins, a sense of foreboding he couldn't shake. Tara had a tone in her voice that Sam didn't like.

"That's kind of why I'm calling. Your mom collapsed and had to be taken to the hospital. She told the doctors not to call you but both Riley and I think you should know. We're here with her now and the doctors are running tests. It might be nothing or... Anyway, we thought you should know."

His mother was the single most important person in Sam's life. Damn right they should have called him. He'd have a talk with Paula. Later. When she was recovered.

His mother had always been in excellent health but she was getting older, a fact that Sam had been conveniently ignoring. He didn't want to think of his life without her in it.

"Give me a few hours and I'll be there. And Tara? You did the right thing calling me."

He only hoped that this time he wouldn't be too late.

CHAPTER
Twenty

RILEY HAD BEEN PREPARING herself for hours to see Sam, but when he burst into Paula's hospital room it was still like a punch to her abdomen. She hadn't exactly been completely relaxed before seeing him, but now it was as if every nerve in her body was at attention and every hair on her head was standing on end.

She'd thought she'd have more time to figure out how to tell him he was going to become a father, but fate had taken over this afternoon. Paula had collapsed while outside doing some gardening and now the decision of *when* had been taken out of Riley's hands. There was no reason to wait. He was here, Paula was okay, and Riley...? She was still pregnant and quietly freaking out as he rushed to his mother's side, peppering Paula and Riley with questions about what happened and what the doctor said.

"I'm fine," the older woman sighed. "I got too dehydrated and my blood pressure dropped. I passed out.

That's the whole story. They're giving me IV fluids and want to keep me overnight for observation. That's why I told Riley and Tara not to call you. There was no need."

After her promise to Sam to look after his mother, Riley had felt duty bound to call him and now here they all four of them were, standing in a hospital room with the tension sky high.

"Jesus, of course they needed to tell me. If you're admitted to the hospital I want to know about it. Thank goodness a few people around here had some common sense."

Paula gave Tara a fierce frown. "And they'll be hearing about that later. I can't believe you left the film and came down here. How did you get here so fast?"

"I chartered a plane and of course I left the set, Mother. I called the director and he can shoot around me for a few days."

"As you can see, I'm fine. They're going to release me tomorrow with a promise to drink more water, especially when I'm outside. Apparently *older* people can become dehydrated more easily."

Riley inwardly winced. Paula hadn't liked it at all when the young doctor had chastised her for not keeping her fluid intake up when she was in the hot sun. Then he'd had the audacity to call Paula a *senior citizen*. He'd left shortly thereafter, having been on the receiving end of a deathly stare that would have scared the bejesus out of most men.

"You have to take care of yourself–"

"I've had about enough of people calling me old in the last few hours," Paula interrupted. "If you don't have anything positive to say then you can get back into your fancy rented jet and fly back to New York. It's kind of been a rotten day."

Sam's expression immediately softened. "Do you need anything? A better room? Some food? I can run out and get you something to eat. Whatever you need. How about some books or magazines?"

"The girls have already taken good care of me. Riley got me some dinner and some reading material for the evening, but they actually have cable here. I'll be fine. Go back to New York."

Sam's lips tightened with frustration. "Is my presence bothering you?"

Watching the back and forth between mother and son was interesting. Clearly Paula didn't want to be a burden and Sam was determined to take care of her.

"No, but I know how you are when you're making a new movie. You're buried in your work and the character, usually. Is coming here going to be a problem?"

"I'm not method, Mother." Sam sighed and scraped his fingers through his hair, reminding Riley of the morning after their night together when his hair had been standing straight up, all tousled and cute. "I'm worried about you and I want to make sure you're okay."

Paula sat up and pressed a kiss to her son's cheek. "I'm fine and I'm glad you're here. Why don't you tell us about the new film? I'd love to hear about it and that's more interesting than television or a book."

Somehow Sam found more chairs - from a few helpful nurses - and they all sat down to listen to his stories from the movie set. He'd barely turned to look at her the entire time he'd been in the room and Riley was growing increasingly angry with him. She hadn't expected Sam to throw himself at her feet, but she hadn't expected to be roundly ignored either. They'd parted as friends but he was acting like she wasn't even alive. Frankly, it was a crappy thing to do.

Her blood pressure had risen and her stomach tumbled with leashed rage by the time another nurse stuck her head in and said that it was time for them to leave. The nurse didn't leave, however, hanging around and standing far too close to Sam. Riley didn't have the right to be jealous but she was.

Paula held out her hand and beckoned to Riley. "Can you wait a moment?"

She nodded to Tara and Sam to go ahead of her while she hung back. "Of course, is there something you need?"

"I'm fine. If you repeat this I'll never admit it, but thank you for calling Sam. I hate to pull him away from work but it was nice to see his face after such an awful day."

"Actually, Tara called him," Riley reminded her.

"It was your idea. I know that he asked you to look after me." Paula's smile was full of love for her son. "He's a good boy. I've tried to be both mother and father to him. Frankly he deserved a better father, but I was all he had."

"You did a great job."

Sometimes a sign from the universe sits on your shoulder softly and sometimes it smacks you across the face.

Riley's baby deserved a chance to have a dad. No matter what, she had to find a way to tell Sam. He'd probably just offer her money and go back to his life, but she had to try. Maybe, just maybe, he'd want to parent this child with her in some manner. She didn't know how they'd work it out but she was sure they could. The nurse eventually came back into the room and shooed Riley out into the hallway with Tara and Sam.

"I need to get back home." Tara checked her watch and then dug into her purse for her car keys. "Hubby should be off work now. Riley, are you going to take Sam back to Paula's?"

Riley hesitated, Sam frowned, and Tara didn't have a clue as to the subtext of the conversation. She'd never told her best friend about her night with the actor.

"Do you have a rental, Sam?" Tara asked when no one spoke up. "If not, either Riley or I can pick up Paula in the morning."

Sam was staring over Tara's shoulder so it looked like Riley wasn't the only one he didn't want to make eye contact with. He was acting so strangely tonight and she was the one with the huge secret. What was his excuse?

"I don't have a rental but I can get one."

"No need." Tara waved away the offer. "We can get her, no problem."

More silence but this time Tara seemed to get the idea that something was going on and she didn't want to be any part of it. Smart.

"Well...goodnight. See you tomorrow."

Tara fled and that meant that Riley had run out of time. Delaying wasn't going to help and Sam's idea of pretending they weren't standing a foot from each other wasn't going to work either.

"I'll give you a ride," she said, turning toward the exit and hoping he followed without too much of an argument. Once they were alone she could tell him. Now that she'd decided she wanted it over with as soon as possible. "It's on my way home."

Not really but close enough. The town was small so it wasn't an imposition.

"I can call an Ub–"

"You'll have to wait for them," Riley replied quickly, not giving him a chance to dispute her claim. "Quicker to just ride with me. Let's go."

She thought he'd argue more but to her relief he followed her out of the hospital without a word. She'd thought so often about what she'd say when she saw him again but now that the time had come all those words had flown straight out of her head. Not knowing how he was going to react, it was difficult to form a strategy as to how to break the news. Gently? To the point? Slip a note in his fortune cookie?

One thing was for sure though...

Sam not liking the news didn't change the reality. He was going to be a father.

———

The ride from the hospital was quiet. Sam didn't know what to say and Riley didn't try and start a conversation, which was a relief. The moment he'd seen her standing next to his mother's bed he'd been hit over the head again with just how damn beautiful she was and how kind, too. For a brief moment he'd thought about what Nate and Paige had said earlier today, urging him to find someone to share his life with. But then he'd realized that once again he wasn't there when a loved one needed him. Luckily

Paula's friends had been here when she'd collapsed, otherwise... He didn't want to think about the alternative endings to this story.

Riley cared for Paula like she would a member of her own family. In Sam's experience, behavior like that was rare.

He'd been knocked almost speechless so it had been easier to not say anything to her at all, focusing his attention and energy on his mother. They were alone now, however, and he needed to say something. Anything.

Maybe he could tell her he'd missed her. Perhaps she'd missed him too.

Stupid idea. You're leaving again.

Riley pulled up into the driveway and cut the engine. "I was hoping we could talk a little bit."

Talk? About what? Did she want to talk about that night? And what did he want?

I don't know. I just wish things were different.

"Sure. Come on in."

He headed straight for the kitchen when they were inside, pulling out a bottle of red from the wine cooler he'd bought Paula two Christmases ago.

"How about we relax with a glass of wine?"

A drink seemed like a really good idea right about now. He was acting like a boy on his first date instead of a grown ass man.

Riley shook her head and perched on the edge of a sofa cushion. "I'll pass, but please, go ahead. You've probably had a rough day."

He poured himself a glass and sat down in the chair next to the couch. Close enough to talk but not so close that he might get an idea to touch or kiss her. Bad idea. He wasn't here to rekindle their romance. Nothing had changed. He was still the wrong man for her.

"So what did you want to talk about? Is it my mom? Is there something else going on that I don't know about?"

Her eyes widened and she shook her head. "No, this isn't about Paula."

She shifted on the cushion, clearly nervous about talking to him which wasn't like Riley at all. It looked like she'd rather be any place but here with him.

Has she fallen for another guy? Is that what she wants to tell me?

Leaning forward, he caught her hand with his own, giving it what he hoped was a reassuring squeeze.

"This is Sam, okay?" he said softly. "It's just me and you and you can tell me anything, right?"

Her fingers pleated the leader strap of her handbag and now it was her turn not to look him in the eye. Whatever she wanted to tell him had to be bad. Shit, was she getting married? For the love of God, had she reunited with Chad the douchebag?

"I'm not sure I can tell you this."

"Sure you can," he cajoled. "Did I become scary in the last couple of months? C'mon, Riley. Talk to me."

Those fingers paused for a moment and she looked up at him, their gazes colliding. Her eyes were bright with tears and he wanted to pull her into his arms and tell her everything was going to be okay, but he didn't have a clue as to why she was upset. He didn't want to lie to her.

"It's just that–"

He waited not wanting to interrupt what was clearly

difficult for her. His own heart had accelerated in his chest as terrible, awful thoughts began to fill his brain.

She had a terminal disease and she was dying.

She was back with Chad-boy.

She'd thought about it and she hated Sam.

She was moving to a sparsely populated island to live out her dream of climbing a volcano.

"It's just that," she began again, exhaling noisily. "I have some news that you need to know. I wasn't sure when I was going to tell you but now that you're here the time seems to be now."

This was it. She was back with that asshole. He braced himself to hear the words but he couldn't help the anger that churned in his gut. That jerk would only hurt her again and here she was going back for a second helping. What was it with women and douchebag guys?

Well, it was her life and he was out of it. If she was the kind of woman that would take Chad back then she wasn't the person he'd thought she was.

He'd thought she was different. Perhaps it had only been wishful thinking.

CHAPTER
Twenty-One

THE TIME HAD COME but Riley still didn't have a brilliant idea about how to break the news about the baby. Once again she was questioning the wisdom of doing this. What if he denied that he was the father? She didn't want a court battle and a DNA test. What if he blamed her and decided that she wanted money from him? Or worse, what if he wanted to be in the baby's life and Riley had to see him with his gorgeous girlfriends all the time? Eventually he'd marry one and have a few children with her.

This attraction needed to run its course in the next five minutes. She'd spent far too long thinking about him and now she was pissed because he had an imaginary girlfriend who was going to become her baby's stepmother.

"What do you need to tell me?" Sam prompted. "You're pale. Are you sick?"

Not exactly, although her stomach was doing gymnastics in her abdomen. It wasn't going to get any better by drawing this out, so she needed to do it before she lost her nerve. Screwing up every bit of courage she had, she took a deep breath.

"So...I'm pregnant."

Sam blinked once. Twice. Three times.

"Pregnant?"

His question came out strained and the shock was clear on his face.

Riley nodded, her cheeks warm and her eyes teary. She couldn't yet tell how he was taking the news. "Yes, I'm pregnant."

"Congratulations. Who's the father?"

Sam's eyes appeared glassy and his skin was pale and covered in a sheen of sweat. The cooler than ice action hero who could face down death with a smile was freaking out right here in front of Riley. It would have been amusing to watch if she hadn't been the reason it was happening.

"You. You're the father, Sam."

She hadn't slept with Chad in a long time, but she and Sam had never discussed timelines. They'd never had to. Until now.

"Okay." He nodded as if he understood but she had a feeling he didn't. He did, however, look like he wanted to flee in a getaway car and then join the witness protection program.

Riley pushed his glass closer to him. "Maybe you should have another drink of your wine."

"Good idea."

He took a gulp but she could see that his hand was shaking slightly.

"You're probably wondering how it happened."

His head came up sharply and he opened his mouth to

speak but no words came out. Yep, he was freaked out alright. She did have sympathy for his plight. She'd been the same when she'd found out. Even now, it didn't quite seem real.

"My doctor said that condoms aren't one hundred percent effective, and I wasn't on the pill after Chad and I broke up. It makes me sick to my stomach so I don't like taking it unless I have to." She might as well talk since he couldn't seem to. She'd been practicing this part although she wasn't sure he was truly listening. "All there has to be is a tiny tear and you did open them with your teeth. Anyway, I think that's how it happened."

Sam appeared to be in some sort of daze and he still hadn't responded. It looked like she needed to be the designated adult. Again.

Alrighty then.

"I want you to know that I don't expect anything from you, Sam. You can be as involved as you like, or you can wash your hands of all of this. I won't tell anyone that you're the father but I'm sure the locals - and your mother - are going to figure it out. I'm guessing everyone is going to be doing math in their head when they find out my due date, but I promise you that I won't tell if you don't want me to. They can guess but I won't confirm." His color was coming back and he didn't seem to be sweating as much. The wine must have helped. Or maybe it was that she'd told him she didn't expect anything. He might simply be relieved. "Are you okay?"

Rubbing the back of his neck, Sam managed a rueful smile. "This is a...surprise. I'm still sort of trying to wrap my mind around it."

"It takes time. I was gobsmacked too. It was the last thing I expected." Her hand automatically went to her stomach. "But I want to keep the baby. I've always wanted to be a mother."

Nodding in agreement, Sam stood and rounded the chair, leaning a hand on the fireplace mantle like it was a lifeline. "Of course, it's your decision. I would support you no matter what."

Riley had to make the difficult admission - if only to herself - that she had been hoping for more from Sam. She hadn't expected him to jump for joy but...

Okay, maybe she had been hoping for that.

He was in shock and she had been too, so it wasn't fair to compare his reaction to some pie in the sky fantasy that was driven by maternal hormones. They weren't in love and they weren't even a couple, so it would behoove her to keep this friendly and a little businesslike. Because that's what it was going to end up being. If he wanted to be in the child's life there would be a legal document that outlined a custody agreement and they would both sign on the dotted line. A parenting contract of sorts. Hopefully they could stay friends during all of this.

"I appreciate that," Riley replied when she realized the silence had gone on too long. "Perhaps I should leave you to mull this over. I've had time to get used to the idea but you haven't. You don't need to make any life-changing decisions tonight."

My life has already changed but you go right ahead and take your time.

"I do need to think about this. Frankly, I'm stunned.

This was literally the last thing I thought you were going to tell me. I thought you were going to say–"

He broke off and didn't finish the sentence. For a moment, Riley thought about asking him to continue but that would detour the conversation and they needed to stay focused.

"It's a big decision," Riley agreed with a small smile, standing and hitching her purse strap over her shoulder. "I'll head home now. I'm so tired these days I fall asleep as soon as my head hits the pillow. Maybe we can talk more tomorrow."

"Let's do that." Sam walked her to the front door and then placed his hand on her arm when she would have walked past him. Her skin tingled where he touched it, warming from the contact. That was the one thing she'd missed since finding out. There had been no hugs of congratulations, no celebratory kisses. She was missing human contact. "Wait...does anyone else know? Tara? Your family? My mother?"

As far as family went, they were close but they didn't intrude in each other's lives. She talked to her parents every couple of weeks and her siblings less so, but they exchanged photos through email or social media. This was going to take them by surprise.

"I haven't said anything to anyone because I wasn't sure what to say. They're going to have questions and I think we need to decide on many of those answers together. Also, I was reading that the chance of miscarriage goes way down after the eleventh week, so I was thinking that perhaps we wouldn't want to tell too many people before then."

That color that had come back into his face completely drained again, his skin ashen. In a matter of seconds he'd gone cold and gray, his features carved from granite.

"We'll talk tomorrow."

She'd been dismissed. Clearly the thought of sharing the news with family and friends bothered him.

"If you like I'll pick you up in the morning and we can go get Paula from the hospital."

He was already a million miles away, barely paying attention. Wherever he'd gone off to wasn't a pleasant place.

"That's fine. I'll see you then."

There wasn't anything left to say so Riley walked to her car and climbed inside, the scent from his aftershave still hanging in the air. It was a reminder she didn't need at the moment.

As she drove away, she glanced in her rearview mirror but he'd already gone back inside and closed the door. Sam certainly had acted strangely tonight but perhaps not. She'd never told anyone they were going to be a father before, so his behavior might be totally normal for all she knew. He just seemed...disturbed. A couple of times he'd looked like he might pass out or at least puke.

Cut him some slack. He's had the shock of his life.

She would do that. For awhile. But eventually he'd need to man up and deal with the situation.

He was either in or out. Which was it going to be?

CHAPTER
Twenty-Two

THE SHOCK of Riley's news followed Sam into the shower and then back into the kitchen where he half-heartedly made himself a sandwich. He wasn't all that hungry, his mind too preoccupied to let him know that his stomach was empty, but he forced down a few bites before giving up and tossing it into the trash can.

Riley is pregnant.

And it's mine.

A baby, and it was his. This was no false alarm like when a crazy fan claimed that he was the father of her kid. That had happened a few times and there'd even been a close call once with a model who had texted him that she was "late" and then a few hours later had said "never mind."

But this was real. Riley wasn't some nutty stalker and the way she'd placed her palm over her belly was pure mother-bear instincts. When he'd watched her do that it had been like taking a roundhouse kick to the solar plexus.

After Trish, he'd vowed never again. He'd failed her so deeply and that last day was ingrained in his brain so he wouldn't forget. He needed to remember that he hadn't been there when she'd needed him.

Now here he was facing fatherhood again. Could he do this? *Should* he do this? Did he even really have a choice, if he were honest?

Sam could be selfish and self-involved. He was in the most narcissistic industry in possibly the entire world except for politics, but he simply didn't have it in him to walk away from his own child.

This was a second chance and he might not deserve one but dammit, he was going to grab it with both hands. It didn't hurt that the mother of his child was a woman that he liked and cared for. He could be a partner with Riley, raise their child together, and create a family. He was lousy at it and she deserved far better but he'd do the best he could. At least financially, she and the baby would want for nothing.

That was one thing he was good at. Making money.

He needed her and the baby where he could take care of them, watch over them all the time, and New Hope wasn't that place. He could take them with him when he worked until the baby started school or better yet, he could just not work for the next few years once he finished this picture.

What would her reaction be to his proposal? They got along well and they liked each other a great deal. They were friends and that was a decent basis for marriage. Plus the sex was out of this world. It was more than many couples had when they started out.

All he had to do was convince Riley to give him a chance, and hope they didn't both regret it.

————

Riley had slept fitfully after her conversation with Sam. It hadn't been easy to tell him the news, especially as she didn't know him well enough to know how he would react. She'd learned many details about the man in the week they'd spent together but how he would react to an unplanned pregnancy? That took a little more time.

At first, she'd been miffed that he wanted to think about things. There was a part of her that wanted him to sweep her off her feet, declare his undying love, and carry her away for some happily ever after that was so amazing she couldn't even imagine it. It was not to be. Sam hadn't been pining for her these last seven weeks, writing bad poetry and love songs.

Now that she'd had some time to think about it she was glad that he hadn't made any quick decisions. It showed a certain maturity that he'd wanted to think things through, mull all the options and figure out what he really wanted. This was better, although it wasn't easy to wait.

They'd picked up Paula this morning and brought her back to the house. Sam had fussed over his mother and tried to make her rest, but Paula wasn't having any of it. She'd been lying down for too long as far as she was concerned. She wanted to sit outside and enjoy the sunshine. No way was she going to bed in the middle of the day.

Sam eventually gave in and set up a small table next to

Paula's lawn chair with everything she could need. A cool drink, her cell phone, the latest bestseller, and her iPad if she wanted to play games. Paula had shooed them out of there, suggesting the two of them get some lunch. She'd said it with a gleam in her eye, clearly not giving up on the idea of them as a couple.

If she only knew. They were going to be in each other's life for a very long time.

They'd grabbed some takeout and ended up at Riley's home, wanting the privacy to talk. All they needed was to end up on social media or be overheard by the waitress while speaking about pregnancy and babies.

Riley studied the contents of her refrigerator while Sam unpacked the food. "I have caffeine-free soda, milk, lemonade, and water. Sorry, there's no caffeine in the house. I cleaned it all out. The less temptation, the better."

Actually, tossing her tea bags and the coffee had been rather traumatic. She loved her iced tea and her morning coffee, but from what she'd read the science was mixed as to how good it was for the baby. If she could give it up, she probably should. It wasn't forever. It just felt that way.

"I'll have whatever you're having."

That would be lemonade. It was a poor substitute but it would have to do.

She poured two glasses and sat down at the table across from Sam, who was parceling out fries onto their plates. She'd ordered a grilled chicken sandwich and her stomach was gurgling with anticipation. She was starving. She'd scarfed down half of her lunch before she realized they hadn't talked yet. Food was becoming increasingly important in her life.

"So..."

Placing his cheeseburger back on the plate, he wiped his mouth before speaking.

"I gave this a lot of thought after you left, and I'm sorry if I seemed so surprised last night."

"You were shocked. I was too when I found out, so it's okay."

"I was shocked," he conceded with a grimace. "I probably should have handled the news better, though."

"You were fine."

Her expectations and fantasies weren't his problem. He'd reacted like a normal human being.

"I want to be part of the baby's life. I know that. I don't know if I'll be a good father, but I can't turn my back on this child."

The room spun for a moment as relief suffused every nook and cranny of her body. She hadn't even realized she'd been holding her breath waiting for his answer. She was fully prepared to do this alone, but honestly, she hadn't wanted to. However, the question still remained as to how involved he wanted to be. Just because he wanted to acknowledge his child didn't mean he'd be going to birthing classes with her and reading baby name books.

"That's good," she replied, getting her lips to work finally. "I think we can do this, Sam."

They'd been friends before, they could be again. She was sure that eventually she'd stop being attracted to him. Once she got to know him better. There were probably dozens of annoying habits that she didn't know about. She did know he snored and that was pretty annoying, although she'd been so exhausted she'd fallen right asleep.

There seemed to be relief in his expression. "I think we can, too. I know it's going to take some compromises on both our parts but I'm willing if you are."

"I can do that."

It might mean some travel for her, taking the baby to see Sam, but it would be doable.

Sitting back in his chair, he appeared happy for the first time since she'd first seen him at the hospital.

"Mom is going to be so excited. She's wanted grandkids for years and is always bugging me to settle down. She's going to be thrilled it's with you. She already loves you like a daughter."

Wait...what? He was settling down with her? Riley must have spaced out and missed something in the conversation. Something really important.

"I'm not following you. What do you mean?"

The pregnancy book had warned her about feeling foggy at times because of the fatigue, but right now Riley felt wide awake.

"She's going to be thrilled about us. You have to know she was trying to push us together."

Riley knew and she'd assumed that Paula was nudging her son as well, this was just confirmation. But his statement raised more questions than it answered.

"Together? Sam, why don't you describe for me how you see us doing this."

Us. That word was powerful. They'd both been throwing it around but what did it actually mean to Sam?

"I think we should do what's best for the baby." He leaned forward, resting his elbows on his knees, his gaze intent. "I think we should create a family for him or her. A real home where he can feel safe and secure."

"A home?"

He nodded, obviously warming to the topic. "A mother and a father. Hell, when the baby is older we can get a dog, too. If I travel you and the baby come with me. I don't know what the rules are in Florida about getting a marriage license, but I can find out. If you want a big wedding, we can do that as well. I'm open to that. But we should probably do it before the baby is born."

She ran his words through her brain over and over again but kept coming up with the same conclusion. He wanted to get married.

Now that was something she hadn't expected.

"You think we should get married?"

She was acting like a parrot, repeating what he said but she was having trouble forming words and sentences.

Sam Collins wanted to marry her.

Those people in hell might want to put on a parka.

CHAPTER
Twenty-Three

"I DO THINK we should get married," Sam pressed. "It makes everything so much easier."

Be still my heart. The romantic fool.

"I'm not sure that's a valid reason for a wedding."

Jumping to his feet, he paced the area between her coffee table and the front window.

"Think about what it will be like if we don't. The poor kid will be shuttled between us constantly, spending way too much time on airplanes and with nannies. Is that what you want for our child? Because that's what it's going to be like. I don't want to be a father that only sees his kid a few weeks every year. If I'm going to do this, I want to be involved."

Be careful what you wish for. It might come true.

She'd hoped that Sam would want to be a father to the baby, and now he did. The devil, however, was in the details.

"I don't want our child pulled from pillar to post," she

conceded with a heavy sigh. There was no clear-cut answer here. "Frankly, the idea of putting my baby on an airplane to you with some nanny is horrifying. I'm not sure I could even make myself do it. But marriage? That's a huge commitment. We don't love each other."

The elephant in the room had to be acknowledged. They weren't a couple and there wasn't love between them. They had respect and friendship and a whole lotta lust but was that enough to build a life on? She wasn't so sure.

"We're committed for life already, Riley. We have a child between us now, which means we're stuck with each other for a good long while whether we like it or not." He came to sit next to her on the couch. "Don't reject this right away. I've spent most of the night thinking about this and it's the perfect solution. If you're my wife, you'd be legally and financially protected if anything happened to me. You once told me that you were sensible and pragmatic. You have to admit that the most practical solution is that we get married."

She couldn't deny it. He'd made a great argument. If she wasn't sort of a romantic at heart.

"That's true..."

"But?"

She wanted to marry for love and romance and passion and all that girly stuff. She wanted to believe that her marriage would last forever and that her husband couldn't live without her.

That wasn't a rational argument, though.

"If you want me to be pragmatic then I need to think about my job and my house. I can't just up and leave. I have responsibilities here."

"I figured we could keep your house and I can just pay it off. We'll want to visit Mom quite a bit and your family is close by, too. The rest of the time we can make our home wherever you'd like, although I do a great deal of business in Los Angeles and New York. If we don't live there I might have to travel more, but if they're just short trips you wouldn't necessarily have to come along unless you wanted to."

Apparently, he'd anticipated all of her arguments. "We would keep my house?"

"Absolutely," he assured her. "And wherever we decide to make our home we can buy a house with a guest cottage so my mother or your parents can visit as often as they like."

" A guest cottage. That's...handy."

He'd thought of everything, essentially knocking the pins out from under her. All she had to do was give in and go with the flow.

"My friend Tyler has one and it's great for when family come and stay. But we'll worry about that when the time comes. I think our main focus needs to be on getting married as soon as possible and then preparing for the baby."

Riley took another long drink of her lemonade, draining the glass and wishing it were vodka.

"Do you want some more lemonade?"

She blinked a few times and then nodded. "I think I do."

What she really needed was more time and space, but they appeared to be in short supply.

Sam refilled both of their glasses but didn't sit down,

instead resuming his pacing that was beginning to get on her nerves.

"Listen, you'll have to take time off once the baby comes, right? Math was never my best subject but I'm pretty sure that you'll give birth this winter in the middle of the school year. So you'd only be going back for part of the year, anyway. You won't even need to work. Whether we get married or not, I'll make sure that you're taken care of financially. You'll be able to stay home full time with the baby for as long as you like."

He didn't get it. He'd been so busy making plans, he hadn't stopped for a minute to think about what she wanted. He'd only thought about what was convenient for him.

Finally. She'd found a flaw in the man. He was a tiny bit self-centered, but then he had good reason to be. People had probably been catering to his every whim for years now.

"You certainly have it all planned."

He stopped pacing and turned to her, his brows pinched together in a frown.

"You don't make that sound like a good thing."

"It could be but you kind of forgot one tiny detail."

He crossed his arms over his chest. "Such as?"

"Me."

"You? I didn't forget you. This is all about you."

Riley shook her head sadly. He really believed what he was saying. "No, it's about you. It's all about me and the baby fitting into your life. There's nothing in there about you fitting into mine."

He opened his mouth but then shut it again. From his

expression, it looked like he desperately wanted to say something but for some reason he didn't.

"No reply?"

Shuffling his feet, he shrugged. "People are always complaining about their jobs. I didn't think it would be a big deal if you quit. I thought you'd be glad."

"Have I ever complained about my job? Because I love what I do, and I've worked hard for the reputation I have as an excellent, caring educator. You're just assuming that I want to throw it all away." She was well aware as to why. "Because you make millions and I make peanuts. Automatically you assumed that your work was far more important than mine."

"No–"

"C'mon, Sam. You've always been honest with me. You just assumed that I would make all the compromises because you're the big Hollywood star and I'm just the knocked-up kindergarten teacher. I should just be grateful that you don't throw a little money my way and go back to your life, right?"

His cheeks were red and he couldn't look her in the eye. Bingo.

"I was trying to make everything easy for you."

"And you," she shot back. If they were going to make this work, she had to set boundaries right out of the gate. She couldn't let him and his fame take over her life. "Let's not forget that all of this would be easier for you."

He looked up then and their gazes clashed, sending a jolt through her all the way to her toes. There was pain and anguish in his eyes, but she didn't know where it came from. As quickly as she saw it, it was gone as if it had never been, but she couldn't forget the haunted expression he'd worn if only for a moment.

"Trust me, nothing about this has been easy for me."

Riley wanted to ask why but nothing about him invited that question. He held himself stiffly. His body language foreboding. The openness he'd exhibited earlier was gone.

She decided to start again and perhaps he would relax.

"I'm willing to discuss what's best for the baby but we need to do this together. No going off on your own and making all the plans, expecting me to just fall in line. If you want us to be a team, let's start now."

He nodded, his entire body seeming to loosen up. "Fine, you've had a lot longer than me to think about this. How did you imagine it would be? What's your vision?"

It was her turn to blush. "Honestly, I wasn't sure how involved you wanted to be, Sam. You have a busy career and you're always traveling."

"Okay, but that doesn't answer my question."

No, it didn't, but then answering wasn't so simple. However, she'd asked him to be honest with her so she had to be as well, no matter how difficult.

"Part of me thought you might offer money."

Sam didn't look angry or insulted. Maybe that idea had crossed his mind.

"And the other part?"

"I guess I thought that you'd be a sort of drop-in dad. You know, come to town when you had time or maybe I'd bring the baby to you now and then."

He sat down in the chair opposite her and took a gulp of his lemonade. "You must have a terrible opinion of me, Riley."

"I don't," she protested. "I actually think you're a good man."

"Who ignores his child?" Sam shook his head, that look of pain back in his eyes. "You know how I was brought up. It was just me and Mom and she did great. She was the best mother I could have ever hoped for, but you actually thought I would walk away from my own child after growing up without a father? I want to be a dad to this baby and I want to care for you, too. I doubt I'll be any good at it, but I want to try if you'll let me."

She remembered the look on Paula's face when she'd spoken about wanting a father for her son. Riley wanted that too, but everything in life had a cost. How much was she willing to give to have a loving daddy for her son or daughter?

Everything. She was willing to give it all.

"Sam, I think I might have an idea we can both live with."

CHAPTER
Twenty~Four

IT WAS the best deal Sam was going to get, at least for now.

Riley had agreed to spend her summer with him in New York City while he finished his latest picture. At the end of July, she'd make a decision as to whether to give up her job and marry him. With Riley living with him, he could take care of her and the baby. If he'd pushed for more, she would have certainly rebelled and he couldn't watch over her. Now all he had to do was make living with him so wonderful she wouldn't want to return to her old life.

Not a small task.

If his ex-wife was to be believed he was difficult to live with and a real pain in the ass, and he'd assumed that he hadn't become any better in the ensuing years since his divorce. If anything, he was probably a hell of a lot worse. Spoiled, set in his ways, and stubborn as hell, he was used to living alone and getting what he wanted pretty much all of the time. If he wanted Thai food for dinner, he called up his favorite restaurant. If he wanted the thermostat set at seventy-two, then by God that's where it would be. If he wanted to stay up all night and watch bad horror movies while eating pizza then he did that, too. Those days were officially over. He had someone else to think about now and that - as Riley had painfully reminded him - was something that didn't come naturally.

He'd handled the situation like he handled most things, by issuing orders and plans to her like she was part of his staff. If things worked out, she was going to be his wife and that required an immediate attitude adjustment. From what he'd seen from his friends' marriages, they needed to become partners and work together.

"How are you feeling, Mom?"

Paula was stretched out, her feet propped on an ottoman while she read one of the books Sam had bought for her. He'd managed to keep her home today but tomorrow was a whole new battle. She was insistent that she was fully recovered.

"Fine, and if you ask me again I won't be responsible for my actions. You'd think I had major surgery the way you're acting. I forgot to drink some water. No big deal."

"It could have been a big deal. You could have died."

Snapping her book shut with a sigh, Paula placed it on the table next to the chair. "Aren't you a bundle of sunshine? Is the movie you're making sad and depressing by any chance?"

"It's a comedy," he deadpanned, resisting the urge to

roll his eyes. "Seriously though, dehydration is nothing to mess with, Mom."

"I know, and I will take it seriously from now on." She nodded to the glass of water on the table. "I'm drinking one of those every hour. I could float around the room like a balloon. Stop worrying."

"You're my mother, I'll never stop worrying about you."

"I have so much to look forward to in my old age. Did you come here to tell me you're leaving? I'll be fine, son. Riley and Tara will check on me and report back to you, I'm sure."

About Riley...

He sat down on the couch and rubbed at his chin, trying to figure out a good way to break the news. He should have planned this better.

"Actually, Riley won't be in New Hope this summer. She's going to spend it in New York with me."

Paula's face lit up with the biggest smile he'd seen in a long time. "Darling, that's wonderful. Just what I'd hoped for you two. She's perfect for you. I think you'll be very happy together."

"Slow down." He held up his hand before she could go too far. "It's for the summer. She wants to see how things go before she makes any more of a commitment so let's take this one step at a time."

Paula clasped her hands together in delight. "It's a step forward and that's the important thing. How did you convince her?"

"My charm, of course. What else?"

He hated lying to his mother but both he and Riley

thought it wise not to spread the news too widely until she was further along. It had actually been her idea, but he'd quickly agreed. There were too many things that could go wrong and it was better to wait.

"I'm so happy about this. Is she leaving with you or following later?"

"With me, but I hope you're still planning to come visit soon. I know that Riley would love the company while I'm working."

He could also trust that she'd be looked after when she was with his mother.

"I wouldn't want to intrude—"

He waved away her protests. "Nonsense, Riley is going to have a great deal of time to herself and she'd love it if you were there. She and I have already discussed it. In fact, why don't you come with us in the morning? I can get another ticket."

They were only worried about Paula guessing Riley's condition, but if she did they would deal with it then.

His mother's cheeks had turned bright pink and for once she didn't seem to have an immediate reply. "Well...I would...but I have plans this weekend. I have...a date."

This was the second time in less than twelve hours he felt like someone had slapped him on the side of the head with a two by four.

A date? Since when did his mother date?

"That's...nice. How did you meet him?" A terrible thought occurred to Sam. "You didn't meet him online, did you? That's not safe."

Laughing, Paula shook her head. "His name is Tom and he moved to New Hope about six months ago. He's a retired aerospace engineer who used to work for NASA. Now he's training for a triathlon and volunteering at the school to help kids with their math. I think you'd like him."

Sam already didn't like this guy. Six months? He sounded like a fast mover. "How do you know he's telling you the truth, Mom? Men will say anything to get a date with a female. You should give me his whole name so I can have him checked out. Find out all the things he hasn't told you yet. He could be a criminal or a con artist."

Awful images of his mother heartbroken, crying and bilked out of her life savings ran through Sam's head. Maybe he should meet this guy before he let his mother go out with him.

"You will do no such thing, Samuel Christopher." Paula had sat up and was now shaking a finger under his nose, her expression tight. Shit. "He can't be a criminal because they do a background check and fingerprint you before you can volunteer in the school system. As for whether he's lying about working for NASA, why would he lie about that? If I were going to lie about what I did for a living, I'd tell people I was a race car driver or a famous surgeon."

Sam still didn't trust him. "Maybe I should—"

"Mind your own business," his mother finished for him. "I am still your mother, and you will not start acting like the parent in this relationship. Do I make myself clear, young man?"

"Very clear," he said through gritted teeth. He might not get to do a thorough background check on Tom but he was definitely going to ask Riley about him. "I'm just trying to help."

"I appreciate that but I'm a grown woman and I've been out on a date before. Now tell me what your plans are for Riley when you get to New York City."

That was easy. Make everything so wonderful for her she'd never want to leave.

CHAPTER
Twenty-Five

RILEY TOOK another sip of the ginger ale Sam's assistant Callie had left by her bedside and found herself relaxing with even the knots in her tortured stomach loosening slightly. Her morning sickness hadn't appreciated the plane ride to New York City.

Like a vengeful god in an old Norse tale, epic morning sickness had hit her today and she'd been blindsided, unprepared for the ferocity. When they'd left for the airport she'd been a little nauseous but nothing terrible, so she hadn't thought much about it. By the time the plane took off, however, she was clutching a barf bag and grossing out all the other passengers in first class. At one point, Sam had apologized to the flight attendant that he hadn't booked a charter.

Now her stomach had emptied itself of not only its contents - decaf coffee and a muffin - but the lining as well. She had nothing left to give and that almost made it worse.

Apparently, her digestive system was extremely pissed off at the moment.

I might live after all.

Cautiously, she swung her legs down from the mattress and slowly stood, testing her jelly-like knees and finding them surprisingly solid. Walking into the ensuite bathroom, she could almost see her reflection in the expensive white marble and shiny faucets. Too cold and sterile for Riley's tastes.

The mirror above the sink told the tale and it wasn't pretty. Her face was pale, her hair limply clung to her skin, and she had nasty dark circles under her eyes making her resemble a panda she'd once seen at the zoo. She needed some damage control and quick. It was bad enough that she'd basically thrown up on Sam for three hours, but she didn't want to look like a zombie afterward.

If we have any future, he's just going to have to take the good with the bad.

Riley rinsed her mouth and splashed some cold water on her face before running her fingers through her hair.

More human.

Time to seek out the other human in the place. Sam.

But first she took her first good look at the bedroom. Was this Sam's room? With the massive bed, it probably was. All done in black, gray, and white, the space screamed that a single man lived here and he had money. The drapes were open, showing off an amazing view of the New York City skyline on a sunny day.

She had an inkling that a condo like this in the Upper

East Side wasn't cheap. It was one more item to remind her how different their lives were, not that she needed it. She'd never flown first class until today either, but it had been clear it was old hat to Sam.

The living room was also masculine with brown leather couches and navy blue throw pillows. The television in here was even larger than the one in the bedroom, resembling a movie screen more than a TV. Her father and brothers would love to watch a football game on this. They'd be in sports junkie heaven.

A phone to his ear, Sam stopped pacing and looked up, giving her a smile. He held up one finger and mouthed *just a minute.*

"Thanks, Bobby. No, just call me if you see anything. I know you'll take care of it."

He pressed a button and tossed the cell into the cushions of the couch.

"There you are. How are you feeling? You look much better than when we got here."

If she looked this bad now she could only imagine how terrible she'd looked about an hour ago, but then she'd been praying for a swift and merciful death at that time.

"Better. That ginger ale and crackers were seriously magic." She walked over to look out of the large windows at the far side of the room. The view was even better from here. "Callie seems nice."

Which was an understatement. She'd been invaluable in the few hours that Riley had been in New York City.

Sam's smile grew wider. "She is. She's the best damn assistant I've ever had but if you tell her that I'll deny it. I can barely afford her as it is, and I swear every year that she works for me she gets more bossy. Sometimes I wonder who works for whom."

"Your secret is safe with me," Riley vowed. "I think I owe you a thank you as well as Callie. I don't think I would have survived that flight without you. As it is, I doubt that we're going to ever be allowed to fly that airline again. I'm sure we've been blackballed. Or at least I am."

Frowning, he came up behind her, placing his hands on her shoulders. She could feel the heat of his skin through the thin cotton of her shirt and the warmth seemed to penetrate her very bones, soothing her even further after the long journey.

"I'll always take care of you, Riley. Don't ever doubt that. If you need something - anything - don't hesitate to ask me. I mean that."

That was sweet but there wasn't much he could do about morning sickness. She was going to have to tough this out. Reaching up, she allowed herself the luxury of stroking his forehead right where his brow furrowed. The skin was smooth under her fingertips and from the way his eyes closed for a long moment he enjoyed it as much as she did.

He *was* hers to touch, after all. He'd said he wanted to marry her.

"I'm still going to say thank you. We're going to have to do battle as a team."

She hoped teasing him a little would garner a smile. He'd been far too tense this entire trip. He should be happy and relieved they'd arrived at his home in one piece.

His lips turned up at the corners and his whole demeanor softened. "We are a team but when one of us is down the other has to pick up the ball, so to speak. If you don't mind the sports metaphor."

"I don't." She nodded toward the expansive view. "Pretty impressive."

"New York is one of my favorite cities. I hope you'll come to love it as much as I do while you're here. Which brings me to my next question. I know you wanted to go sightseeing the minute you got here but maybe you should take it easy today and try again tomorrow?"

He'd said it like a question, but she had a feeling she'd have a fight on her hands if she didn't agree. Riley already felt much better but still less than a hundred percent, so she wasn't going to argue. In fact, she might spend the rest of the day in this beautiful home reading and watching television. Sam had assured her they had nothing that needed to be done until he had to be on the set tomorrow morning.

"I think that sounds like a good idea. I have plenty of time to see the sights and I am a little worn out."

Hopefully morning sickness would indeed stick to only the morning hours and she'd be recovered very soon.

"If you feel better later, we can go out to dinner."

"I'd like that. Callie said you were talking to your publicist. Has anything been published on social media?"

"Not yet, but he's keeping watch. I asked the flight attendants to ask the other passengers not to post anything but of course no one can stop them. I didn't notice anyone taking our picture while on the plane but that doesn't mean someone won't just post on Twitter that they saw us and that you were sick. That would be enough to start the conjecture and rumors. I think we may need to tell your family and my mom sooner rather than later. Especially as we have the doctor's appointment day after tomorrow and you'll want to do some baby shopping while you're here. The news is going to filter out whether we like it or not."

She didn't like it. It was too soon, but then would she ever really be ready for the world to know she was having Sam Collins's baby? She doubted people would care all that much about her, but they would be curious about the child. If it resembled Sam, and if he or she had inherited their father's talent. He did, however, have a valid point and the last thing she wanted was for her parents and siblings to find out about her pregnancy from a supermarket rag.

"You're right," she sighed. "Although I wish you weren't. Maybe after the doctor's appointment we can call them."

"Sounds like a plan. Now is there anything I can get you? More ginger ale or crackers? Maybe make you some tea?"

He had that anxious look on his face as if she were going to pass out on the floor at any minute. Of course, he had good reason after their flight.

"Thank you but I'm feeling much better. I'm going to get a refill of ginger ale and then maybe sit down and read a good book. The light from those windows is perfect."

Holding up his phone, Sam grimaced. "I have several more calls to make, if you're okay with that. If you need anything—"

"I'll be fine." Riley waved away his concerns. "I know that you're here to work. Believe me, nothing is more luxurious to me than a day spent lounging around and reading.

This is heaven and I'm all happy. Go make your million dollar deals."

"I'll go in the office so I don't disturb you."

Settling on the couch, Riley stretched out her legs and opened her e-reader. She had a massive to be read list and the biggest decision she wanted to make for a few hours was which book was she going to choose.

The other more important decisions about her life would have to wait. Taking it one day at a time here in New York with Sam was the most prudent course. This could work out, but it might crash and burn. This was all shiny and new to Sam, but in a few weeks would he still be all in? Only time would tell.

CHAPTER
Twenty-Six

SAM STOOD in the center of his bedroom listening to the water running on the other side of the bathroom door. Riley was preparing for bed and that was what he needed to do as well, but instead he was frozen in place contemplating multiple scenarios and grading each one as to how likely it was an outcome.

He had been nervous many times in his life. His first audition. His first day on a movie set. His first date. His first time having sex. And that was just a few from the very long list.

But nothing in his life to date had him as nervous as bedtime now that Riley was staying in his home. She'd agreed to spend the summer with him and really think about his marriage proposal but that didn't mean she'd agreed to share a bed with him. It also didn't mean that she was interested in having sex with him, especially as she'd been so sick this morning. Physical intimacy was probably the furthest thing from her mind and he wasn't a jerk that was going to press the issue. He'd let her come to him.

But...

The question of where he was going to sleep tonight was still wide open. He'd placed her suitcases in the master bedroom when they'd arrived and she hadn't objected. He'd even showed her where he'd made room for her clothes in the closet and the dresser so she was able to unpack. But it didn't mean that she expected him to sleep there. She might assume he was bunking in one of the guest rooms.

Except that all of his clothes and toiletries were in there.

I'll just stroll in like this is totally normal. Act like we do this every night.

If his friends could see him right now they'd be howling with laughter. Sam had a reputation as a cool, smooth operator but he was sweating through his t-shirt and hoping his heart didn't jump out of his chest.

This was ridiculous. He was a grown man, well-experienced with women of all kinds. He couldn't remember the last time a female had rejected his advances. In fact, he rarely had to do the chasing. The women came to him.

Riley, however, was different. She'd never come on to him or even flirted really. She was honest, straightforward, and she didn't play those head games that so many of his other girlfriends had played. She wasn't here because she wanted fame or diamonds. She was here...because of the baby. Whether any attraction to him had played a role, he didn't know. If he'd asked her to join him before she knew she was pregnant, then he might have a clue into her psyche but right now all he had to go on was that she wasn't sure whether to marry him or not, so this was a trial run. Technically he was on probation, so he didn't want to screw this up.

So here he was. Still standing in the middle of his bedroom like a fool. He didn't have any more answers now than he'd had ten minutes ago. All he knew was that he wanted to share that bed with Riley. The sex wasn't the important part. Okay, it was important, but it wasn't required. He could control himself.

He simply wanted to be close to her. He'd spent so many long, empty nights thinking about her and now she was here. The fact that his emotions were so diverse and all over the place spoke to a greater issue than where he would lay his head tonight, but he could only take one problem at a time.

He took too long, however, and the bathroom door swung open. Riley stood there looking so absolutely, stunningly beautiful that he had a difficult time sucking oxygen into his lungs. Speaking was out of the question.

A lump lodged in his throat as his gaze ran from her pink-painted toes, up her shapely golden limbs, to the hem of the oversized t-shirt she was wearing. Gray with pink letters across her breasts, it read "New Hope Beach, Florida" and he lingered a little too long right there. Hopefully she'd just think he was a slow reader and not that he was checking out her rack.

Because he totally was. Like a randy teenage boy who had never been laid, he was staring at her with his tongue hanging out. Not exactly the mature and laidback image he'd been honing in Hollywood for years.

"Sam?"

Don't just stand here like an idiot. Say something.

"How are you feeling?"

Better than nothing but hardly original. He'd been asking her that all day.

She smiled and he couldn't help but notice how her eyes lit up when she did. There was no pretending she was happy or even a halfway grimace. When she smiled, she was all in.

"I'm good. Much better than this morning." She held up her wrists which had round dents in the flesh from the elastic bands she'd worn most of the afternoon. "Those pressure bands are magic right along with the ginger ale. I didn't even have to try the lollipops."

Thank God. He didn't think he could have handled watching her licking and sucking a lollipop. He was only human.

"I bet you're tired."

Wow, scintillating conversation. She had to be questioning his intelligence right about now.

"Actually, I'm a little too keyed up to sleep," she confessed. "I did rest earlier and now that I feel better I'm kind of excited to finally be visiting New York City. I'm looking forward to doing some sightseeing tomorrow and that reminds me...thank you for letting Callie spend so much time with me. I know it's her job to take care of you."

"And you," he corrected. "We're a team now, remember? What's mine is yours."

"You might not want to say that," she giggled, her hand flying up over her mouth. "Because I'm not sure you want anything of mine unless you've had a deep-seated need for a used Honda Accord with low mileage."

"They're sensible automobiles." He realized they were still standing in the middle of the room. At some point, one of them needed to make a move toward the bed. Did he dare? "We can watch some television if you're not sleepy."

"That sounds good." She moved to one side of the bed but then stopped abruptly. "Um, is this side okay? I can sleep on either."

From her pink cheeks and the way she avoided his gaze, Sam was beginning to get the idea that she wasn't totally comfortable about all of this either. They'd always been honest with one another and their quickly burgeoning friendship had reflected that. He should have been up front in the first place instead of standing here like a dolt wondering what he should do.

"I usually sprawl in the middle but I'm fine with either side." He finally caught her gaze and he could see the nervousness she'd been trying to hide. "We haven't talked much about this. I don't want you to feel pressured about anything this summer. If you need me to sleep in the other room, I can do that."

I just don't want to.

"Do you want to sleep in the guest room?"

"No," he replied firmly. He didn't want there to be any doubt in her mind. "I'd like to share this bed with you. I meant what I said about us being a couple and committing to a future. As for sex, well, you can decide about that. I won't push especially as I know that you're not feeling a hundred percent."

"Then we should start as we mean to go on." Riley lifted the covers and slid in, so he did the same on the other side before reaching for the remote. "I want this to work, Sam. I'm just cautious by nature."

"I respect that. It's just when I want something I tend to go all out until I get it, but I won't pressure you about marriage right now. I know that you want the summer to see how we do."

He was determined she was going to love living with him, although he wasn't sure how. She couldn't be wooed like other women with gifts and parties.

He handed her the remote control. "Your choice. I'll watch anything."

It was the first step in the campaign to make life so wonderful for her that she'd never want to go back to Florida and live alone. Whatever Riley wanted, he'd make happen for her. But he had a feeling that the biggest problem would be that she didn't want anything from him.

There was nothing that he could give her that would make her want to stay.

CHAPTER
Twenty-Seven

THE NEXT DAY, Callie stuck her head into the kitchen where Riley was preparing lunch. Sam had headed off to the set before the sun was even up but he'd left his assistant behind. The two women planned to see some sights today if possible. After more tea, crackers, and a pregnancy nausea lollipop, Riley was feeling pretty good and anxious to get out of the condo and breathe some fresh air.

Callie wasn't what Riley had expected. Somehow she'd pictured a young person, probably female and probably beautiful. While Callie wasn't old she looked to be in her late forties or early fifties perhaps, although her dark brown hair didn't have a single gray in it. Attractive and energetic, she was tall, whip-thin, and dressed casually in blue jeans and a Ramones t-shirt.

"You have a visitor," Callie said, motioning towards the living room. "It's Sam's attorney. I told him you'd be out in a minute."

Sam's attorney. Was Riley being thrown out already with nothing but a check and a warning to say nothing? Sam had said he wanted them to have a future, but Chad had said that, too. Placing the pan of soup on a cold burner she wiped her hands and joined Callie and the lawyer in the other room.

"Riley, this is Alexander West. Alex, this is Riley Bridges." Callie stepped back and gave Riley an encouraging smile. "I'll be in Sam's office if anyone needs me."

They shook hands and Riley took a seat in the chair next to the couch where Alex West sat. He was dressed in a dark charcoal gray suit and light blue silk tie, and appeared to be about Sam's age. Despite her apprehension, he had a kind expression on his face. If he was here to say Sam wanted her gone then he was clearly enjoying the task.

"It's nice to meet you, Ms. Bridges." He began unpacking documents from his attaché. "May I call you Riley?"

"Sure, that's fine." From this angle she couldn't read the papers that were beginning to stack up in front of her. A pit had begun to form in the bottom of her stomach. This obviously wasn't a social call. "Sam didn't mention that you would be by."

"I wasn't sure I would be able to make it today but I had a cancellation in my schedule. Here we are. I think this is everything he and I discussed." He dipped into his jacket pocket and pulled out a pen. "You just need to sign everywhere there's an x."

Hold your horses, buddy.

"Um...I don't get to read them first?"

His brows flew up but his smile grew wider. "You may absolutely read through them but I'm happy to explain what each document is. I can assure you it's nothing nefarious or even that secretive. Sam asked me to put some papers together to ensure that you and the baby would be protected and taken care of in case anything happened to him."

With a jolt, Riley realized that she wasn't being swept under a carpet or sent back to Florida. She hadn't scared off Sam by being violently ill on the flight. She was staying, at least for now.

But what had Sam done here? And just what was she signing?

Riley was a fish out of water and gasping for breath. Nothing was the same and she had a feeling that they never would be again. Time to get used to her new reality.

———

"You should have warned her, Sam."

Callie's tone was slightly scolding despite the fact that he was the one that signed her paycheck. Or at least his accountant did.

"By the time I read Alex's text it was too late. We were shooting the fight scene today."

Consequently, he felt like an old punching bag that needed to be thrown to the curb. The other actor was a total jerk and was supposed to pull his punches. It was all make believe, after all. Yet, somehow Sam was going to be black and fucking blue for the next week. Even the director had lost his patience with Sam's co-star, finally bringing in a stunt man to finish the scene, and sending the sniveling little shit to his trailer so he could bang one of the interns.

"She was shocked and almost didn't sign the papers. I think it would have been easier for her if you'd talked about your reasons for doing it." There was a quiet pause before Callie continued. "She doesn't want people to think she's here for the money or the fame."

Anybody that thought that didn't know Riley Bridges at all. She was the most honest, straightforward woman he'd met in years, and she didn't give a shit if he had a million dollars. To her, it was about how he was inside as a person. If he'd been a dick, there was no amount of money in the world that would have made her spend time with him.

"I'll talk to her tonight. I promise. But she did sign?"

After a long talk with his attorney, Sam wanted to make sure that she and the baby were taken care of no matter what happened to him. Fate was a fickle entity and he'd seen younger and healthier men unexpectedly kick the bucket after a freak accident. At least now, he could sleep easier knowing that his child and Riley would be okay without him.

"She did," Callie confirmed. "I told her that she would be doing a lot of shopping for the nursery and things like that. Plus, I reminded her that just because she had a credit card didn't mean she had to use it. That seemed to calm her down. I thought you should know because I think you're going to have a fight on your hands to get her to spend any money."

He'd expected that, but he hadn't thought it would be so soon. Once they were married she wouldn't have any more room to object, but until then he would have to assure her that it was perfectly normal for a father to spend money on his baby. And his woman.

"Thanks, Callie. As usual you handled everything better than I could. Will you let her know I'm going to try and be home in time for dinner? I think the director is going to call it for the day here in about an hour. If she wants to go out, we can do that."

"I think she'll want to stay in. She and I walked all over midtown today seeing the sights. She's taking a nap now. I can order something and have it delivered, if you like."

Sam wished he was curled up with Riley, her warm little body pressed against his. It had been sheer heaven last night to sleep beside her. It had also been hell not being able to make love to her. He didn't want to press his luck. Better to woo and court her than to assume she was immediately ready to resume their sexual relationship.

Or that even if she wanted to that she could. She'd been so sick yesterday that the last thing she needed was some guy pawing at her, even if that guy was him. He was trying to impress her, convince her that she should take a chance and marry him. The last thing he needed to do was clue her in as to how much of a horn dog he really was. She'd take the first plane back to Florida.

"That sounds great. Whatever Riley wants. You know that I'm not picky." He could hear a rapping on his trailer door. Back to work. "They're calling me back to the set. Thanks for taking care of her. I appreciate it."

"No problem, Sam," his assistant assured him. "We're becoming good friends. I haven't had this much fun since your mother and I took that cruise a few years ago."

Sam still had a few gray hairs from that. He'd sent Callie to be the voice of reason on the trip. The joke had been on him.

"Just don't end up in jail and needing bail money. *TMZ* will be all over that."

"Sam Collins, I wouldn't take your pregnant girlfriend anywhere that we might be arrested. Mostly we just walked around and did some shopping. You're a suspicious man."

For good reason.

"Just take care of her. I'm trying to convince her to marry me. Throw in a good word now and then, will you? I could use some help here."

Callie chuckled. "You don't need any help there, hot shot. She's head over heels for you. She just doesn't want to admit it. And honestly, I've never seen you look happier. It's much better than that brooding Hamlet you were doing before she came here."

He was happy, and he wanted them to be a family. He could only hope that Callie was right.

Because now that Sam had Riley here with him, he wasn't sure he could let her go.

CHAPTER
Twenty-Eight

UNFORTUNATELY, there had been a snafu on the set and the final camera setup and lighting took far longer than Sam had anticipated. He'd called Riley apologetic and sounding exhausted. She'd assured him she wasn't upset and hoped he'd be home soon.

That was six hours ago.

She'd eaten the dinner that Callie had ordered and packed the leftovers in the refrigerator for warming later when Sam arrived. Except that the time kept ticking away as she watched television and tried to stay awake. She was sure he was fine but she felt badly that he'd had such a long day. He'd warned her about the crazy hours on a movie set but she hadn't thought she'd see it so quickly.

At some point she must have fallen asleep because her lids felt heavy but she could hear a key turning in the lock. Rubbing her eyes, she could see Sam trying to tiptoe into the condo, probably hoping not to wake her.

"What time is it?" He whirled around, clutching at his chest. "Oops, didn't mean to scare you."

Chuckling, he bent down to brush his lips over her forehead. He'd done that same thing this morning before he'd left. "I thought you were asleep. It's about one. Why aren't you in bed?"

He'd kept his tone hushed as if they already had a little one sleeping in another room.

"I must have fallen asleep watching television." She didn't recognize the show that was currently playing and it definitely wasn't what she'd been watching. "You look tired."

He had dark circles under his eyes and his shoulders sagged with fatigue. If he leaned against the wall, he'd probably fall asleep on his feet.

"That's because I am tired. We were working on a fight scene all day. I'll be black and blue by morning."

"I thought they had stunt men so you wouldn't get hurt."

Scraping his fingers through his hair, he rubbed at the back of his neck. "They don't want me jumping out of an airplane but pretend fighting is okay. Except that my idiot co-star is trying to macho-up his image and wasn't pulling his punches and kicks. Eventually I had to return the favor. He didn't act so manly then."

Riley was more than a little fascinated by the glimpses she received from Sam regarding the backstage moviemaking. It was far more work than she'd ever imagined.

"Did he cry?"

Sam chuckled and shook his head. "No, but I think he wanted to. He muttered something about how it wasn't fair, which took nerve since he'd been smacking me around for twenty takes."

She couldn't stop herself from speaking her mind. "I'm not sure what it says about you that it took twenty takes for you to put a stop to it."

"I was following direction." Sam shrugged, not taking offense to her words. "He wasn't. After twenty takes I didn't give a shit if I got in trouble with the director."

"But he didn't get in trouble?"

Groaning, Sam fell into a chair and propped his long legs up on the ottoman. "Every goddamn take the director yelled at him but he kept doing it. So I decided that if he wanted to act like a badass, I'd be happy to help him out with that."

"Because you're a badass."

Sam snorted. "Being a badass is too damn much work. I'm just a guy that needs to soak in a bathtub until it's time to get up in the morning."

"I hope you get to go in late since you worked so many hours today."

Pushing himself to his feet, Sam sighed loudly. "That's not how it works, honey. They have a schedule and a budget that they're trying to stick to. My quick trip to Florida for a few days didn't help. I have to be on set bright and early tomorrow. Oh-six-hundred."

"That's in five hours," Riley gasped in shock. "That's cruel and unusual punishment."

"That's moviemaking. Now I'm seriously going to take a soak in the tub. You should go to bed and get some sleep. You're resting for two now."

She could climb into bed but she was wide awake now

after her nap. "How about I go warm up some dinner for you? There were lots of leftovers. Are you hungry?"

"Starving, but you don't—"

His denial was interrupted by a huge yawn that had her yawning in return when she wasn't that tired. It really was contagious.

"I'll warm something up and you go take a bath."

She used the same tone with Sam as she used with her kindergarten students. No nonsense and assumptive. She expected to be obeyed and it worked. He grumbled a little but did as she directed, kicking off his shoes and padding on sock-covered feet into the master bedroom.

Riley headed into the kitchen and pulled out the myriad of food containers, placing them on the counter. Callie had ordered enough food for an army and by the time Riley had emptied the shelf in the refrigerator she'd filled all the space on the countertop.

Not sure what he wanted to eat, she decided to heat up a little of everything. She piled his plate high with warm food and her own with just enough for a snack, then grabbed a bottle of beer, Sam's preferred beverage when eating dinner. Just in case though, she also added a bottle of her ginger ale. He did have to be at work in five hours so he might not want to drink. Caffeine also seemed like a no-no as he'd want to fall asleep as soon as possible.

She quickly set the table, her own stomach growling to be fed again. It was one of those rare moments when she wasn't nauseated and food sounded and smelled like nirvana. The home was quiet, however, with not a sound from the bedroom area. Riley peered around the corner of the doorway but the room was empty. Sam must still be in the bathtub. Softly, she knocked but there was no answer. Concerned, she cracked open the door and peeked in only to see Sam fast asleep, his head pillowed on the edge of the tub, snoring away.

Poor guy.

She couldn't let him sleep in the bathtub, though. It wasn't good for the back and he might slip down and drown. Trying not to stare at his exposed chest, she tiptoed across the marble floor so as not to startle him - again. Calling his name, she lightly placed a hand on his damp shoulder, the muscles firm under her palm. He jerked awake, his lids snapping open before relaxing when his gaze landed on her.

"Damn, I fell asleep. How long have I been in here?"

He held up his hand and rubbed his prune-like fingers together.

"Not too long but dinner is all warmed up. Do you still want to eat or do you want to go straight to bed?"

"Eat then bed." Sam rose out of the water, sending a wave over the side and splashing at her feet. Not one bit self-conscious, he stood there with rivulets of water running down his magnificent body as he reached for the towel he'd placed nearby. Images of their night together flashed through her brain and the room suddenly felt way too hot. Escape was the only thing on her mind. "Thanks for waking me up."

She backed toward the door, averting her gaze so she could only see him from the knees down. It didn't matter. He had great calves and feet, which was weird for her to notice, but then she was fascinated by everything with this man. "You're welcome. So...I'll see you in the kitchen."

Turning and not realizing how close she was, she smacked her forehead right against the hard wood of the door, knocking her a few steps back. For a moment, she stood there too stunned to move or speak as she processed the fact that her head hurt. But not nearly as much as her pride. She'd been caught out as a creeper and embarrassed herself.

"Hey, are you okay?"

Sam twisted her around and bent down so he could look at her head more closely. His gentle fingers grazed the goose egg that was beginning to form above her temple along with a king-sized headache that she couldn't take anything for.

I am so stupid.

"I'm fine. I guess I'm a little tired, too."

Sure. Yeah. Blame being a horn dog on fatigue. He might buy that if he happened not to see the lust in her eyes. This is what happened when she started to feel normal. She went from puking to lusting in seconds. Damn hormones.

Rubbing at the knot, she ignored the pounding in her head to instead stare into Sam's blue gaze. For a long moment the world seemed to fade away, their breaths co-mingling as she took in every detail of his face. The slight scruff at his jaw, the way his damp hair curled slightly, the sharp tang of his skin that made her want to run her tongue up the center of his chest. Because she knew from experience that he tasted as good as he looked and smelled. She turned her face up slightly, just enough to cue him that a kiss was welcomed. She'd spent last night lying next to him but not touching.

It had been far too long since they'd kissed.

A knife of disappointment sliced through her heart when he instead stepped back, hitching the towel around his waist. He didn't want her anymore. All the morning sickness had turned him off. She shouldn't have expected anything else. It was hard to keep the romance alive when one person in the couple was sick as a dog and about to blow up like a balloon in a parade.

"Let me get dressed and we'll put some ice on that."

And now she'd been dismissed.

Fleeing from the bathroom, she tried to hide the hurt by tucking into her meal and ignoring Sam when he came out to join her. Dressed in a pair of gray sweat pants and a form-fitting black t-shirt, he looked gorgeous as always. Being together like this in such a domestic scene...it felt warm and cozy. The two of them together hanging around the house and eating a late night supper after a long day. Then after eating, they'd climb into bed and cuddle, maybe even make love. It was like they were a *real couple*.

This is getting bad. What is my problem?

She'd gone much longer without sex before without blinking an eye. Now back with Sam, it was all she could think about. According to the pregnancy book, this rush of hormones shouldn't be happening for a few weeks.

Was it pregnancy or was it Sam?

Dumb question. It had to be Sam.

This might be one long and tortuous summer.

CHAPTER
Twenty~Nine

SAM HAD BEEN SO close to kissing Riley earlier but he'd backed away at the last minute, not wanting to presume too much. He'd invited her here to show how great they could be together. He'd vowed to woo and court her but as usual his career wasn't making it easy. The long hours and the physically demanding shoot weren't a good mix for a robust romantic life, too.

Now he was sitting across from her at the kitchen table wishing he'd gone ahead and kissed her. At least he'd know one way or the other. She would have either smacked his face or kissed him back. As it was, he didn't know where they stood and that was maddening. She was sharing his bed, but she wasn't *sharing* it.

In the carnal sense. They were like an old married couple who didn't care about sex anymore. Except that he cared a great deal. He hadn't thought it could be possible, but Riley was even more beautiful than when he'd left her over two months ago. He wanted her with a strength he'd never experienced before. It scared him and energized him in equal measures. If he had any sense at all, he'd be running away. Turns out he was dumb as a stump.

The silence had begun to feel awkward so he tried to fill it. "This is good and just what I needed."

"I have a feeling that Callie knows all the good restaurants in town."

"She does," he confirmed with a chuckle, thinking about the mass amounts of data his assistant kept in her head. Callie had the best memory of anyone he'd ever met. "She's got this town under her thumb. Anything you need, just ask her. She knows where to get it."

Riley set her fork down and dabbed at her lips with a paper napkin. "I have a doctor's appointment coming up."

She didn't say it like it was a good thing.

"I know you probably wanted your regular doctor–"

"It's fine," she said, shaking her head. "I just wish you would have talked to me about it first. It's becoming a...habit."

He didn't know what she meant by that.

"A habit? Making an appointment?"

"No, doing things without discussing it with me."

Ah, he knew what they were talking about now. But she couldn't be angry with him for wanting to provide for his child?

"In my defense, I didn't know Alex was going to be coming over today. I thought we'd have time to talk about it before he did."

Sighing, she rubbed her temples before she spoke. "I shouldn't have brought this up now. You're exhausted."

But...she had brought it up.

"It's been bothering you all day."

"Yes," she admitted, her shoulders slumping. "I know this is going to sound stupid because I should be thrilled that you want to make sure that the baby is taken care of - and I am - but I just kind of feel like you're off making decisions about the future and I'm sitting here."

She didn't mention that others might think she was here for his money. An idea that was so silly it couldn't even be contemplated. Riley wasn't that type of person and he would know. He'd had more than his share in his life and she wasn't even close.

"You have a point and I should have discussed it with you. I guess I don't know much about being partners or a team."

Sam pretty much did whatever he wanted when he wanted to. Clearly, that wasn't going to work going forward. He had Riley to think about now.

And hopefully for a long time.

"That makes two of us. I've never actually lived with a man before so this is all new. I just want to make sure that we make the big decisions together. The small ones I'm not so worried about."

"What would you classify as small?"

Tapping her chin, she smiled. "If you want to buy the baby a stuffed animal, that's small. If you want to buy him a pony or a car, that's big."

Fair enough.

"And if I want to buy you a pony or a car?"

"We would need to discuss that."

It was probably lack of sleep but he was feeling brave.

"What about a wedding ring?"

Riley's cheeks turned a lovely shade of pink and she didn't throw her leftover food at him. This was real forward progress.

"We'd need to discuss that too. But you said you'd give me the summer, remember?"

"I do. I was just checking to see how things were going a couple of days in."

She giggled at that and his chest tightened in response. "It's going good. I just want to see how I can integrate into your life, Sam. If we're going to make this work I want to be a true partner to you. Not just the mother of your child who's off in a corner doing her own thing."

"That's exactly what I want." Their gazes locked and he could feel the awareness between them build. She definitely wasn't indifferent to him. "Callie is going to take you to the appointment tomorrow and I'll meet you there. Then if you want, we can go back to the set where I'm filming. I'd love to show you around and introduce you to my co-stars."

It might sound corny and stupid but he wanted her approval of his chosen career. In simple terms, he wanted her to be proud of him.

"I'd love that. I have to admit that I'm sort of fascinated by the whole movie making process when you talk about it. There's much more involved than I ever realized."

"I felt the same way when I got my first role," he agreed, remembering back to the bit part he'd taken in a low-budget horror movie. "Just be sure to tell me if you don't feel up to the visit. If you don't feel well, I can bring you right back here afterward."

Wrinkling her nose, she shook her head. "Is it awful that I'm already tired of morning sickness?"

"I think that sounds normal. We can talk to the doctor about it tomorrow."

"If men got morning sickness they'd have cured it a couple of generations ago."

"Of that I have no doubt." He stood, picking up their empty plates. "Are you ready to head to bed? We have a big day in just a few hours."

Riley stood as well but she surprised him by taking the dishes from his hands and heading to the sink. "Fine, but I'll clean up in here. You go ahead."

"But–"

"No arguments," she said firmly, in that schoolteacher voice he was beginning to love. "You need your sleep and I've already had a few hours. I'll be there in ten minutes. Go."

It would be churlish to refuse. "Thank you. I will."

Sam could get used to this. Someone other than his own mother fussing and caring over him. Someone who would occasionally put his needs ahead of her own. That wasn't something he experienced often in Hollywood. He'd make sure that he returned the favor often. He wanted this to work and for more reasons than just the baby.

Riley. She was so different than any woman he'd ever known even before he'd made it big. She was honest, trustworthy, caring, and positive. She made him happier than he could remember being in a long time. Even just sitting and eating leftovers with her was better than just about anything else with some other woman.

She might be the one.

CHAPTER
Thirty

THE BEDROOM WAS STILL DARK when Riley opened her eyes the next morning. She could hear Sam moving about somewhere else in the condo and the space on the bed next to her was already growing cold. In just a few nights she'd become so used to sleeping next to Sam that she missed his presence when he wasn't lying beside her.

Knowing not to move too fast, she carefully sat up in bed and switched on the bedside lamp. Her stomach was churning but not as badly as it could have been. Quickly she slipped on the nausea wristbands that she'd placed on the nightstand and crossed her fingers that they would work fast so she could get out of bed.

"I know you're not hungry, but Callie said that this would help in the mornings."

Twisting toward the door, Sam stood there showered, dressed, and carrying a small plate of dry toast and a cup of tea. This was above and beyond the call of duty. He needed to be at the studio and instead he was toasting bread for her pissed off tummy.

"I can't believe you did this for me."

Chad would never have done it. But then he was a douchebag and Sam most decidedly was not.

"It only took a few minutes." He set the plate and cup on the nightstand. "I need to get going but I'll see you in a few hours, okay?"

Her mother had once told her that she needed to look for a partner that would care about her wants and needs as much as his own. Riley had but until this moment she hadn't realized that a man didn't have to make a grand gesture to show what kind of a person he was. He could simply make tea and toast. He could hold her hair when she was puking and put a cold cloth on her face. He could hand over his own assistant to show her around a new city. He could show up and talk about his career to a bunch of five and six-year-olds.

This was a man worth keeping in her life. Whether it was as her husband or as a friend that remained to be seen.

Completely unaware of the direction of her early morning thoughts, Sam leaned down to kiss her forehead again, all chaste and disappointing. She probably looked a sight this time in the morning, hair like a rat's nest and breath like a coyote. Hardly a vision that would strike lust into the heart of a man who could have just about any woman he wanted. Her stomach wasn't exactly on board for any sort of kissing or cuddling either, doing another somersault in her abdomen and reminding her to put that toast and tea to good use.

"Have a good day," Riley said, lifting the cup from the

saucer and blowing on the steaming liquid. "And thank you again. This was really thoughtful."

Sam smiled that movie star smile that had graced a million screens and made women swoon everywhere. She wasn't immune either, and her pulse kicked into a higher gear.

Sam glanced at his watch and sighed. "I hope you feel better. I'll see you in a few hours. I have to go or I'll be late."

With a wave, he was gone leaving Riley to her tea and toast. She sipped the hot liquid slowly, interspersing bites of dry toast in between. By the time she finished, she was feeling almost human. A shower would take her the rest of the way.

Thank you, Sam.

This just might work out. Her and Sam. And eventually their baby. They could be a couple and raise a family. They could have a future together. Was it selfish to want love, too? Wasn't it enough that he respected and cared for her?

She wasn't sure of the answer but she'd have to figure it out. Soon.

———

Riley checked her reflection in the mirror one last time to make sure she didn't have lipstick on her teeth. She and Callie were heading to her very first doctor's appointment and the usual nausea in her belly had been replaced with hundreds of nervous butterflies. She already knew that she was pregnant but somehow it made it more real when a bona fide doctor confirmed it.

This is really happening. I'm having a baby.

Throwing her purse strap over her shoulder, she joined Callie in the living room. Sam had ordered a car service to take them to the appointment and it was waiting downstairs by the curb.

Callie turned from the front window and walked over to Riley, placing a hand on her shoulder. "We have company out there. Are you ready for this?"

Riley wasn't sure what the assistant was referring to.

"Company?"

Frowning, Callie nodded. "Paps. Photogs. Whatever you want to call them. They're lying in wait out there hoping to get a picture of you. Seems the word is out that Sam has a live-in girlfriend. Normally the tabloids leave him alone, especially in New York City, but he's never lived with a woman before so this is big news."

The paparazzi were camped outside hoping to get a photograph of her. It was kind of surreal. She was still just a kindergarten teacher and nobody special, but dating Sam had cast a spell. Now people wanted her picture and maybe a quote. She wasn't completely naïve. She'd known this was a possibility, especially if they stayed together as a couple past this summer. It had simply happened a little more quickly than she'd thought.

I can do this.

"I'm ready. I assume I should just ignore them."

Callie nodded in agreement. "Keep your head down so they can't get a good shot. They'll throw out questions, some of them deliberately nasty, to try and get you to respond. Whatever you do, don't. That's exactly what they want so they can get their money shot. They want to see you upset or crying or yelling so they can have a lovely front page with your picture and a headline about Sam Collins's emotional girlfriend. Don't give it to them."

Riley did not want to be on the front page of some tabloid if she could help it.

"They sound like a pack of rabid wolves."

Callie laughed and guided them toward the door. "Actually, some of the photographers are good people and Sam rewards them by stopping to pose when he can. Some, however, are assholes and they're the ones you have to watch out for. They'll invade your personal space, push you around, and generally be jerks. All they want is to get a picture and sell it. They don't care that it might be the worst day of your life that they're interrupting. Just stay close to me and I'll get us to the car."

Riley had thought she was prepared. Ha. How naïve. Nothing in her life up to now had prepared her for the shitstorm that awaited her on the sidewalk. It was only a few feet to the dark-windowed black SUV that Sam had ordered for her, but it might as well have been a mile.

The sidewalk was filled with shouting people, mostly men, but a few women as well. Flashbulbs blinded her as they went off in rapid succession, like fireworks on the Fourth of July, disorienting her as she tried to shade her eyes. Her pulse accelerated and adrenaline kicked in as her fight or flight response was triggered. Turning back, however, wasn't an option. She could only move forward.

Callie's arm was tight around Riley's waist, keeping her close as the paparazzi jostled her, almost knocking her to the pavement at one point. She had to keep her right elbow pointed out and her hand in front of her to push away the crush of bodies that threatened to overtake them.

Breathless but determined, she put her head down and plowed through the crowd, ignoring the questions being pelted at her. Some innocuous, and others rather mean, just as Callie had predicted.

Are you and Sam engaged?

Are you and Sam married?

Are you pregnant?

Was Sam dating Lucinda when he was dating you?

Is Sam still dating Lucinda?

How did you meet Sam?

Are you and Sam in love?

Who in the hell was Lucinda? Apparently, that was one of Sam's girlfriends that Riley had missed. Did these guys actually think that Riley would admit that Sam was dating her and this Lucinda at the same time?

Magically the back door of the black SUV opened and Riley dove in, followed closely by Callie. The door closed and the driver swung into the front seat, pulling away from the curb, parting the sea of paparazzi until they were safely away.

Riley didn't have the vocabulary to describe the last few minutes.

"That was..."

"Intense?" Callie asked, her brows lifted. "Annoying? Crazy? Surreal?"

"I'll go with all of that and a few other adjectives to be named later. I guess I didn't think that anyone would truly care about me. Not really."

"You're the woman who stole Sam Collins's heart.

That's a front page story. You're lucky that no one knows your other little secret or it would have been five times worse. They'd be following us to your doctor's appointment and bribing nurses for the ultrasound pictures."

Stole Sam Collins's heart.

Callie didn't know how loaded that sentence was. With each passing hour with Sam, Riley was hoping that was indeed what she'd done but then she wasn't completely sure of her own feelings.

Would I be hesitating if there weren't photographers on the sidewalk? Is his fame an issue?

If Sam were her friendly neighborhood dentist or accountant the situation would be much simpler. They'd be left alone to figure out their relationship and their feelings, but now she had no such luck. They were going to have to do it within sight of the American public. Riley was by nature a private, quiet person so this wasn't going to be easy but for the baby's sake she was going to have to strengthen her spine and do it.

Don't give those photographers any power over your life. Screw 'em.

The drive to the posh offices of the best obstetrician in New York City didn't take long. Honestly, they could have walked it but then the paparazzi would have trailed behind them and that would have been a disaster.

The lovely brick building on the Upper East Side screamed money along with the plush waiting room that was nicer than any doctor's office Riley had ever been in. In fact, it looked more like someone's living room than it did a place of business. She signed in at the front desk and the smiling receptionist handed her a clipboard and a stack of papers to fill out. She hadn't even finished when they were calling her name to see the doctor.

A moment of panic ran through Riley as her gaze darted for the dozenth time to the door.

"Sam isn't here."

Callie held up her phone. "He's on his way and he'll meet you back there. It's okay to go on."

She hadn't thought she might have to do this alone. She hated going to the doctor in general and this was a new one she'd never met. Presumably Sam hadn't either so at least they would have been in the same boat.

The nurses, however, appeared determined to make her as comfortable as possible. Riley had to do the usual things like pee in a cup, have her blood pressure taken, and oh joy, stand on the scale for her weight. She'd read in the pregnancy book that all of this would be done every time she came to the doctor.

"I have a feeling that in a few months I'm not going to enjoy stepping on the scale," Riley observed as the friendly nurse named Diane wrote down the number displayed on the digital readout. It was about right, give or take a few pounds. Riley hadn't worried much about her weight until now when it was out of her control.

"You don't have to look if you don't want to," Diane replied with a smile. "You can close your eyes. Some women do and if the doctor doesn't mention their weight then they know they're fine."

Riley wouldn't be able to stand not knowing.

"I'm not that bothered by it."

Not much anyway.

"That's the spirit. Now let's get you ready to see Dr. Kate."

Getting ready to see Dr. Kate involved taking off all of her clothes and putting on a cotton gown that opened in the front. To be fair, it was one of the nicer hospital gowns that Riley had ever worn. Her own gynecologist used paper gowns that were disposable and quite drafty, so this was a step up.

Diane handed Riley a remote control and pointed to the large screen television on the wall.

"Dr. Kate shouldn't be long but you're welcome to watch while you wait."

There was no way she was calmly watching daytime television while she waited. Her heart was practically beating out of her chest and so loudly she could barely hear anything around her. This was it. She was pregnant and the doctor was going to confirm that today. She might even get to hear the heartbeat.

Or was it too early?

Quickly shedding her clothes before the doctor came in, she shrugged into the gown, tying the lone tie at the neck, leaving her boobs and butt hanging out of the skimpy frock. Luckily the exam room wasn't over air conditioned. She hopped up onto the table and waited, her thoughts scattered.

The baby. Sam. The paparazzi. A possible marriage. That would mean a wedding. And then there was the whole did she love him? She was definitely falling in that direction and it scared her. She hadn't had the best of luck with men but then Sam wasn't like anyone else she'd ever dated. Did he love her? Even a little? Was he feeling the same fear that was holding her back? She couldn't blame him if he was. Caution had ruled most of her life except for that one night she'd thrown it to the wind and slept with Sam.

That hadn't turned out too badly. She was happy about the baby, although the timing was less than ideal. But she wasn't going to complain about a gift just because she didn't care for the wrapping paper and bow.

A knock at the door jerked her back to the present and she tugged the gown more closely around her body before calling out, "Yes?"

"It's me, Riley. Sam."

Relief flooded her body and she blew out a slow breath. She wasn't going to have to do this all alone. Sam would be there holding her hand the whole way.

This partnership stuff was pretty cool.

"Come in and join the party."

Sam stepped into the room wearing an unhappy expression. "Sorry I'm late. I had to speak with Callie before I came back here. She told me what happened this morning. I'm going to have Bobby try and put out the message that you're off-limits."

"Will that work?"

"Doubtful but I'm going to try. That shouldn't have happened this morning and I'm sorry you had to go through that."

It wasn't his fault. He was famous and this was a byproduct of that.

"It wasn't that bad. No big deal." Even as she was saying it she realized it was the truth. The whole thing had lasted about a minute and then it was over. "Who is Lucinda, by the way?"

His cheeks flushed and he rolled his eyes. "A woman I dated for about five minutes right before I met you. I haven't seen her since then. God, I really am sorry. Did they ask about her?"

"They did," Riley confirmed. "But Callie warned me they'd try to get a reaction out of me. Spoiler alert. They didn't. Seriously, you don't have to apologize. I admit it was a new experience for me but for the most part if was fine. I can handle it."

"They're going to go crazy when they find out about the baby."

"And then they'll move on to the next story when they find out that we're boring as hell. Well, at least I am."

A sharp knock sounded and then a dark-haired woman stuck her head in. "Hi, I'm Dr. Kate. Are you ready?"

As ready as I'll ever be. I'm going to be a mommy. And maybe a wife.

CHAPTER
Thirty-One

"SO WOULD you like to get a look at your baby?"

Riley's fingers squeezed his own tightly and their gazes met. They were both eagerly nodding yes.

The doctor's appointment had gone well with only a minor hiccup during the internal exam. Riley had nudged him so he was standing near her head and holding her hand, which was far better than his earlier position near her feet. Since they hadn't been intimate in a while it felt a little strange to be a party to something so personal but it had been over quickly.

Dr. Kate had patiently answered all of their questions, even the stupid ones. He didn't know which of his questions met that criteria but he was sure there were more than a few that did. The doctor, however, had her game face on and didn't bat an eyelash when he asked about foods, exercise, and travel. When answering, she'd taken the opportunity to assure both of them that sex was perfectly fine and that Riley might experience a sharp rise in her libido in the second trimester. Neither of them had asked but it was good to know.

Lucky me. Hopefully.

Sam and Riley were moved into the ultrasound room and he settled into a chair next to the padded table, holding Riley's hand. This was really happening. He was going to see his baby for the very first time. His chest had tightened painfully and he could barely draw a breath. He had to grip the arm of the chair with his free hand to keep it from visibly shaking.

Please let the baby be okay. Please let him be alright. I'll do anything, give up anything. Just let him be healthy. That's all I ask.

Tears pricked at Sam's eyes and his stomach did flips in his belly as he waited for what seemed like days or years for the gray screen to flicker to life. This was the verdict that he'd been hoping and dreading.

Please, please, please.

Riley looked almost as tense as he felt. He was trying to be the strong man for her but inside it felt like he might crumble into a million tiny pieces. He was that vulnerable. This baby hadn't even been born yet, didn't have a name, and he hadn't even seen it but already he loved it more than anything in the world. He'd do anything for it. He'd give up his own life for Riley and the baby, without question.

And he was helpless. Riley had to be the tough one and carry the child. All he could do is stand by her side. She was the hero and he was the sidekick.

Dr. Kate pointed to a round thing on the screen. "There he is. There's your baby. Of course, it's too early to know if it's a boy or girl but that light there? That's his heartbeat. Nice and strong."

Strong. He kept repeating that word over and over again in his head because speaking was out of the question. He couldn't even begin to try and form words. It was too overwhelming.

That was his baby. And he was *strong*.

"He's healthy?" Riley asked, a huge smile blooming on her beautiful face. "He looks normal and everything?"

Even the doctor was grinning. "Looks good in there. We'll take another look at your next appointment, of course. Should I print you a few pictures to show your family and friends?"

Riley answered for him, vigorously nodding yes. The doctor printed off the photos and handed them to Sam who couldn't stop staring at the murky images. That light was his child's heartbeat. That round thing was the head.

These blurry pictures were such a simple thing but their effect was profound. And the funny thing was, no one in the room but Sam seemed to recognize it. He'd been changed forever and the doctor and Riley were chatting as if nothing miraculous had happened. Couldn't they see that he would never be the same person ever again? He wanted to look into a mirror and see if he'd physically changed as well.

For the first time in Sam's life, he knew what it felt to be truly fucking terrified.

———

Sam had been strangely quiet during Riley's ultrasound and no chattier on the way to the movie set. He didn't seem as...*excited* about seeing the baby as she did. His smile and laughter seemed strained, almost forced as they'd chatted about the appointment. Had the reality of what he was getting himself into hit him when they'd seen their child?

He certainly had much to lose. He was a renowned bachelor and could basically have any woman he wanted. Getting married and having a family was going to cramp his style. No more jetting off to the south of France for champagne-soaked parties and beautiful French models. There would be midnight feedings, diapers, and crying. None of that was glamorous and it was a far cry from the life he'd led so far. She could only assume from his remote expression that he was rethinking it all.

She could, of course, simply ask him what he was thinking but she hated to be that woman...that female that asked, "What are you thinking?" It was so cliché and almost as bad as asking if her butt looked big when trying on jeans.

But then she remembered his face when the baby had first appeared on the screen. He'd appeared almost in awe, completely gobsmacked. Not that she wasn't as well. They'd both been amazed and dumbstruck. Maybe he was simply processing those emotions. Men didn't always do *feelings* like women did.

It was in that moment when she and Sam had seen the baby that she'd moved a mile closer to agreeing to marry him. This baby deserved the best they could give him or her. Was she being selfish by hesitating? He was a wonderful man and she'd have to look far and wide to find another half as good.

If their relationship kept on going this well, she was going to say yes.

CHAPTER
Thirty~Two

MAKING a movie was truly a marvel of technology. Currently Sam was acting in front of a giant green screen that would later be changed into a computer-generated backdrop and the only reason Riley would know it wasn't real was because she'd been on set today. He had listed several of her favorite movies and she'd been shocked to find out that some of the amazing action sequences were partially created by a machine.

"Impressive," Riley remarked as they toured the set. There were so many people milling about, carrying heavy equipment or shouting at one another. That was something else she'd learned today. It took a heck of a lot of people to make a movie. "The lighting alone is amazing, and the kitchen set is so real and detailed all the way down to the coffeemaker on the counter."

"It's just for show. It doesn't work. None of the appliances do, but they did wire the refrigerator so that the light comes on when we open the door."

"I'm one of those movie watchers that would notice if it didn't turn on."

"Let's head to my trailer," Sam said, pointing off to the left. "It will be quieter there."

Anyplace would be quieter than where they were standing. Sam had explained to her that they were doing construction on the sets and props in preparation for filming that day.

"Sam," a woman's voice called from behind them. "I've been looking for you. Did you get my texts?"

Riley turned and saw that the voice belonged to Ivy Parker, an up and coming actress in Hollywood. Riley had seen her in a romantic comedy where Ivy had played the lead's best friend who was constantly trying to give advice, most of it bad. It had been a cute film and she'd enjoyed watching it, although Ivy certainly looked different today. In the rom-com, her looks had been played down, and she'd worn clothes that didn't quite fit. Today, however, she looked like she'd stepped out of a fashion magazine. Every hair in place and her outfit - a little black dress - hugged every line of her slim figure.

"I had an appointment this morning, Ivy. What did you need?"

Ivy rushed forward but stopped short in front of them. Riley had a feeling if she hadn't been standing there, Ivy might have given Sam a hug.

"I was hoping you could help me with the discovery scene this morning. I wasn't sure how to play it. Sad or angry." Ivy stuck out her lower lip and pouted. "You didn't answer any of my texts. That's not nice."

"The appointment was important. I turned off my phone."

Sam didn't sound perturbed, more like he was talking to an indulged child. Riley was the one who was annoyed and she didn't know why. Sam talked and texted lots of people and until this moment she hadn't cared who. But something about the entitlement of this one woman bugged her. Like Sam was just waiting around to get Ivy Parker's texts.

"I had to do the scene this morning all on my own."

"I'm sure you did great." Sam put his arm around Riley. "Riley, I'd like you to meet my co-star Ivy Parker. Ivy, this is Riley Bridges, my girlfriend."

Ivy's brows shot up but to her credit she didn't verbalize her shock that the mousy kindergarten teacher had caught one of the biggest stars in Hollywood. Riley couldn't help the rush of satisfaction as the actress pressed her lips together as if to keep from saying something nasty or mean.

I'm becoming a terrible person. Just awful.

It wasn't right to be happy that someone else was mad and Riley wasn't proud of herself in the least. She needed to keep her head on straight and not become someone she didn't like or respect.

"It's nice to meet you," Riley replied, extending her hand. She was going to be the bigger person here. "I've seen some of you work and enjoyed it very much."

There was a moment that she thought Ivy was going to snub her but then the other woman shook her hand and murmured thank you.

A shout from across the room had Sam sighing. "The

director needs to talk to me for a minute. Just wait here and I'll be right back, okay?"

Riley nodded, still watching Ivy from the corner of her eye. She didn't trust this woman at all. "Sure, take your time. It's fine."

Sam strolled away, leaving her with Ivy. Oh joy.

"Are you an actress?"

Gone was the simpering sweet tone that Ivy had used with Sam. This one was petulant and demanding. This might get ugly.

"No, I'm a kindergarten teacher."

Keep your answers short and to the point. Don't let her get under your skin. And if she does, don't let it show.

"A teacher?" Ivy's mouth hung open in amazement. "How did a little teacher meet Sam Collins?"

A little teacher? Screw you.

"I work with his mother."

Riley hadn't thought her answer was all that funny but Ivy seemed to think it was hilarious, throwing back her head and laughing.

"So you were handpicked by Mommy. That explains a lot."

There was so much Riley could say but she kept her mouth shut. It wasn't easy. She was becoming rather fond of speaking her mind, but she just had a feeling that today was not the day to do it. Chad and Ivy were in far different leagues and didn't play by the same set of rules.

"I hope you're fine with sitting at home by yourself and waiting." Ivy was smiling now, confident and happy. "Sam and I will be...working late every night. You know, co-stars so often fall in love with each other because there is a certain intimacy between the characters. There's an undeniable chemistry that can become an overwhelming passion."

Was this supposed to be a warning? Riley should let it go but she wasn't that good of a person. Blame it on the pregnancy hormones but she'd had it with this young woman.

"I've seen that but sadly those relationships never seem to last," Riley replied, her gaze swinging to Sam who was approaching them. "White hot and then fizzled out to nothing. I think at this point in his career, Sam knows better."

But this did remind Riley as to why she'd hesitated saying yes to Sam's marriage proposal. It would always be like this. Women - young and beautiful - would want him and it would take a strong man to say no every time.

Rubbing his hands together, Sam gave her a smile. "Ready to see more? I have a few minutes before I have to report to makeup."

"Sounds perfect."

Ivy wasn't giving up, however. She pushed herself forward so she was in between Sam and Riley. "I was hoping–"

"Can't," Sam cut in, his gaze firmly on Riley. "I only have a little time and I still need to show Riley around. Catch me later between takes."

Reaching around the starlet, Sam wrapped his arm around Riley and led her away, leaving the seething woman standing there. He hadn't said it out loud but he'd made it clear - he didn't have any interest in his co-star.

This time. But there would always be another movie,

another woman. It felt like two steps forward and three steps back and the dance was ceasing to be any fun. She needed to make a decision and stick to it, but after her behavior today she was beginning to think she already had.

She was jealous and that was not an emotion she had much experience with. Had she already fallen in love with Sam? It might simply be too late to save herself any heartache.

————

Sam could barely concentrate on work, his thoughts busy with the appointment this morning and seeing his baby for the first time. The overwhelming need to protect Riley and the child had him contemplating ideas that a few days ago would have seemed outlandish and completely insane.

He was thinking about retiring.

After he finished his contractual obligations, of course. Breaking a contract wasn't something he did lightly and if he'd committed to do a role he needed to see it through. But afterward, he would be free to do as he pleased.

Acting, producing, and directing were his passion but he couldn't allow history to repeat itself. It might be irrational - and he was pretty sure it was - but he felt that the only way he could care for his family was to be with them all the time.

Money wouldn't be an issue. He had enough to never work a day in his life again. He hadn't been extravagant and purchased a dozen houses, collected cars and jewels, and partied with drugs and alcohol. He'd seen enough in

Tinsel Town to know the pitfalls. He'd watched some good and talented people go down the wrong road and ruin their career. He'd been determined from the beginning not to become one of them.

But he couldn't imagine not working. It was one thing to have some time off in between projects, hang out around the house and rest, maybe even travel a little. But every single day for the rest of his life sounded like true boredom. He'd need two hundred hobbies just to fill the time so he wouldn't go stark raving mad. His needs, however, weren't what was important here. He had to put his family first.

"Sam?" Ivy poked her head in the doorway. He hadn't bothered to lock his trailer door. "I brought you a coffee."

Ivy held up two paper cups with lids and then handed him one. He hadn't slept much the night before so the caffeine was welcome. She plopped down on the sofa next to him and stretched out her legs so that her feet were propped up on a small table.

"Thanks, I could use this. Shouldn't you be in wardrobe?"

"I have forty-five minutes. They're moving the lighting again. I thought I'd come see how you are. You've been wearing a scowl all day long." She leaned closer and placed her hand on his thigh. Alarm bells started going off in his head. Danger. "I can tell that you're unhappy with your girlfriend, Sam. You know, you can talk to me about it."

It was almost comical. Ivy thought that Sam was unhappy with Riley when it was actually the opposite. He was only unhappy at the thought she might not stay.

"I'm very happy. I'm hoping that Riley and I get married."

He wanted to make sure that Ivy knew there was no way anything...intimate was going to happen between them. She'd been dropping hints the entire shoot, but meeting Riley seemed to have pushed her into playing all her cards. Not that she had any. Sam wasn't interested. The only woman that existed for him was Riley.

Christ, I'm in love. When did that happen?

He waited for the panic to set in along with a feeling of suffocation but it didn't. Instead a warmth filled his chest and spread through his limbs. He was in love and it was good. Riley was the woman he'd been waiting for his whole life and now they were going to have a baby together. This was what he'd wanted but never in a million years thought he'd have. He sure as fuck wasn't going to toss it aside for a quickie with his co-star in his trailer. If he didn't screw this all up, he could have a wonderful life with the most wonderful woman on the planet.

But first, he had to get Ivy out of his trailer. Then he could worry about how to make Riley fall in love with him. She'd already said that she wasn't.

But you said that too. Maybe it's changed.

Ivy sat straight up, her mouth hanging open wide enough to catch flies. "Married? You're getting married? Since when?"

The last person he was going to discuss his love life with was his shallow co-star.

"Ivy, don't you have someplace you need to be?"

Standing and then stomping to the door, Ivy looked like she wanted to be anywhere but with him. Her face was bright red and her lips were pressed together so tightly there was a white ring around her mouth. Yep, he'd pissed her off good.

"Have fun with your little teacher," she spat, her lip curled in derision. "She can't do anything for your career."

He almost...almost...reminded this young woman that she couldn't do shit for his career either, but he could do a hell of a lot for her, which he assumed was a major part of the attraction. If he'd been a ditch digger or an accountant, he doubted Ivy Parker would have given him a second look. She was like most of the women he met on a daily basis. She wanted what Sam could give her.

Riley, on the other hand, didn't want anything from him. If he was lucky he might get her to want his love.

"Thank you for the reminder. Close the door on your way out."

Chuckling, he felt the trailer shake as Ivy slammed the door behind her, still muttering under her breath. He had a nasty feeling that she was going to make the rest of this shoot fucking miserable.

It didn't matter though. All that mattered to Sam was sitting in a condo on the Upper East Side. Riley, his baby, and their hopefully soon to be family. He'd do whatever it took to make her fall in love with him. Except that he'd never had to work that hard before.

How did a man get a woman to fall for him?

CHAPTER
Thirty-Three

SAM PACED BACK and forth across the small space of
his trailer, his agitation and anger growing with every
passing minute. Bigger problems had kept Sam from
concentrating on plans to romance Riley. His publicist had
sent him photos of Riley from this morning that were
splashed all over the internet. The headlines were
predictably lurid, conjecturing that he'd slept with Riley at
the same time as his last girlfriend, whether he and Riley
were married, and an especially maddening picture of
Riley's tummy which at the angle the photo was taken
looked slightly pooched out. That last one was paired with
the headline "Is that a baby bump we spy?"

Riley's tummy was still flat, but the wily pap had
known that the awkward angle would fire up the public
with questions.

If Sam lived to be two hundred years old he would
never learn to like the phrase "baby bump". It sounded
stupid and juvenile and now he was pissed as hell because

some tabloid was going to get so-called credit for breaking a story before he'd released it.

But the worst of it was all the comments underneath these articles and blog posts. Most fans were supportive, sweet, and kind, congratulating Sam on finding someone to share his life with. There were always a few, however, that seemed to live to spew hatred and venom and they'd done a number on Riley. They'd questioned her looks, her intelligence, and her motives. She'd been called plain, ugly, fat, ordinary, common, and a few more adjectives that made him so angry he wanted to punch a hole in the wall of his trailer. She was the kindest and loveliest person he'd ever known and all these people had to do with their time was to tear her down. It was pathetic, really.

It also terrified him. If Riley saw these, and he'd already contacted Callie to keep Riley away from the internet, she might decide that he was too much work to be with and not marry him. She definitely wouldn't fall in love with a man that managed to have her name and likeness dragged through the mud. He was trying to show her how wonderful life could be for them together, not chase her away.

His phone buzzed and he glanced at the screen, hoping it wasn't his publicist again with more bad news.

His mom. The way his day was going she'd probably gone out on that date, fallen in love immediately, and they were currently on their way to Vegas to get married. Oh, and his new stepfather was Sam's age with no discernible means of financial support.

"Hey, Mom. How's it going?"

"Fine. I was just calling to tell you that I think I'll fly up the day after tomorrow. If that's okay?"

It was perfect. Riley would have Paula to help deal with all of this craziness.

"That sounds great, Mom. I'll have Callie book the flight and the transportation. We'll all be glad to see you."

I have big news for you.

"I can book all of that myself. Callie has better things to do." There was a long pause. "You sound a little strange, son. Is anything wrong? Did I call at a bad time? I know you're probably working today."

Sam had intended to say that nothing was wrong. Everything was fine and he couldn't wait to see her.

That's what he'd intended to do. The best laid plans and all...

Instead he found himself pouring out the whole story - minus the sex parts - and even about the baby. He admitted to his mother that he was scared, too. Scared that something would happen to the baby and scared that Riley wouldn't fall in love with him.

She'd listened quietly, not interrupting, which was Paula's way. She'd done the same thing since he was a boy. Let him get it all off of his chest before saying a word. Half of the time he'd figure out what he needed to do just by explaining the situation. His mother was smart like that. She wanted him to think for himself before she rushed in with the answer.

No such luck this time. He was fresh out of easy solutions.

"Well...first of all...I'm thrilled that I'm going to be a grandmother," Paula replied slowly when he was done.

"And I can't think of anyone I'd want as the mother of the child more than Riley. You know that I've wanted the two of you together. I think you and she could be very happy."

"I think so too but I have to convince her of that, Mom."

Another long pause, the silence building. Sam knew better than to interrupt his mother, though. She was about to say something he wasn't going to like and was trying to find a nice way to tell him. Eventually she'd give up and just say it. So he waited.

"Son, you have a bigger problem."

The press? His career?

"I'm listening."

"You need to deal with your past. Sooner rather than later. Frankly, you've put it off way too long and I've let you. But it needs to stop now. It's not your fault Trish lost the baby. It was just one of those things that happen. It was sad and awful but it wasn't your fault. There was nothing you could have done even if you'd been home."

He didn't want to hear this and he sure as hell didn't want to discuss it. Life had given him a second chance with Riley and he wasn't going to screw it up. He was going to make sure that his family was safe and protected. All he had to do was convince Riley to let him take that place in her life.

"I'm concentrating on the right problem, Mom. I need to convince Riley to fall in love with me."

He could hear Paula's sigh through the phone. "You're a bright boy, I'm sure you can figure out how to do that, especially as I think she's halfway there to begin with. She was unhappy after you left, Sam, although she tried to hide it. Haven't you been in a few romantic movies? What did the leading men do?"

"She wouldn't fall for all that corny romance. She's too smart for that."

"Then don't make it corny," Paula answered promptly. "Riley won't be impressed by an expensive restaurant and extravagant gifts. Sending her flowers isn't going to make her swoon. Just show her a good time. Have fun. Take her somewhere that she'd like to go. Are you so rich and famous that you don't remember how to do that?"

It was so simple and obvious he ought to smack himself in the head. Maybe he had been famous too long with people catering to all his whims.

Put Riley first. Think about her needs. He could absolutely do this.

Hold on to your hat, Riley. You are about to be swept off of your feet.

———

Riley had known something was up. Callie kept trying to pull her from her laptop, and it had become clear that the older woman didn't want Riley to see something on the internet. It didn't take a genius to figure out what it was.

The photos weren't the worst part. Candid shots had never been kind to Riley and this morning had been no exception. She'd been photographed from all angles and some of them were downright terrible. One even seemed to show a pregnant belly which made her laugh. She wasn't showing...yet, but it wouldn't be long.

No, the photos sucked but they weren't horrifying. That

had to be saved for comments on the photos and articles. Not even the incendiary headlines could compete with the hate and vitriol she'd found. On Twitter, Facebook, and blogs, people seemed to come out of the woodwork to bash her and they didn't hold back. They thought she was stupid, ugly, and a gold digger. All from actual human beings who had never even met her. But they acted like they knew her well and they sure as heck didn't like her. She wasn't good enough for Sam and he could do far better.

"Those women are just jealous." Callie sat across from Riley at the kitchen table. They were both having tea and cookies while Riley tortured herself with the internet. "They're upset because somewhere in their brains they got the idea that Sam could be their boyfriend. This doesn't have anything to do with you personally."

"I know that intellectually..."

"But emotionally?"

"It hurts," Riley admitted. "These people don't even know me but they already think the worst. They were just plain nasty, too."

"These were the kids that bullied in school. You probably know all about that."

Rarely did Riley have to deal with a bully in her kindergarten class but it wasn't unheard of. Usually they were bullied themselves by their parents or they observed it in their home life. They didn't feel heard or respected so they lashed out at others.

"I have, and I understand the psychology around it in children, but these are grown adults."

Callie slapped her cup onto the table, making it shake

on its legs. "That's right. Supposedly grown ass, mature adults who have nothing better to do than troll articles on the internet and write mean, nasty shit about people they've never met and never will. It's easy to be brave when you're hidden. They'd never in a million years say that to your face. Believe me when I say that there are some disturbed individuals out in the world and I know this because I've read some of Sam's fan mail."

"I'm afraid to ask. That bad?"

Shaking her head, Callie reached across the table and pressed the lid on the laptop shut. This time Riley let her.

"It ain't good. People can be lovely and nice and some are mean as snakes. I'm going to be up front with you and just lay it on the line. If you're going to live this life, you're going to need to toughen up. There are always people that want to rip others down and when you're successful like Sam you become a target." Callie pointed to Riley. "Now you're a target too. There will be people who are jealous or angry or sad or frustrated or whatever. This is about them, not you. Don't get mired in all the negativity. You could be the most perfect person on the planet and they'd find something to complain about."

A thicker hide. That's what Riley needed. She shouldn't be letting the opinions of strangers bother her. If she was going to be with Sam - and that's what she wanted - she'd have to get used to this.

Fair was something that came to town in the summer. It wasn't something she should expect from life.

Riley stood and carried her cup over to the sink. "I'm going to lie down for a little while. All the drama has worn me out. Thank you for talking to me. I really do see what you're saying and you're right. I need to learn to ignore this."

Callie tapped on the laptop. "Stay away from the internet. It's a jungle out there."

Words to live by. Riley wouldn't make the same mistake again and seek out pictures of herself. She already knew the truth and she didn't need a blog or a tabloid to explain her life in a hundred and forty characters or less. They were just trying to sell papers and get clicks. They weren't worth her time or attention.

CHAPTER
Thirty-Four

RILEY HAD BEEN UP to her neck in steamy bathwater by the time Sam had arrived home. He'd been grinning and hyper, excited like a child for Christmas, and she'd allowed him to railroad her into getting out of the tub and dressed. He had a surprise for her.

At first she'd balked, still rather tired but his enthusiasm was infectious and when he'd said that she didn't have to dress up, do her hair, or even put on makeup she was beginning to get excited too. A little casual fun sounded like just what she needed to shake off her afternoon.

After throwing on shorts, a t-shirt, and some mascara, she'd trailed after him to the dark SUV parked at the curb. They'd climbed in and were off to their mysterious destination, Sam still smiling widely and then chuckling to himself every few minutes. He certainly had something up his sleeve and she couldn't wait to find out what it was. She loved surprises.

"Are you even going to give me a hint?"

Arching an eyebrow, he seemed to ponder her request. "Alright, your hint is we're going to Brooklyn."

"Brooklyn?"

That would explain the bridge they were currently crossing. It didn't, however, help her figure out at all where they were going and what they were going to do when they got there.

"Yes, Brooklyn. I do have one question before we get there. How is the nausea? Do you need any ginger ale or your lollipops?"

She held up her wrists, wrapped in the pressure bands. "I'm fine. I had a lollipop while I was getting dressed plus these, so I should be good to go. Thankfully I'm usually better in the evenings. Are we going to a restaurant?"

She could definitely eat but she hoped it wasn't some fancy place with gourmet food. Looking down at her attire, it didn't appear that she was dressed for anything other than a burger and fries.

With cheese. And bacon. And lots of ketchup. Was this her first craving?

"We'll eat," Sam assured her. "But we have something to do first."

"You're being very mysterious."

She kind of loved it. He'd planned this all for her and it made her feel...special.

"No one has ever accused me of being mysterious," Sam laughed. "Not even the press."

"You're being mysterious now. You're lucky I like surprises."

It wasn't long before they pulled up to the curb and

Sam opened the car door, sliding out first before helping her out as well.

Trees. People. A beautiful view of the river and the bridge.

"It's a park."

Maybe they were going to have a picnic.

"The Brooklyn Bridge Park," Sam confirmed, taking her hand. "I hope you like this. Follow me."

They walked hand in hand deeper into the park, under a canopy of trees. There were many people about, adults and children, and a few did give them strange looks but no one approached them. Sam had been right. People in the city didn't bother celebrities. They had also clearly lost the paparazzi tonight. They hadn't been in front of the building when they'd left which had been a huge relief. She'd have to ask Sam if he knew why they'd suddenly backed off. Maybe an even bigger star had done something newsworthy.

Lights and music captured her attention and her gaze traveled to her right, toward the bridge. There was a beautiful carousel nestled near the river and she found herself pausing to watch it as it twirled slowly, the horses prancing up and down as if by magic.

"That's Jane's Carousel. It's famous in this area. It's the reason we're here."

Riley couldn't quite believe her ears. Sam Collins, movie star and sex symbol, was going to ride a carousel? On purpose?

"We're going to ride the carousel?" She pointed to Sam and then herself. "As in you and me? Both of us?"

He nodded, a smile on his too handsome face. "If your

tummy feels up to it. I remember you telling me that you loved carnivals as a kid. I thought you might like this."

She loved it and she loved that he'd remember some off the cuff, throw away remark she'd made a few months ago. She hadn't even remembered that she'd said it until now. He had though, and it made her heart do flips in her chest.

Sam, I'm falling in love with you. Stop being so wonderful.

They did ride the carousel. Twice, with a rest in between.

It was a perfect evening. Warm and a little humid but not uncomfortably so. The sun was beginning to set and the sky had turned a brilliant pinkish-orange. For the first ride, Riley had chosen a noble steed with a red saddle while Sam had chosen the one beside hers, a black horse with a blue saddle. Riley had promptly named her mount Buttercup.

"Buttercup, huh?" Sam helped her onto the horse, her heart tight in her chest with only his touch. When he dropped a kiss on her cheek, she almost fainted like a schoolgirl. "I see you're a fan of *The Princess Bride*. Good movie."

"It is. What are you going to name yours?"

Swinging his leg over the horse, he settled into the saddle before answering. "Is it important that my ride have a name? What if he already has one and we confuse the poor thing?"

"I don't see any name plaques." Riley looked the carousel horses over well. "A name is very important. How else are you going to tell him when to go faster or slower?"

She was only teasing Sam now but he was being such a

good sport tonight. Perhaps one day they would bring their child here - together - and tell him the story about how Mommy and Daddy rode the carousel when she was pregnant. The only thing that would make that story better would be a happy ending.

Ultimately that's what Riley wanted with Sam. A happily ever after. She simply wasn't sure if it was too much to ask of the universe.

Sam just laughed and shook his head. "He'll know, but you're welcome to name him."

"Midnight," she replied immediately. "I think that's a good name for him."

"Midnight it is."

The carousel began to move slowly and then faster. To Riley's delight, Sam reached across the empty space between them and captured her hand in his, holding it the entire ride. The sensitive flesh tingled and electric sparks shot up her arm. Fighting against her feelings was becoming exhausting.

I love him so much.

It was one thing, however, to admit it to herself. She wasn't ready to tell him yet. It meant the world to her that he'd planned this romantic evening but she couldn't - wouldn't - read too much into it. He might do this all the time for all she knew. He might have brought dozens of females to this carousel over the years.

After a brief break, they rode a second time. Riley chose a white horse with a gold saddle and Sam once again chose the horse right next to her own so he could hold her hand. She would have happily ridden that carousel all night but there were other people waiting so she allowed Sam to lead her away from the carousel where they could speak without having to yell over the music.

"Are you hungry?" Sam asked. "There are several restaurants around here. Pizza, burgers–"

"Burgers," she said, cutting him off the minute he mentioned what her stomach was screaming for. Her mouth was watering just thinking about it. "I have a craving for a bacon cheeseburger."

She thought Sam might be annoyed but instead he looked delighted, a big grin on his face and his brows lifted in surprise. "A craving, huh? Well, we definitely have to make sure you get what you want. The place is a short walk from here. It's one of those chain places but it's supposed to be very good. I think from their name that they have shakes too."

"I want a chocolate one."

Suddenly she was ravenous. Hungry and happy. She was holding the hand of the man she adored and he was taking her out for an evening of fun. But not his style. There was no flowing champagne or yachts. No fancy restaurant or expensive outfits. He'd thought about what she'd like and enjoy and he'd come up all aces. It was perfect, and even if they didn't work out together, she'd think about this evening for a long time to come.

"You can have whatever you want. Just eat slow like the doctor said so you don't get sick."

So far that advice seemed to be helping. The problem was her hunger snuck up on her and then was like a raging beast until it was fed and sated.

"I will. You take good care of me."

His fingers lightly squeezed her own. "I always will."

Riley wanted to count on those words. She wanted to believe.

The moon was high in the night sky when the driver pulled up in front of Sam's condo. Riley had been telling him a funny story about her students but she paused when they arrived, turning to give him a smile that was part innocence and part sin. They'd been flirting with each other all evening but now they were home and the tension between them was high. He was nervous. He wanted her. He couldn't pretend that he didn't. Her feelings were more of a mystery, however.

But they'd had a good time tonight. He'd made progress in winning her heart. Her cheeks were pink from laughter and her eyes sparkled with happiness. She'd enjoyed the park, the carousel, and even the bacon cheeseburger with a thick chocolate shake. Such a wonderfully simple date that didn't require a tuxedo and camera lights flashing. Tonight they were just two people out for the evening and enjoying each other's company. They might even be two people in love.

"The date isn't over yet." He stepped away and flipped a switch on the discreetly hidden sound system, having set it up in advance. He remembered well the song they'd danced to their first night together. Their song. "We could dance a little. A club would be too noisy but we can do it right here without the prying eyes."

He didn't want the paps or his fans watching him romance Riley. This was private, intimate, only for the two of them. There wasn't much in his life that he could claim was only for him but this...he wouldn't share.

She smiled when she recognized Billy Vera and the Beaters and he pulled her unresistingly into his arms. Her head rested on his chest and her arms had snuck around his waist, splaying on his lower back. He could feel the heat of her touch through the thin cotton of his t-shirt and his skin burned from the contact. They barely moved at all to the romantic tune, their bodies brushing and sending messages of arousal through his veins.

Riley had never looked more beautiful than she did at this moment. Her skin glowed in the soft light, her lips plush and pillow soft.

"Riley..."

Her name came out strangled and hoarse but she seemed to understand, her mouth turning up at the corners. Her hands slid up his chest until her palms were right above his pounding heart. There was no hiding what he was feeling now. It had to show in every line of his face. His desperate need for her. This love that he couldn't hide any longer. She could laugh in his face but he had to speak the words. His heart was too full of emotion to keep quiet.

"Riley, I...I love you."

She stopped then, her eyes widening in...surprise? Shock? There wasn't dismay or disgust to his relief, but clearly she hadn't been expecting a declaration of his feelings. Maybe she thought he was trying to get her into bed. Which he did want but that wasn't why he was saying it.

"I swear I'm not just trying to sweet talk you into bed,"

he said, holding up his right hand as if taking an oath. "I wouldn't do that."

This waiting wasn't easy. Riley still hadn't said anything and he was beginning to panic. She might be trying to find the words to let him down easy.

Shit. Fuck. Damn. I should have kept my big mouth shut.

"I'm not expecting you to say it back or anything." Great. Now he was starting to babble. "I know this is soon but–"

"I love you, too."

The words came out of her mouth quickly and her fingers pressed against his lips. He had to lift her hand away so he could speak.

"Say that again."

Because I don't quite believe that I heard it. I can't be this lucky.

She swallowed hard and that look was back in her eyes, the one he'd thought he'd seen earlier. "I love you, too."

They simply stared into one another's eyes, time seemingly standing still as they absorbed the enormity of the moment and what they'd revealed. They'd made themselves vulnerable and this time neither of them would walk away with a broken heart.

"Sam," Riley said, cupping her hands around his face. Christ, her skin was so fucking soft. "Sam, take me to bed."

His sluggish brain took a moment to wrap around her request. She wanted them to make love. From her expression, this wasn't that she was tired or wanted to watch television.

She wanted him, and she was going to get him. All of him. Body, soul, and heart.

Look out, Riley Bridges. I'm going to make you the happiest woman in the world.

The bedroom was a pretty good place to start.

CHAPTER
Thirty-Five

THE MOON SHONE through the partially open curtains and played peekaboo with the bedroom, spots here and there bathed in light while others were cloaked in shadowy darkness. Sam and Riley tumbled down on the bed, impatient fingers tugging at their offending garments. She didn't want any barrier between them and she couldn't get him naked fast enough. In between pulling down zippers and sliding off panties, they kissed, their tongues tangled and vying for dominance. But it was only a game and they were both winners.

Riley's bra melted away and Sam cupped her breasts, his thumbs brushing the now extremely sensitive nipples and sending shockwaves of electricity straight to her clit. It wouldn't take much to send her over tonight. They were both starved for one another. It had been too long.

"Yes," she whispered as his lips closed over a pebbled nipple, his tongue running circles around it. Trembling with the force of her arousal, she carded her fingers through his silky hair to anchor his head. "I think they're bigger."

The changes in her body weren't major yet, a little thickening at the waist but it felt like her chest had gone up a full cup size and they didn't appear to be stopping there.

Lifting his head, he gave her a wolfish grin. "They're more sensitive, too. I barely have to touch you."

To demonstrate his point, he leaned down and swiped at a nipple with his tongue, watching her entire body quiver in reaction.

"Is that a bad thing?"

Her question came out breathless but she was finding it hard to take a deep breath.

"Absolutely not. It's a good thing. Like when I do this."

His callused thumb grazed her swollen clit and she gripped his shoulders as a wave of heat ran through her veins like liquid fire. She wanted to make him feel as amazing as he did her. Sliding her hands to the front of his chest, she pressed back against him. At first he resisted, his brows pulled down in confusion but then he acquiesced, falling back on the mattress.

She met his puzzled expression with a determined one of her own. "I didn't get to do this last time."

She didn't leave him wondering for long, insinuating herself between his muscular thighs so she could easily reach his cock. Lapping at the crown, she ran her tongue up and down until his ass lifted from the mattress and he was groaning her name. His hand went to the back of her head and she obliged him by taking him as far into her mouth as possible while her fingernails scraped lightly over his balls. His grip tightened on her hair and then suddenly went lax, his hand cupping her chin and gently tugging her up so she was looking into his eyes.

"That's not where I want to come. I want to be inside of you, babe."

So far gone, Riley wasn't going to argue. If things worked out between them, and it was looking more and more like that would be the case, they'd have a lifetime to explore and pleasure one another.

To her surprise, Sam didn't move from his position on the bed, instead urging her to straddle him with her palms braced on his chest. A frisson of arousal ran through her when Sam raised his hips, running his cock up and down her slit while his strong hands gripped her around the waist.

"Ride me."

His huskily spoken command was all she needed, lifting up and then slowly lowering herself down taking him inch by inch until he was in to the hilt. Her walls stretched but the discomfort was drowned out by the pleasure of being so incredibly full. She paused for a moment and closed her eyes to savor the sweet sensation before beginning to move, a little at first but then more boldly as she gained confidence.

"That's it, honey," Sam praised, his hands sliding up her torso and cupping her breasts. At some point, she'd leaned forward and now her hands were planted on the mattress on either side of his wide shoulders. "Are you close?"

Not waiting for her answer, he snaked his hand down between them and began running circles around her clit. Crying out with the sensation, her forehead dropped down to rest on his damp chest as their bodies moved in perfect synchronicity. The tightening coil in her abdomen was ready to explode and their movements became even more frenzied as they both neared completion.

When she fell over the precipice the world spun and tilted as white lights sparkled behind her eyelids. Flames ran through her veins like dragons licking at her damp flesh. She barely registered his climax so caught up in the pure pleasure of her own, but she could feel his fingers tighten on her hips and knew there would be faint bruises there in the morning. They would match the crescent moons her nails had made in the flesh of his shoulders.

Collapsing together, their sweaty limbs tangled in the sheets, Riley was content to lay her hand on Sam and feel the racing of his heart and the rapid rise and fall of his chest. Knowing he was as affected as she somehow made all of this easier. Falling in love was scary but she wasn't alone.

She had Sam. They were a team. Partners. And now they were officially lovers, too. In love and wanting to build a future together. Her, Sam, and the baby. It felt right, warm, and cozy.

She wanted a family with him more than she'd ever wanted anything in her entire life.

CHAPTER
Thirty-Six

SAM COULDN'T STOP WHISTLING and grinning the next morning as he placed two pieces of dry toast on a plate for Riley, right alongside a cup of ginger tea. He was going to take her a little snack so she could settle her stomach before she got out of bed. Not that he wouldn't be glad to keep her in bed all day long, but they had a phone call to make to her parents and some shopping to do.

Sometime last night as they'd cuddled close together whispering silly things to one another, they'd decided to take his morning off from filming and spend it together. They would call her parents and tell them the news, plus head to the stores and do a little shopping for Riley. She wasn't ready for maternity wear but she was beginning to complain that her waistbands were a little snug. They'd buy her a few outfits to bridge the in-between.

He was so excited about the prospect of being a father he couldn't wait to furnish the nursery and buy the baby lots of stuffed animals. It might sound crazy but he was even looking forward to the day to day baby care like diaper changes, baths, and reading stories. Never having thought he would have this, he'd been given a precious second chance and he wouldn't mess it up. He'd enjoy every minute of it.

Sam had another hope as well. Maybe they might visit a jewelry store and look at rings. Just look. He didn't want to scare her off, but he did want her to know how serious he was. This was it. He'd found the one he wanted to be with for the rest of his life.

Carrying her tea and toast into the bedroom, he stopped in the doorway to just look at the woman who had stolen his heart. Riley was still asleep, twisted in the sheets, her arm flung overhead and the other clutching the comforter. Her chest slowly rose and fell with each breath and he almost hated to wake her from her slumber.

Almost.

Placing her breakfast on the nightstand, he sat on the mattress and leaned over her like he was the prince and she was Sleeping Beauty. Brushing a stray strand of hair from her silken cheek, he lightly pressed his lips to hers as his fingers trailed down the bare flesh of her arm. He was about to pull back when one of her fingers tangled in his hair, allowing him to deepen the kiss. They were both flushed and out of breath when he lifted his head.

His thumb caressed her swollen lips. "Good morning."

"Good morning." Her voice was husky and her smile told him there was no regret about last night. "That's a lovely way to wake up."

"Play your cards right and I might do that every day."

"I look forward to it."

As far as commitments went, it was decent. They hadn't spoken about forever, but they were talking about the future.

"I brought you some tea and toast for your tummy." He helped her sit up against the pillows, the sheet slipping down and giving him a glimpse of her perfect breasts. With a giggle and a blush, she tugged the covers higher before accepting the steaming mug of tea.

Down, boy. Now is not the time.

"Thank you. You're spoiling me, you know."

That was entirely the point.

"It's all part of my devious plan to make you want to stay with me forever."

She took a sip and then licked her lips, a sensuous gesture that made his groin tighten painfully. Riley knew exactly what she was doing too from the witchy smile on her face, but he wouldn't be tempted. She needed to deal with her morning sickness first.

"It's working."

Now in addition to a hard cock, he could barely draw oxygen into his lungs. Leaning forward, he planted a hand on either side of her torso, effectively caging her in so they were almost nose to nose.

"I love you, Riley. More than you can ever imagine."

"I love you, too." Her lashes swept down to hide her gaze. "I was trying to show you that last night. Words are good but actions..."

Yes, they meant more. He'd heard the words too many times but when they came from her pretty lips they actually had meaning.

Leaning even closer, he brushed his lips over the shell

of her ear, delighting in the shiver she couldn't hide. "Last night was amazing."

"Yes, you are."

Sam was as susceptible as any man to praise from his woman and today was no exception. Puffed up with pride, he chuckled as he recalled just how satisfied she'd been last night. Several times.

"Just think about it. If you say yes, I'd be all yours. Exclusively."

"You're making it hard to say no."

"Then don't."

Their gazes met and held, and the world seemed to stop for the two of them. Nothing mattered but how they felt and the world inside his home. He could happily lie in her arms until the day he died.

The vibration of his phone shattered their intimate moment, drawing a groan from Sam and a giggle from Riley. She popped a piece of the toast into her mouth as he dug his phone out his front pocket.

"Go take your call. I need to get ready for our morning." She playfully shoved at his shoulder. "Go on. I bet it's your agent, or your publicist, or your business manager, or maybe a director that desperately wants you in his next film."

It was his agent, returning Sam's call about not accepting any more commitments for a few years. Maybe five or ten. If Riley agreed to marry him, he'd never work again if she didn't want him to. His family would always come first.

————

It had taken some doing but Riley finally had persuaded Sam that she didn't need an entirely new wardrobe. There was no point buying a bunch of clothes she wouldn't be able to wear long, although he'd argued that she might be able to wear them after the baby was born. Luckily, she'd countered with the logic that they didn't know where they would even be location-wise then, so she might need a completely different season of clothes. He'd given in, but she could tell that when it came time to actually buy maternity outfits she was going to have to leave him at home or he'd buy out the store.

Now they had just enough time to eat a late lunch before Sam had to be back on set this afternoon. He'd had the morning off since the director was working on some background shots around the city.

Riley's stomach growled loudly after the waitress walked away, apparently anxious to be fed. The slight nausea she'd experienced this morning had worn off and now she was ravenous. She'd ordered spaghetti and meatballs and planned to eat every single bite. Carb heaven.

"Your parents were very nice on the phone this morning," Sam said, tucking his phone away. She appreciated the gesture, although she'd assured him that if he needed to take a business call it was fine. "Considering I knocked up their daughter and all."

They'd called Riley's parents this morning after breakfast to tell them the news since Paula now knew. It would simplify things if the tabloids got wind of their secret and printed anything. Better to get in front of the story than try to catch up. Sam and his publicist Bobby were already working on a plan to break the news to the public.

"Knocked up?" Riley laughed at the statement. "We're not two kids in high school who got carried away on prom night. We're adults. I'm pregnant. We're in a committed relationship. Of course, they were polite."

She especially liked the *committed relationship* part. She'd felt slightly giddy when she'd explained to her parents that she and Sam were a couple and in love.

Rubbing his chin, Sam grinned. "It was kind of like prom night with both of us dressed up. And we are adults, but that doesn't mean that your daddy doesn't want to grab his shotgun and march us down to the nearest justice of the peace so I can do right by his little girl."

"My father is not a violent man."

Her father had been quite restrained on the phone call. Riley's mother had done most of the talking. And the crying. Catherine Bridges had been overcome with joy that she was going to get a new grandchild.

"To be honest, I expected them to ask if we were getting married."

Riley had expected that too, which was why she'd headed those questions off at the pass by first explaining that she and Sam were together as a couple. She could feel that her mom and dad wanted to ask more but they'd held off. It was enough for now that Sam was stepping up to the plate and caring for their daughter and future grandchild. The question, however, would be posed at a future date.

"They will ask," she admitted. "But not when you're on the phone. They would never embarrass me like that. They also trust me to make good decisions and I think they can tell that I'm happy."

"They might be amused to learn that it's you holding

out on the wedding band, not me," Sam observed with a chuckle.

She wanted to say yes. But there was something inside of her - that damn cautious part that kept her from having fun and taking chances - that was speaking the loudest.

Take it slow. There's no rush.

Then the opposing voice would pipe up in her other ear.

He loves you. You love him. Go for it. He's the one. Take a chance.

It was enough to give her a gigantic headache. She was constantly going back and forth, unable to make the commitment. Because this was the big one. The forever kind. It would be one of the biggest decisions she'd ever made in her life. This was her Achille's heel. She was a big fraidy-cat. She just wanted...a little more time.

"They might be surprised but they also might predict my behavior. I've never been the daredevil type."

"Marrying me is such a risk?"

Change was always a risk. "It's a big deal and you shouldn't rush into it. We haven't known each other long. My siblings all dated their spouses for over a year before they got married. My oldest brother dated his wife for five years."

"And they're happily married?"

He'd effectively caught her in her own trap. Damn. She needed to think this stuff through more.

"Well...no. They split up recently but they were happy. You know, at the beginning." Riley was aware that Sam had been married but he never talked about it. If she was going to marry him, she probably needed to know more about his past. "How long did you date your wife before you got married?"

Sam stiffened, his easy smile disappearing and leaving in its place a grim line for a mouth.

"Trish and I dated for awhile."

Trish. His ex's name was Trish. Was it short for Patricia? Was she beautiful? Had she also been an actress? Riley had so many questions, but it was clear Sam didn't want to talk about it. This was part of what held her back from plunging into marriage with him. His avoidance of discussing his first marriage made her wonder if he was still in love with her.

"How long were you married?"

His long fingers played with the silverware. "Almost four years. Now let's talk about something important. I spoke with my agent today about scheduling and it looks like I'll be finishing my next film about six weeks before you're due. After that, I'm not accepting any roles for the foreseeable future."

Riley noticed the deft way he changed the subject and she wanted to call him on it, but his last sentence was way more important. He wasn't going to take any work. Just how long was the foreseeable future?

"I'm not sure what that means," she said, watching his expression carefully. "I know you wanted to take some time off after the baby's born."

The waitress appeared at the table with their food, the aroma of tomato and garlic reminding Riley that she was starving. Sam didn't answer until she was gone.

"I've been thinking about retiring."

"Retiring," Riley repeated slowly. To her, he seemed far

too young to retire. "You don't want to be an actor anymore? Is it that you want to direct instead?"

He'd mentioned moving more behind the camera, but he hadn't said he never wanted to act again. If anything, he'd expressed how much he loved what he did and how lucky it was that he was able to do it for a living.

Sam shook his head, digging into his lunch. "No, I mean retiring altogether. That way I'd be home with you and the baby all the time."

"You want to be a stay at home father. I didn't realize that."

He wouldn't look at her, concentrating instead on his salmon. "I don't want to miss anything."

"We talked about me traveling with you until the baby starts school."

They hadn't made any decisions but it had been one option. They were luckier than most in that they had several different ways they could go with this.

"It's not important right now." He finally looked up but his expression was guarded and shut down. "Have you told Tara the news yet?"

This was the second subject today he hadn't wanted to discuss. Riley didn't want it to be like this. Sam making all the decisions about their life and her simply along for the ride. Apparently, he'd been doing a great deal of thinking and keeping it to himself.

"I thought I'd call her this afternoon while you were on the set."

"You can invite her out here if you'd like. You might get bored sitting around while I'm working."

"Your mother will be here tomorrow," she reminded him. "And it's never dull around Paula Collins."

"That's true. It's up to you. How's your spaghetti?"

Kind of ruined since Sam had made his retirement revelation. The delicious pasta and sauce tasted like sawdust in her mouth.

"It's good. Will you excuse me for a moment? I need to run to the ladies' room."

Grabbing her handbag, she headed straight for the bathroom. Once inside, she pulled out her phone and sent a text to Paula.

Need to talk to you. Sam's talking about retiring from movies completely.

Paula's answer was almost immediate.

Yes, it's time we talked. There are things you should know.

Riley's caution was looking pretty smart at the moment. Clearly there were things that Sam didn't want to talk about, and she couldn't rush into a marriage with a man that had secrets in his past. Before she said yes, she needed to talk to Paula and find out what Sam was hiding.

CHAPTER
Thirty-Seven

THE NEXT AFTERNOON, Riley sat on the bed in the condo's spare bedroom while Paula unpacked.

"Even Callie doesn't know this story," Paula said, tucking her clothes into a drawer. "She met him long after he and Trish divorced."

Riley hated this. Going behind Sam's back to find out personal details felt distasteful, but if she was contemplating marrying him she needed to know what demons were driving him to make such rash decisions. After all, she was physically having a baby and she hadn't even entertained the idea of giving up everything she loved and sitting home for the rest of her life. If she wasn't a teacher, she still wanted to do something productive. She wasn't sure what that would be yet but she wouldn't stop looking until she found it.

"I tried to ask him about his marriage but he shut down. Changed the subject and made it clear he didn't want to talk about it."

Paula sighed and hung up her last blouse in the closet. "No one wants to talk about their failures. Not that Sam failed in my eyes. I don't think that he did, but he does and that's what matters. After the divorce, Sam swore off love, marriage, and family. He planned to be a happy go lucky bachelor for life."

"Which would have worked if I hadn't gotten pregnant."

Chuckling, Paula came to sit down on the bed. "No, my dear, it would have worked if he hadn't *met* you. The baby is just a bonus. He was falling for you long before he found out you were pregnant."

Riley had a hunch that meeting Sam had been completely engineered by Paula. "You threw us together on purpose, didn't you?"

The older woman couldn't quite meet Riley's gaze. "I wanted to help you."

"And?"

"And I wanted to show Sam that not all women were the same. You two are perfect for one another."

Crafty old woman. Riley would need to keep on her toes or Paula would have the baby's entire future planned out. "It didn't hurt that you would get to choose your daughter-in-law."

Tapping her chin, Paula seemed to consider Riley's words. "I never thought of that but you're right."

Sure you didn't, Paula. It was all a happy accident.

Riley couldn't hide her grin at Paula's innocent facade. Her son was the actor in the family.

"Never occurred to you? Not once?"

"Maybe once. But what you really want to know about

is Sam and Trish, and that's a story I can tell you. Sam won't. He doesn't even discuss it with me."

He wouldn't even talk about it with Paula. That slapped Riley right in the face, making her think clearly for the first time that day. She'd been so worried about what she needed that she hadn't been focusing on what Sam needed.

He needed her to respect his privacy. Going behind his back to his mother to find out things he didn't want to discuss wasn't respect. It was slimy and she just couldn't do it. She did indeed desperately want to know what was driving him to ask so strangely, but this wasn't the way to find out.

"He and Trish met when he first went to Hollywood–"

"Stop, Paula." Riley held up her hands and shook her head. "I can't do this. I want to hear the story but I need to hear it from Sam."

"He'll never tell you."

Never is a long time.

"I cannot imagine that he wouldn't tell his future wife about his previous marriage. I think I have the right to know, but he needs to be the one to tell me, Paula. I just can't go behind his back like this and let you tell me. Sam would be livid."

"He might be relieved."

Riley didn't believe that for a minute and she didn't think Paula did, either.

"I'll talk to him again tonight when he gets home. I need to make it clear that if he can't open up to me then I can't marry him. Does that seem harsh? Am I being unreasonable? Because if I am–"

"You're not," Paula waved away Riley's concerns. "Sam should tell you about his first marriage, especially as he has apparently lost his mind and decided to retire from acting. I have to admit that I know the story and I didn't see that one coming. It's a major overreaction but Sam, much like his actor friends, tend to be drama kings. He was like this when he was little boy too, everything was a big damn deal. I'm just sorry that you're caught in the middle of all of this. But I do respect your decision, although I think it's more than my son deserves right now. He's been carrying this around far too long and letting it fester. In his mind Trish is blameless and believe me when I say that she isn't some innocent here. There were issues on both sides of that marriage. Neither one of them were very happy."

"So I simply need to get Sam to finally talk to me about his past. Piece of cake, right? I'll just give him an ultimatum. I won't marry him until he tells me. That should go over wonderfully. Maybe I should have Callie make a hotel reservation for me tonight after he throws me out."

Paula crossed her arms over her chest. "If you go, I go."

This wasn't going to be easy. In fact, it might be impossible. By taking a stand tonight, Riley might bring an end to her relationship with Sam. She was asking a great deal from him, more than he might be able to give.

She could lose it all.

———

When Riley and his mother had to be prompted to speak during dinner, Sam knew something was going on.

Normally they chatted away and he could barely get a word in edgewise, but tonight he had to ask them questions to get them to talk. The two women were exchanging glances and fidgeting in their chairs as if they couldn't wait for the meal to be over. They'd ordered in Chinese, and if Sam read his fortune cookie he had a feeling it was going to tell him that his mother and girlfriend were up to no good.

Perhaps they were plotting together to get him to live in Florida after the baby was born. They didn't need to conspire, however; if that's where Riley wanted to live then it was fine with him. He wouldn't be working anyway so he didn't need to be in Hollywood or New York City.

Sam pushed his plate away and patted his full stomach. It was nice to come home to a house that wasn't dark and empty. This was something he intended to get used to.

"Do you and Riley have anything planned for tomorrow?"

Another furtive glance. Yep, they were definitely up to something.

"Not much," Paula finally replied. "I wanted to show Riley some of my favorite places in the city like Serendipity and Radio City Music Hall. She also wants to see the Statue of Liberty, but we have all week to decide. It depends on how she's feeling tomorrow."

Riley had been doing so well with her morning sickness, but of course it would hinge on how she was feeling. Thankfully his mother was here now to keep an eye on Riley.

"Are you feeling okay now?"

"I'm fine. We're just being careful." He must have

looked like he didn't believe her because she rolled her eyes. "Seriously, it's all good. The tea and toast in the morning help and then the wristbands and lollipops keep me good through the day. If I even start to feel queasy, I drink some ginger ale and it goes away."

"Good. That's good. But now Mom is here to help if you have any issues while I'm working. I'm trying to get the director to push all of my scenes together on the schedule so I can finish early. Then I can be here all the time."

Those glances again. Sam was getting tired of it. If they had something to say, they should just damn well say it.

"Does anyone want to tell me what's going on? You two are obviously plotting world domination. Should I be scared?"

Paula dabbed at her lips with a paper napkin. "I think I'm going to take a nice, long, very long bath. I'll even have my earbuds in so I won't hear a thing."

Sam frowned, not sure what his mother had in mind. Obviously she wanted Sam to have some privacy with Riley but this was strange. He wasn't going to have sex with his girlfriend in the kitchen or living room when his own mother was staying here.

Riley was wringing her hands together, the fingers almost white where she was twisting them. This was not good. A bar of fear began to build in his gut as he watched the woman he loved fret and worry. She clearly wasn't happy at the moment and he had no idea as to why.

Did she want to leave?

"I think Mom wants us to talk."

She looked up and he could see the war going on

behind her eyes. Whatever it was she wanted to discuss, she was of two minds about it.

"I need you to do something for me," she finally said, taking a visibly shaky breath. "And you're not going to like it."

"There's isn't anything I wouldn't do for you, Riley. You have to know that."

He couldn't think of one single thing he'd refuse her. He'd walk buck naked over hot coals if that's what she wanted him to do.

"I need you to tell me about your first marriage."

Except that. He couldn't talk about that.

"No."

The word came out reflexively, no thought required. His whole being rejected the idea, his brain and heart in total mutiny.

Folding her hands, her expression turned sad, her lips drooping downward. "I thought you might say that. Paula offered to tell me the story but I told her I couldn't go behind your back like that."

Righteous anger at his mother welled up inside of Sam, making him see red. She had no business blabbing his life story to anyone that asked. It belonged to him and he would decide whom he would tell.

Riley wasn't just anyone, though. He wanted her to be his wife and that small part of him that was still sane knew it wasn't unreasonable to want to know about his past before she married him. Hell, for all she knew he'd been a wife beater and cheated on Trish, and she wouldn't want to marry him if he was like that. He just...couldn't tell her. If she knew, she might think less of him. She might not marry him.

"I can assure you that I'd be the best husband to you that I possibly can be. I'm ready to devote my entire life to you and the baby."

Leaning forward, she reached out for one of his hands, her skin chilly when it should have been warm. "That's what this is about, Sam. I'm not asking you to devote your entire life to me. I'm not asking you to retire from acting. I'm not sure why you'd want to. You love what you do and you enjoy it. You keep talking about watching over me and making sure I'm safe. I'm worried about you. I don't think it's healthy to obsess like this. I realize now that I've barely been alone since I got to New York. Either you or Callie have been here, and now you're talking about your mother watching me. It is not necessary to babysit me twenty-four-seven. I'm a grown woman and I can take care of myself."

She didn't have a clue as to what could happen. He wasn't going to enlighten her, instead lobbing the ball back into her court. He could argue and debate with the best of them.

"You know, some women would be overjoyed that I was willing to put my career aside for them. They'd be grateful that I put my family first."

Her brows shot up and she straightened in her chair, her hand falling away from his. Shit. That might not have been the smartest thing to say.

"You're right. Some women would be glad to have you hanging around all hours of the day admiring them and bringing them tea and toast. If you want one of those women, I suggest you call one. I'm guessing you have dozens of phone numbers of females just like that. You said you loved me because I was different. Was that a lie? Just a line to get me into bed?"

"No," he said, jumping up from his chair, anger beginning to build again. "I've never used a line on you."

"Okay, then...you were telling the truth. But you're lying to me right now, Sam. I can see there's something you're not telling me. So let's get this out of the way so we can move on."

That sane part of his brain was drowned out by the chorus of voices in his ears telling him to say nothing. Never tell her his shameful past. He had to convince her to drop this now.

"If I tell you, you won't marry me. We love each other. Isn't that enough?"

From the look on her face the answer was a resounding no.

"I do love you but that's only part of the equation. I have to be able to trust you, and that's something I've been burned on in the past. You know that. I'm not trying to make this an ultimatum, but I don't see how I can move forward with you unless you're honest with me." She stood as well, walking to him so she was standing close. He could smell the vanilla scent of her shampoo, and it was all he could do not to sweep her into his arms and kiss her until she forgot all about this crazy subject. Make it so nothing mattered but the way they felt when they were together. "Sam, did you cheat on Trish? It's okay. You can tell me."

That's what everyone assumed. That he'd been unfaithful. He'd never corrected anyone, preferring it to the truth.

He opened his mouth to say yes, to admit to a deed he'd never committed but his innate honesty wouldn't let him tell the lie. It was one thing to stay silent but a whole other thing to blatantly tell an untruth. He couldn't do it.

Riley was looking up at him, love in her eyes but anguish, too. She wanted his story and he'd gone to great lengths to keep it from her, but he could also see the resolve behind the sadness. She would never marry him if he didn't tell her the truth. Of course, she probably wouldn't marry him afterward, either.

Frankly, his mother had already inserted herself into this dilemma, so it was only a matter of time before she spilled the beans to Riley. He was cornered like a wounded animal, no way out.

"I didn't cheat on Trish. Ever. I swear."

Blinking a few times, Riley nodded and smiled. "Well...that's good."

Scraping his fingers through his hair, he groaned in surrender. The woman he loved looked so hopeful and he was about to knock her rose-colored glasses off. So much for protecting her from the harsh world. He was about to throw her headlong into his dismal past.

"You better sit down. It's a long story."

CHAPTER
Thirty-Eight

RILEY HATED herself for putting Sam through what appeared to be some kind of horrible and painful torture. His skin had gone an ashen gray shade and his blue eyes were almost black with emotion. Anger? Fear? Clearly whatever memories he was about to dredge up weren't pleasant.

She, however, needed to understand why he was acting so strangely. The Sam Collins she'd met a few months ago would never have thought to retire and give up his career just because he was becoming a father. It was a major over-reaction and there had to be a logical explanation for it. What if he went even more overboard and decided that the child shouldn't attend school or play with other kids?

They settled on the couch, her on one end and Sam on the other. He'd sat there on purpose and she didn't say a word. If he needed a little distance to be able to do this, it was the least she could do.

"I'm listening," Riley said, folding her hands in her lap

and waiting for Sam to gather his thoughts. "And I'll try not to interrupt. I can see this isn't easy."

He didn't answer, his gaze lost somewhere in the past, a place she couldn't get to and was no part of. It was hard to simply wait and keep her mouth shut but eventually she was rewarded when he began to speak.

"Trish and I met when we were both struggling actors in Hollywood. We both had a small part in a movie and the first time I saw her we were in wardrobe. I remember thinking that she was beautiful and had great legs. She smiled at me and later I asked her for coffee. That was pretty much it and we were married about a year later. Just a small ceremony at the courthouse but we had a big party afterward for all of our friends. It was a double celebration because I'd just landed a decent role in a pilot for television."

Pressing her lips together, Riley kept from voicing all the questions whipping around her brain. Sam had been in love with Trish. That alone made Riley curious as to what the woman was like.

"The pilot wasn't picked up but I was getting pretty steady work. Just small roles but I was working. Trish, on the other hand, hit a dry spell and believe me when I tell you that there is nothing worse as an artist. She had a day job at the cosmetic counter of a department store and she was promoted to manager. That's when she decided to take a break from acting for a little while. All the rejection was getting to her. Of course, that meant that when I had to travel, she couldn't go with me anymore. She had to stay for her job."

A picture of Sam's marriage was beginning to emerge.

An up and coming young actor, running all over the world and a young wife stuck at home in a job she probably hated. It was a recipe for disaster.

Leaning forward, Sam propped his elbows on his knees. "I was a lousy husband. I was hardly ever home and when I was all I concentrated on was the next role. I was trying to make connections in the business, and that meant going to parties and meeting as many people as possible. That town is all about who you know. I encouraged Trish to go back to acting and she did audition for a couple of roles, but when she didn't get them she decided to quit show business altogether. It was pretty tense that year, although she tried to hide how unhappy she was."

Riley couldn't stop herself from commenting. "That wasn't your fault. You were just chasing your dream."

He gave her a lopsided smile. "I'm telling this story with the benefit of hindsight. Looking back, I doubt I was truly even aware that she resented it every time I was cast in another production. Or maybe I did realize it but didn't want to admit it, because then I'd have to deal with it. I wouldn't say either of us were all that good at communicating. I did know she wasn't happy but frankly, I didn't know how to help her, and if she'd asked me to give up acting I wouldn't have. I wouldn't have done that to make her happy, Riley. I was too selfish and self-absorbed."

It would have been far too much to ask of him. Riley loved Sam and there was no way she'd ask him to give up his dreams because it was inconvenient for her. She'd always known that he wouldn't be a nine-to-five kind of guy, kissing her goodbye in the morning and coming home to dinner in the evening.

"When we're young and climbing the ladder, we often are," Riley replied, reaching out and rubbing his hand. "And if she didn't tell you how she felt..."

"That wasn't Trish's way. Mine either, to be honest. I think we both thought that if we just ignored it, it would go away."

Sam went silent, once again far away and long ago with his thoughts, reliving some drama and misery if the expression on his face was anything to go by.

"I was in Toronto working on a new movie when she called me. She was pregnant, and for the first time in a long time she sounded really happy. She was giggling and laughing and I had my wife back. I could tell that she was thrilled that she was going to have a baby."

A shock rocketed through Riley's bones and her fingers curled onto the arm of the couch for support. Sam wasn't a father to any children.

None that you know of.

This was his secret. He had a family somewhere. Had he been a terrible father and that's what he didn't want her to know?

"I was happy, too," Sam went on, not seeming to notice her surprise. He was lost in the past, his lips a grim line as he told his story. "I truly was. We hadn't really talked about kids in any concrete way. We were both young but we'd both said that we wanted them...you know...someday. Well, that day had come and it was all good. But I had to finish my commitment to the film in Toronto while she was still in Los Angeles."

A lightbulb went off over Riley's head. Sam had been *away* from Trish when she'd been pregnant. A heaviness settled into her chest and tears pricked the backs of her eyes.

There was a reason she didn't know about any child. This...This was what drove Sam Collins.

Staring down at the hardwood floor, Sam finally raised his head and she could see unshed tears in his eyes as well. A lump grew in her throat and she had to swallow a few times to be able to breathe. Speaking was out of the question, but Riley ached to reach out and pull him into her arms. Comfort him and take away the pain that was etched in his face.

Oh Sam. I love you so much.

"I guess it was about three weeks later when Trish called me. She'd started bleeding and her friend had taken her to the hospital."

She waited for the words she knew were coming. Sam wanted to protect Riley for a good reason. It all made sense now.

"She'd lost the baby."

This time Riley did reach out but Sam shook away her touch and stood, walking over to the front windows to peer out, but she doubted he was really seeing anything. He was still back there with Trish. With a loss he'd clearly not dealt with.

"Then she just hung up. I tried to call her back but she didn't answer. I called her best friend but she hung up on me, too. I managed to finish my part in the film and got home a few days later. Trish had moved out. This time I drove to her friend's house and wouldn't leave until Trish talked to me."

Sam's hands were clenched into fists, his entire body stiff and tense. He was alone, not letting her comfort him, but even from this distance she could see that this had been torturing him for years. Riley's pregnancy had brought it all up again.

"She was crying and yelling at me that it was all my fault. That if I'd been home she would have got to the hospital in time. She said she'd never forgive me and she never wanted to lay eyes on me ever again after what I'd done, putting my career before our child. Then she said that I never wanted the baby, but that isn't true, Riley. I did want the baby. I already loved it."

His words came out choked and the tears he'd tried so hard to keep at bay were sliding down his cheeks. Riley's body shook and she didn't care if he pushed her away. She had to be close to him, holding him and protecting him from these memories. He'd carried this albatross around his neck far too long. Time to cut that cord. He hadn't done anything wrong.

Wrapping her arms around his lean middle, she pressed her cheek into his back. "You didn't do anything wrong. Trish was upset, understandably so, and she took it out on you. But I bet in a few days or a few weeks, she regretted saying them. I'm not a doctor but I doubt there was anything you could have done, and even if you hadn't been in Toronto you might not have been home."

"I could have taken her to the hospital. Made sure she got the best care."

His tone was resolute and he wasn't buying what she was selling. He was too invested in the narrative.

"You were a young man," Riley reminded him. "Yes, you would have taken her to the hospital as quickly as possible but were you honestly going to march around the emergency room demanding the best specialists in the world?"

His body had stiffened and he was trying to extricate himself from her arms but she simply tightened her hold. He needed this whether he realized it or not.

"I wasn't there when she needed me. She'd never needed me before and the one time she did, where was I?"

"Getting a paycheck that I suspect paid your rent," Riley countered. He was determined to be the bad guy in this scenario. "Doing your job and following your dream. There is no way you could have foreseen what happened."

"Exactly." He sounded like she'd just confessed to a crime and he was the detective on the case. "We don't know what's going to happen with our baby. We can't see the future. It's better if I'm around as much as possible, and if I can't be here then Callie or Mom can take care of you."

She loosened her grip and allowed him to turn around. Cupping his jaw in her hands, she gazed into his stormy gray-blue eyes, still watery from his tears. "If I'm alone and I start bleeding or have contractions, I'll call 911."

His brows shot up as if she'd responded in a shocking way. "You'd call 911?"

"Of course. That's what people do."

As a teacher, Riley had been trained to handle emergency situations and part of that training was when to call 911.

"What if the ambulance got caught in traffic? What if it took too long to get to you?"

Riley nodded. "All good arguments. But if someone was trying to drive me to the hospital, they'd probably get stuck in that same traffic jam so I'm no better off. We all take chances every day, Sam, just walking across the street. There's no such thing as a risk-free pregnancy. It doesn't exist. You didn't cause Trish to miscarry and it wasn't your fault that she didn't get to the hospital in time. For all you know, it was too late before she even picked up the phone to call her friend."

"You can't know that. There might have been time."

He wasn't going down without a fight.

"Why don't you talk to Dr. Kate about this? She might have some insight into whether there was anything you could have done." Riley sucked in a breath, knowing her next request wasn't going to be popular. "I also think you should talk to Trish. I'm guessing she has a different outlook on this situation all these years later."

Sam was looking at her as if she'd lost her mind. "Talk to Trish? She said she never wanted to see me again and I've made that happen. I haven't seen her since that day."

"How could that even happen? Didn't she have to show up in court for the divorce?"

"We did everything through our lawyers. I made sure she was taken care of, though."

What?

"You mean financially?"

Sam nodded. "We didn't divorce right away. By the time we did split up officially, I was starting to make good money. I just wanted to be sure she didn't have to worry about anything."

That was sweet and wonderful and just like the man that Sam was.

"And you've never heard anything from her? Not a thank you or a fuck you? Nothing?"

His lips twisted and he shook his head. "She basically said fuck you that last time I saw her. She didn't want anything to do with me and I get that. I ruined her life."

Riley wasn't going to give up on this. Her life with Sam was too important.

"Perhaps...and I'm just throwing this out there for consideration...perhaps Trish was upset and hurting and she needed someone to blame it on? Because there was no one to blame. These things sometimes happen. I've had friends that had miscarriages and then go on to have one or more successful pregnancies. There's no rhyme or reason to it, but she wanted someone to be at fault. So she chose you since you were conveniently not there when she needed you to hold her hand. Yes, that is something that you needed to apologize for, but you did not ruin her entire life. I hate to break it to you, but you're not that powerful, Sam."

"You don't understand—"

"I don't?" Riley broke in. "Because I think I do. If you went off on location to shoot a movie and something bad happened, I would be upset. I might scream and cry. I might yell and curse. But it wouldn't be your fault, Sam, and you wouldn't have ruined my life. I bet Trish knows that now, too. She was sad and hurting and she lashed out at the person she loved. That's normal. But you've been carrying this around with you for far too long and it has to stop. This isn't healthy or productive. You can't wrap me and the baby in cotton wool and protect us from the big, bad world. I won't live that way. You need to talk to her about what happened and come to some peace about the past. Only then can you and I move forward."

A muscle jumped in his jaw and his hair stood on end from scraping his fingers through it.

"Is that an ultimatum?"

Was it? She didn't do them often, if at all, but she couldn't see how they were going to be together for any length of time if he couldn't deal with her living her life in a normal manner. She loved him - more than she'd ever thought possible - but he'd been punishing himself too long and she wasn't about to join in and martyr herself as well.

"It's simply the truth. I want us to have a happy life and family together. When our child wants to sleep over at a friend's house, what are you going to do? Or when it's his first day of school? What if we decide to have more children and I get pregnant again? Will you just follow me around twenty-four hours a day? What's the plan?" She threw up her hands in frustration. He wasn't hearing her. He was too caught up in the past. "Just call and talk to her. Don't you think it's time? Aren't you even a little curious as to how her life turned out when you supposedly ruined it?"

For a brief moment it looked like he might say yes, but then he turned on his heel and marched out of the house, slamming the door behind him. Closing the door on the dream of them being together. It sounded so final.

She almost followed but then stopped when her hand touched the doorknob. He needed this time. She'd thrown so much at him and he was too hurt and confused to make logical decisions. Hopefully in a few hours he'd come back, ready to face the past so they could have a future.

Or he'd end things, once and for all.

CHAPTER
Thirty~Nine

AFTER SAM STOMPED out of his own home he'd walked around for a little while, not really going anywhere in particular but definitely not heading back to Riley. He was still angry and defensive, which didn't make the best combination to speak rationally about the situation they'd found themselves in.

A standoff.

She wouldn't marry him if he didn't talk to Trish, and he wouldn't talk to his ex-wife. Neither one of them was going to budge.

Somehow he found himself at his friend Nate's front door, although he hadn't consciously gone there. But it wasn't a bad decision. Hanging out with a buddy and talking business was a great way to relax.

Nate invited Sam in and retrieved a couple of beers from the refrigerator, handing him one.

"Drink up. It looks like you could use it. You look like shit."

Thanks, I feel that way, too.

They settled on the couch and Sam asked Nate about the twins - who were currently sleeping - and the movie that the couple was working on while in New York City.

"Shooting is going great," Nate said with a huge smile. "And the kids are sleeping for longer stretches which is a miracle from heaven for us. At night we get a good seven hours and it's awesome. I never realized just how much I loved to sleep until I became a dad."

"I'm going to become a father," Sam heard himself say before he could stop the flow of words. He needed to tell someone as if it would make it more real. "Riley is pregnant."

Nate's brows shot up to his hairline and his eyes grew round. "Bloody hell...she's...and you're...shit...I'm just so surprised. Congratulations, you must be over the moon. When you described her she sounded like a wonderful woman and now you're having a baby. That's great. Truly fantastic. I highly recommend being a father despite the lack of quality sack time."

"Thank you. I'm...*we* are excited. We got to see the baby on the ultrasound and it was great."

Nate held up his pointer finger. "Just one? Trust me when I say that you need to check that."

Chuckling, Sam had a vivid memory of when Nate showed him the ultrasound photos with two babies. "Just one. I made sure."

"That's wonderful. You must be very excited."

"I am."

Nate rubbed his jaw, those shrewd eyes taking in everything around him. "You're so happy that you showed up at my front door unannounced, looking like hell. Try again, my friend. What's going on? Did you and Riley quarrel? Let me give you some advice about pregnant women. Just give them whatever they want. It's easier."

That was the problem. The one thing Riley wanted he couldn't give.

Do I want to talk about this? I wouldn't have ended up here if I didn't.

"We didn't really have an argument so much as a disagreement," Sam finally admitted. He needed to talk to someone and his mother had already taken Riley's side. Nate was Sam's friend and would hear him out and understand his reasoning. "No one raised their voice or anything."

Nate took a long draw from his beer bottle. "What did you disagree about? Is there a way to compromise on this? A way you can both call this a win?"

"It's kind of a long story."

Nate laughed and took another drink of his beer. "The best kind. I'm in for the night and have no plans except to try and get some sleep later. But you better talk fast because the babies will be up in about forty-five minutes wanting to be fed for the last time tonight."

———

Riley could have used a drink but she was stuck with decaf tea, and it was not doing the job. Paula's calm and unruffled facade wasn't helping, either.

"You have to be patient with Sam. He has to come to the right conclusion in his own time."

"How old will I be when that happens?" Riley pushed her teacup away and grimaced. "That tea is terrible. If I drink any more it's just going to come right back up."

Shrugging, Paula picked up the cup and emptied it in the sink. "Because it's decaf. It might as well be colored water. How about a nice ginger ale? That might settle your stomach. Don't worry about Sam taking forever. He's stubborn but he's not stupid. He knows that this has to be dealt with, but he hasn't had any reason to do it before now."

"Am I a good enough reason?"

Riley wasn't sure she really and truly wanted an answer to that question. When Sam had walked out of the condo her heart had broken into a million little pieces that were scattered all over this home. Every place she looked, she could see Sam laughing and smiling. She wanted to make a home and a life with him, but she couldn't do that until he stepped out of the shadow he'd been living under. Never mind her feelings, it wasn't fair to him. He'd been blaming himself for something that wasn't his fault.

"You and the baby are the best reason ever," Paula assured her, handing Riley a can of ginger ale. "My son loves you and that's a powerful motivator. He wants to spend the rest of his life with you so eventually he's going to come around to the fact that he's out of options. He's ignored this for years and his time is up. But until then, he's going to act like a real jerk."

"I'm not proud of the fact that he feels cornered. There was probably a better way to handle it."

Paula sat across from Riley, a dubious expression on her face. "Really? What would that have been? I didn't hear what you said but I'm sure you were as gentle as you could be. Sam's been deeply in denial about this for a long time, Riley. There was no soft landing here for him. He has to come back to earth with a thump. When you told me that he was thinking about retiring from acting so he could be with you all the time, I knew that he'd finally gone overboard. He knows it too, but he's fighting it tooth and nail."

There was still a part of this that Riley didn't understand, that she simply couldn't wrap her mind around.

"How could Trish do that?" Riley asked, her hands cupped around the cold can of soda, her fingers going comfortably numb while her mind worked overtime trying to make sense out of what had happened tonight. "Throwing everything on Sam and then walking away. It seems so cruel."

"What you really want to know is if Trish was always like that."

Apparently, there was no fooling Paula. That was exactly what Riley wanted to know.

"I haven't talked to Trish since they split up but I always liked her. She was a good person and she seemed to love Sam." Paula seemed to choose her words carefully. "They had their problems like all couples do. They were both young and headstrong, and neither of them were good at compromising, although Sam has become better at that over the years like most of us do. When Sam told me what she'd said...well...all I can say is that Trish must have been in a great deal of pain to lash out like that. It's the only explanation that makes any sense."

"Why didn't she ever reach out to Sam then? You'd think she'd want to clear the air."

"I don't know. Maybe she was scared, maybe she just

wanted to put it all behind her." Paula sighed and shook her head. "Only Trish knows and that's why Sam needs to talk to her. Purge all of these demons that had been driving him since that day. I've urged him over the years to do it but he's never listened. Hopefully he will now."

That's all Riley had at the moment. Hope.

"Just how stubborn is your son?"

"Let's just hope the baby takes after you in that department."

It was going to be a long night waiting for Sam to come home.

CHAPTER
Forty

"YOU'RE the biggest fucking idiot I may have ever known in my entire life."

Nate's rather crude declaration didn't help Sam's already nasty mood. He'd just poured out his story and his friend had basically shit on it.

"And you're a big British asshole. Fuck you."

Nate didn't take offense, simply throwing his head back and laughing. "Paige probably wouldn't argue with you, although not all the time, I hope. But I stand by my statement. You're stupid and delusional. You're not thinking about this right, mate. There's no way you can keep Riley and the baby safe all the time. It's not even practical to try and be with her every minute, nor do you want to do it. Marriage thrives on a little mystery. Some-times you need to go do your own thing and then come back together. If Paige and I were together all the time we'd be at each other's throats constantly."

Sam was only beginning to admit that his plans might

be flawed. He wasn't ready to admit it out loud yet, though.

"How do you do it every day?" Sam marveled at his friend's relaxed posture. He appeared like he didn't have a care in the world. "I'm fucking terrified all the time and you look like you could fall asleep in your chair. You have a family. Two kids and a wife. How are you not worried all the damn time?"

Nate placed his beer bottle on to the coffee table and looked Sam straight in the eye. "Listen close because I'm about to lay some deep wisdom on your ass. Are you listening?"

"Jesus, yes. You don't have to be so dramatic."

Except that they were all actors and Nate loved nothing more than an audience.

"To be in love is to be vulnerable. To be a father is to be completely and totally vulnerable. Before it was just me, but now anyone can hurt me by hurting someone I love more than my own life."

That sounded utterly horrifying. Yet, Sam was right there with Nate and there was no way out.

"How do you deal with it? Doesn't it make you crazy? I don't want to be scared all of the time that something is going to happen to my family."

"I just don't think about it."

Sam sucked in a breath at the seemingly bald statement. One sentence that sounded so simple and fucked up at the same time.

"You don't think about it," Sam echoed in disbelief. This night was actually getting worse. "This is your plan? That's not a plan, that's denial. Christ, I came to you for advice and this is it? Just don't think about it? Fuck. I'd have got better advice from a random stranger."

Nate, however, seemed to find the situation hilarious. "I think it's great advice. Some of the best I've ever given, in fact. Let me ask you a question. How did you get here to the city from Florida?"

This was stupid.

"I flew."

"And when you arrived at the airport, how did you get to your house?"

And becoming even more stupid by the minute.

"A car service."

"And you didn't worry about the danger of flying? You didn't ponder the intelligence of getting in a vehicle driven by a complete stranger? You didn't worry and fret about the dangers on the highways? Come on, the world isn't an oasis of personal safety. There's always going to be an element of danger in whatever you do and wherever you go. We take chances every day just living our lives. Do you spend your time worrying about that?" Nate didn't give Sam a chance to answer. "No, you don't. You live your life and savor the happy times and do your best to get through the crappy ones. That's the plan. Live and enjoy your life because you don't want to get to the end of it and find that you were so busy being an asshole that you didn't appreciate the gift of your family."

Sam hopped up from the couch and began to pace in front of the fireplace. "It's not the same. Crossing the street isn't the same as keeping Riley safe during her pregnancy. They're not equivalent."

Shrugging, Nate grinned. "Okay, let's say they're not.

But let me ask you another question, although you'll ignore this one the same as you did the others. Do you honestly believe that you can protect Riley and the baby by being there all the time? By quitting a job that you love? You're not some all-powerful being. You're not a doctor. We play badass heroes on the movie screen but we're just normal guys in real life. You're only human and you can't fix everything. Something bad could happen to Riley in your own home. Hell, she could slip in the shower or cut herself with a knife cooking dinner. You can't stop life from happening. No matter how much you want to."

Sam threw up his hands in frustration. "So you just give up? You don't even try?"

Nate stood and walked up to Sam, poking a finger in his chest. "Riley is absolutely right. You're not being rational about any of this. Are you listening to yourself? You're talking about trying to control life, which we both know is stupid. You need to talk to someone about this and right away. You're not thinking straight. Then call your ex-wife and tell her you're not going to carry the blame for this anymore. She should never have put this on you."

Sam wanted to argue with Nate. Debate the question back and forth but clearly his friend had sided with Riley.

It was becoming a pattern. First his mother, now Nate. What did that say about Sam's case? Nothing good.

"You've been no fucking help at all," Sam growled before stomping toward the front door. "I'm sorry I came here."

"So you're going home?" Nate asked, still smiling as if nothing was wrong in the world. "Or heading to a bar?"

Alcohol would be nice but wouldn't solve his problem. Going home wasn't an option, either.

"I don't know," Sam admitted. He felt lost and out of control. He couldn't make people understand and he was beginning to wonder if it was because he wasn't making any sense. "I can't go home. Not yet."

Maybe not ever.

"You're welcome to stay in the guest room. But be warned that Paige probably won't have an opinion much different than mine."

"I'll take my chances. She's smarter than you."

"And if she agrees with me?"

Paige was a wise woman. A widow and a single mother before meeting Nate, she'd been through the wringer and come out the other side, happy and healthy.

"Then I'll think about following your advice."

"You are such a bloody idiot."

Sam had no evidence to dispute Nate's claim. He'd never felt more stupid in his life than he did now. He was dug in and didn't want to change his mind but that was the least of his worries. The one big one wouldn't leave him alone.

What was Riley doing right now? Had she washed her hands of him? Was she making plans to go back to Florida? There was only one way forward if he wanted to be with her and have the family of his dreams. He simply wasn't sure he was capable of it.

CHAPTER
Forty-One

AFTER A SLEEPLESS NIGHT in Nate's guest room, Sam sat down in the chair on the opposite side of the desk from Dr. Kate. Since this wasn't a medical visit, they were meeting in the physician's office and not the exam room.

"Now tell me, Sam. What brings you here today?"

Shifting uncomfortably in his chair, he cleared his throat before speaking. "First off, thanks for seeing me on such short notice. I appreciate it."

Dr. Kate nodded but didn't respond, clearly waiting for him to get to the damn point.

"I have a few questions," he finally said, the words not coming easily. He was already conflicted about even being here, still not ready to admit that he had a problem. "I was hoping you could help me."

Except that deep down he knew he had an issue with his past. Admitting that was simply hard to do. If he admitted it, then he had to deal with it.

That's why I'm here.

"I'll do what I can to answer your questions," Dr. Kate assured him with a cool, professional smile. "What concerns do you have?"

"I'm not sure where to begin," he admitted with a humorless laugh. He wasn't in the best of moods and all he wanted to do was go home to Riley and the baby. "This isn't really about Riley's pregnancy."

A brow arched in question and Sam realized he'd fucked up. He should have had that second cup of coffee before coming here. "It's not what you're thinking. This is not about another woman."

Shit. "Well...it is about another woman but from a long time ago. I'm asking about something that happened over fifteen years ago."

Dr. Kate sat back in her chair and folded her hands in front of her. "How about you start at the beginning of the story? I'll just listen and answer your questions along the way. How does that sound?"

Painful. It sounded horribly painful.

He'd been avoiding this for years. Afraid to find out that Trish had spoken the truth. Now he'd know for sure.

———

Riley slammed down her empty teacup and wished it was filled with coffee. Beautiful, deep, dark, and rich caffeinated coffee. Nectar of the gods and the one thing guaranteed to make her feel slightly more human this morning after a sleepless night.

Sam had never come home.

He was a grown man and he could take care of himself,

so she wasn't worried that he was lying dead in a ditch somewhere. Especially as New York City didn't seem to have a plethora of ditches and Sam had a black Amex card so he could check into any five-star hotel in the tri-state area. She doubted he'd bunked down on a park bench last night, although she hoped whatever mattress he'd slept on last night had been lumpy. She'd spent most of the night hours pacing the floor worried about what he was thinking and what stupid thing he might do.

Paula reached for the offending cup and placed it in the sink. "Did you get any sleep last night?"

Tapping the dark patch under one eye, Riley asked, "Does it look like it?"

"Sadly...no. But I have just the solution for our rainy day blues."

To make matters worse, the heavens had opened up about five in the morning and it was now raining cats and dogs, the sky as gray and stormy as Riley's mood. At least she wasn't wasting a sunny day feeling like crap.

"Did you hear from your son?"

Paula's smile fell and she shook her head. "I'm very angry with him. I had to send him a text early this morning to tell him that he's worrying us unnecessarily. It's one thing to decide not to come home last night, but he should have at least sent a message to you or to me. It was very thoughtless. He did send a text back a few minutes ago that he's fine. He stayed at Nate and Paige's last night."

No park bench. No ditch. Or morgue. Or emergency room.

"Did he say anything else?"

"No, but then I didn't expect him to. He's still in his

stubborn mode and it may take a while." Paula gestured toward the large windows, the rain dripping down the glass. "I'm not going to let you sit around here all day and brood about what my idiot son is doing. We're going to have a spa day. You and me. I've made all the arrangements so don't even think about saying no. We're going to have a wonderful time. And Sam is going to pay for it."

Standing, Riley set her plate in the sink. "I did a lot of thinking last night. I think that Sam is going to end things and send me back to Florida."

Wrapping her hands around her coffee mug, Paula nodded. "You think he doesn't have the strength to face the past? I think he does."

"That isn't it at all." Riley thought the world of Sam. Possibly more than he thought of himself. "I think he has the strength but doesn't have the will or desire. His world is comfortable and easy. Facing this, dealing with it, well...that's hard. He never has to if he doesn't want to. He can slide on by for the next fifty years."

"He's never been the one to take the easy road. He's always been willing to do whatever is necessary. However, you have a point that so far he hasn't had to deal with this, but that's changed now. He can't go on pretending he can control the fate of the world." Paula suddenly grinned and laughed. "Especially if you two have a girl. Can you imagine those teen years? He'll give himself a coronary trying to micromanage his daughter. I think he's finally come up against a wall and he's going to have to face the past. Once and for all. He's just going to do anything and everything he can to avoid it until he can't anymore."

That sounded good but Riley wasn't convinced.

"You say that he's stubborn and I believe it. Just how long can he avoid this?"

"I don't know," Paula admitted with a soft sigh. "But I do know that he loves you very much. He won't be able to stay away too long."

Riley could only hope Paula was right. Despite being angry with Sam, she missed him.

"I just wish I could do something to help him. I feel so useless."

"He has to do this himself. I don't think this is something that either one of us can help him with. But I'm sure he knows that we love him and that we're here if he needs us."

Waiting. It wasn't a particular skill that Riley excelled at but she needed to settle in for the long haul. Sam needed to take that all important first step. The rest she was sure they could do together.

———

Sam's twenty minutes with Dr. Kate had been educational, but she hadn't answered the one most important question.

"You know I can't answer that," she said gently, her voice low. "I don't know enough about the circumstances and I never examined your ex-wife. It would be pure conjecture on my part, Sam."

He swallowed hard, dislodging the lump that made it difficult to speak. All these years later he wasn't immune when telling this story. He still felt the loss even though he'd never held the baby or heard the heartbeat.

"I only want to know if I could have saved our child."

Such a simple, straightforward query that seemed to have no answer.

"It doesn't work like that." Turning in her chair, Dr. Kate motioned toward the row of file cabinets against the wall. "Those are filled with the files of my patients. I've delivered thousands of babies in my career. Every pregnancy is a little different, just as every woman isn't like any other. I do understand where you're trying to go with this, and I cannot make a definitive medical conclusion here. But I will say, Sam, that if a doctor couldn't save the pregnancy then you probably couldn't have, either. Getting your ex-wife to the hospital may not have made any difference at all. She could have been there for a doctor's appointment and started to miscarry and there might not have been anything anyone could do. If the pregnancy wasn't viable... That's out of medical science's hands. And out of yours."

Disappointed, he stood, wanting to bring the conversation to a close. He was grateful that Dr. Kate had taken the time to speak to him but he wasn't going to get the answers he sought today. She didn't have them.

"Thank you, Doctor, for seeing me. I appreciate your time and your detailed explanations."

Dr. Kate stood as well. "I'm sorry I couldn't be more specific."

What she was really saying was she was sorry she couldn't take away his guilt. He could see it in her eyes, that sadness and pity.

"You helped. Thank you."

She didn't believe him but then, he wasn't sure he believed himself. She did help in a small way, slowly but surely pushing him toward seeing his ex-wife.

Talk to Trish. Only she had the answers. A woman he hadn't seen in over fifteen years. He didn't even know where she lived or what she was doing.

If she still hated him.

The two choices in front of him were clear. He could go back to the condo and tell Riley he wasn't going to do it. Let her return to Florida or whatever she decided to do. But he'd have stood his ground and not given in. That would surely be cold comfort when he was alone.

What was the saying? Pride goeth before a fall.

Sam had his share of pig-headed pride. He didn't want that to be the reason that Riley left him.

His second option was to go talk to Trish. Not because Riley had urged him to do so but because it was something he should have done years ago. Put this all behind him. The worst thing he could find out was that he truly was responsible for Trish losing the baby and since he kind of already thought that - and had been living his life as if it were true - it couldn't be the terrible thing he'd made it out to be. It would confirm what he'd always thought to be the case, but the sliver of doubt had been something he could hold onto. That sliver had kept him sane right after it happened.

He could lose that scrap of hope, and that was why he was so chicken shit to go see her. To ask her the questions that he needed answered. Because deep down he didn't want to be responsible.

Jesus, he was fucked up. Pushing people away because he thought one thing but a part of him didn't want to believe. Consequently, he'd stayed frozen in time, not moving forward or looking back. Just standing there like a statue.

And everyone knew what happened to statues. They got shit on.

He needed to speak to Trish, not because Riley or his mom wanted him to. Not because he was going to become a father. He had to do this long overdue deed for himself. So he could take a step forward and leave all of that baggage behind. It wasn't fair to Riley to ask her to take him on for life when he was carrying a large set of luggage full of his crap past.

There was only one thing to do. See Trish. But first, he had some apologizing to do to Riley for walking out.

CHAPTER
Forty-Two

RILEY DIDN'T KNOW whether to slap or kiss Sam when he walked in the door several hours later. She was angry with him. Really, really mad. She understood the need that drove him to leave but it didn't stop her from being royally honked off. He could have called, sent a text, or even a smoke signal over the New York City skyline. She'd been worried as hell. The only thing that kept her from going off on him right then and there was the fact that he looked far worse than he had when he'd left last night.

He looked horrible, pasty with a growth of beard and his eyes red-rimmed, as if he'd been up for days instead of one night.

"You look awful," Paula said bluntly, her arms crossed over her chest and her lips pursed. "I'd better go make some coffee. Have you eaten?"

"Not really but I'm not all that hungry, Mom."

"You'll eat because you need to and I won't hear another word about it."

Paula strode into the kitchen, leaving Riley alone with Sam. They simply stared at one another for a minute or two before he broke eye contact and looked away. His entire body language was unsure, his shoulders slumped in defeat. It was a far cry from the confident man that she was used to seeing. Her own stomach twisted in sympathy. Just because she was mad didn't mean that she couldn't feel badly for him. He'd had a rough night, but then again so had she, so she wasn't ready to fall into his arms and forgive.

She'd thrown down the gauntlet last night and started this ball rolling, but he was the one that had chosen to walk out.

"I'm sorry."

If Riley was a better person she might let him off the hook, but sadly she wasn't. He'd made some bad decisions along the way and he needed to own up to those.

"For?"

"Leaving the way I did," he replied, rubbing his stubbled chin. "You were probably worried too, which I certainly don't deserve. I am really sorry, babe. I'm all fucked up and I need to fix a few things."

Admitting it was a start.

"Thank you for the apology. I was worried." She gave him her best mean look and he had the good sense to look ashamed, color suffusing his pale cheeks. "Are you working on a plan to fix those things?"

"I am," he confirmed with a nod of his head. "I know what I need to do next, anyway."

"All by yourself?"

His eyes widened in surprise, which made her want to smack him on the forehead. He didn't understand. Still.

"You want to help me?"

Sighing, she tried to explain. "I want to support you, Sam. You talk about wanting us to be together, be a team, but the first time we came up against a huge hurdle you walked out. You didn't give me a chance to be a partner, did you? I love you, despite the fact that you sometimes act like an idiot, and I hope you love me even when I do something incredibly stupid as well. I want to stand by your side and help you through the bad times, not just the good ones. I know some monsters you have to face on your own, but that doesn't mean that I can't be there to cheer you on. I don't want to just be there to walk the red carpets and pick up the awards. I want to be there for it all, no matter how ugly it might get."

"This might get pretty bad." Sam's throat worked and he scraped his fingers through his already disheveled hair. "I need to see Trish and talk to her. She might not like that very much."

While Riley had sympathy for the other woman she'd never met, she also felt strongly that Trish had thrown out some serious and cruel accusations. It wasn't unfair for Sam to want to question the veracity of her claims. Even if what she said was true, and Trish still hated him, he had to find a way to forgive himself. He hadn't hurt anyone on purpose and he'd lost a child, too. They'd both suffered, and neither one's grief was more important than the other's.

"I think you should. I can go with you if you like," Riley

offered, her chest tight with hope. Sam was ready to face the demons from his past. Finally. "Not to talk to her, but just to hold your hand before you do. Do you even know where she is?"

Fishing his phone out of his pocket, Sam held the screen up for her inspection. "My agent was able to track her down. She lives in Connecticut. I've been walking around pretty much all afternoon with her address in my pocket trying to get the courage to go see her. I promised her she'd never have to see me again."

"You made that promise under duress."

His smile was crooked and his chuckle humorless. "I'm not sure she'd see it that way. She seemed pretty adamant that day. But I have to do this. I know that I have to face this if I want a future with you and our baby. And I do want that. I love you more than you can possibly imagine."

Her heart shattered into a million little pieces and then whirled around in her chest before fusing together again, this time stronger than before. This man...what was it about him that could make her feel this way? Weak and mighty at the same time. Angry and happy. But loved. So very loved.

"I sincerely hope this doesn't become a habit."

"Talking to my ex-wives? I only have one."

She smiled, her first one of the day. It wouldn't be her last, though. "I was talking about how you can get me to forgive you just by saying you love me. That's going to be darn inconvenient for me if it keeps happening. I want to be mad but all I can think about is kissing you."

Sam looked up at the ceiling, his eyes closed. "Please let that keep happening."

Reaching for a handful of his cotton t-shirt, Riley pulled him closer. "Just kiss me."

Their lips met and it felt like coming home after a long journey, despite the fact that it had only been less than twenty-four hours. There was promise in the kiss as well. A promise that they would try harder, work together, become that team that so far they'd only talked about. As usual, doing it was far more work.

They weren't out of the woods yet, but Sam had taken the first tentative step. There was still much more to get through before she could call this a success. Next stop?

Trish.

CHAPTER
Forty-Three

THE HOUSE LOOKED like every other suburban home in this well-to-do neighborhood. Two stories, white with black shutters, and an inviting front porch that spanned the entire front. The lawn was a lush green and the walkway from the sidewalk was lined with flowers, red and pink. Obviously cared for and loved, it was a home for a family.

Or maybe it was the blue bicycle leaning up against a wall of the open garage door that clued him in. The garage that housed a minivan.

I should have asked if Trish had remarried.

Somehow in his mind, his ex-wife had never changed from the last day he'd seen her. Frozen in time, Trish was still the young wife he'd taken for granted and left for weeks or months on end. Clearly, she'd made some changes in her life.

Double checking the address on his cell phone, he turned to Riley who had made the trip to Connecticut with him. He'd waited all week to do this, finally getting a day off from filming to make the trip. It wasn't far from New York City but it might as well have been a million miles. This place had nothing in common with the bustling metropolis they'd left behind. It was quiet and serene, only a dog barking in the distance or the faint laughter of playing children. Even the air smelled sweeter here, not filled with exhaust fumes or the grit of Manhattan.

Sam felt out of place here. He didn't really belong. He certainly didn't belong on the sidewalk in front of his ex-wife's home, but here he was.

Shaking like a leaf, barely able to draw breath. If it weren't for this amazing woman beside him, he couldn't have done this. He would have drifted through the rest of his life letting his past dictate his future.

Today...that stopped. It had to. He needed to face forward and look to his future with Riley. His partner.

Sam glanced at the vehicle parked at the curb, engine running but all of the windows closed. The car service driver was still sitting behind the wheel, giving the couple their privacy. Whatever they were saying, he couldn't hear.

"Are you sure you're okay waiting for me?"

It had been decided that she would bide her time at the coffee shop just down the road. He could call her and she could be here within a few minutes if his conversation with Trish turned contentious.

"I'm fine. They might even have some decent decaf." Riley laid her hand on his arm. "I think the bigger question is are you going to be okay? You don't have to do this today if you don't want to."

His lips twisted in self-derision. "I think we both know

that the longer I put this off the more reasons I'll find not to do it. I need to get it over with."

Try as they might, they'd both been on pins and needles for days waiting for him to get it done. They needed some peace in their lives and the only way there ran straight through his ex-wife's front door.

"Just call me if you need me."

"I will."

Riley climbed back into the car and it pulled away from the curb. He watched until the vehicle disappeared before turning back to face Trish's home. He hadn't called first, hadn't wanted to hear her say she didn't want to see or talk to him. Better to surprise her, not give her the choice. It wasn't necessarily a kind thing to do but he'd waited to speak to her for too many years. He was bringing up parts of her past that she'd probably buried long ago but that was a luxury he hadn't allowed himself.

Heart in his throat, he climbed her front porch steps and knocked on the door, wanting to turn and flee when he heard movement inside the home.

This is a bad idea. Run! Run for your life!

No, stay. Get this over with. Talk to her.

Indecision kept him rooted to the spot and the door swung open, revealing a woman that looked like Trish's mother Jane. It took a moment before it dawned on his addled brain that it was Trish. A little older, but Trish. A few gray hairs and some lines around her eyes, but still the same woman he remembered.

Standing in front of him, her mouth hanging open in shock. Of course, she hadn't been expecting him. Ever.

Her hand flew to her mouth and she made an

exclaiming noise. "Oh my God, Sam. I can't believe it's you– I mean– It's been so long." Her cheeks grew pink and she stepped back from the doorway. "Come in, for heaven's sake and tell me what you're doing here. It's so wonderful to see you."

Her expression immediately turned from surprise to alarm and she grabbed his arm, her grip strong. "It's not Paula, is it? Tell me she's okay. Is she alright?"

Trish thought he was here to tell her Paula was sick or worse.

"She's fine," he assured her, his own voice unsteady. So much emotion was running through him at the mere sight of Trish. All the past came crashing down at once. The good, the bad, the funny. Things he'd forgotten but were now so clear in his mind. "She's fine. Retired now and having a ball."

Trish still didn't look sure, but she'd loosened her hold on his arm. "She's okay?"

"Healthy as a horse. She's here in the city. You should have lunch or something."

He didn't know why he'd made that offer. It was laughable as they hadn't spoken in years.

Trish blew out a breath and smiled. "I'm glad."

Now that was over, neither seemed to know what to say. Standing awkwardly in her foyer, he was once again questioning the decision to come here.

Finally Trish spoke, her gaze on his face, seeking the reason behind his appearance. "Were you just in the neighborhood?"

For a moment - a short one - Sam thought about lying. Making up some story about how he was shooting a movie in Connecticut and he got the wild idea to visit, but when it all came down to it he couldn't lie. He was here for a reason and that reason was sipping really awful decaf coffee a few blocks away.

His future.

Time to release the past.

"Actually...I came to see you. I know I should have called first..."

But I thought you would tell me no.

Waving him in, Trish smiled in welcome. "It's wonderful that you're here. Come in. Would you like a cup of coffee?"

What he really needed was a shot of Patron but he nodded in agreement and followed her through a large living room decorated in red and taupe before entering the kitchen. Trish pulled out a chair at the large table before bustling over to the half-filled coffee pot.

The kitchen was a sunny yellow, bright and cheery. Before he could stop himself, the words seemed to tumble out of their own accord.

"Your favorite color is yellow."

She didn't answer right away, finishing pouring his coffee first. Her smile was gentle but there was a look of surprise in her eyes. "You remembered. Do you still drink this black?"

She'd remembered, too.

"I do. Thank you."

He accepted the steaming cup and took a sip as she sat down opposite him.

"You actually timed this just right," she said, taking a drink from her own cup. "My husband took the kids to the park and they shouldn't be back for a little while. We'll have some time to talk and catch up."

Husband. Kids. Maybe her life hadn't been ruined after all.

Still it was strange and awkward. He hadn't even thought about a husband when he'd come up with this scheme. The last thing he wanted to do was cause problems for Trish.

"Does your husband know...?"

Shit. Was that too personal a question? Was there such a thing as too personal a question when two people had once been married?

Smiling, she nodded and laughed a little. "Dan knows, although I had to show him pictures before he believed me. He's a big fan. The kids are, too. You've done well for yourself, Sam. I'm so proud of you."

She sounded sincere and not angry at all.

His chest tightened painfully and with a shaky hand he placed his cup on the table before he dropped it. Too many emotions were running riot inside of him and he could barely contain the agony he was digging up by seeing her. He hadn't been prepared for how much this was going to hurt. So many memories that he'd buried deep enough he'd thought to never see them again.

He had to speak, though. That's why he was here. But he couldn't shake the curiosity of just what had happened to her these last fifteen years or so. She wasn't yelling and screaming at him, or kicking him out of her home. Perhaps he was forgiven. But he needed to hear her say it.

"You said you have kids?"

Her smiled widened and she clasped her hands

together. He could see the pride shining in her eyes, the love, too.

"I have three. Two boys and my youngest is a girl. Jacob, Liam, and Hannah." Her phone was sitting on the table and she reached for it, fumbling at first but then holding it up triumphantly. "Here we are at Disney World a few weeks ago on our family vacation."

His hand trembled as he too the phone, bringing it closer. His throat closed up as he studied the five smiling faces in the photo. Trish, of course, looking happy and carefree in her Mickey ears. Her husband, a nice-looking man, although Sam wasn't much of a judge on that. Then the three children, the oldest looking around ten or eleven. They'd all inherited Trish's dark hair and stubborn chin.

"You have a beautiful family."

Trish let out a shaky breath and a silvery tear ran down her cheek. She was as affected by their reunion as he was, but probably for different reasons.

"Thank you, Sam. I'm a lucky woman."

"That's great. Really great."

He didn't know what to say. He hadn't expected this.

"The divorce settlement made it possible for us to buy this house," she went on to explain, her gaze running lovingly around the room. "It's a great school district for the kids. I've never said thank you for that but I am very grateful. You made things so much easier for us so I want to thank you now. You didn't have to do it but then you were always a generous man."

"You deserved it. I know I wasn't a great husband."

Trish's gaze came to rest on Sam, and her smile faded. "No, I wasn't a good wife. I was a pretty terrible wife if the truth be told. Sam, it's wonderful to see you, but I have to ask...why are you here? We haven't spoken in more than fifteen years. Is everything okay?"

He didn't understand why she would say that she wasn't a good wife. She'd waited patiently every time he'd gone on location. Not every woman would have done that.

"I did as you asked that last night. You said you never wanted to see me again." He was here now, though. "But I had to speak to you. I know I'm bringing up–"

"Wait," Trish commanded, holding up her hand. "Yes, I said that and my apology is many years overdue so please let me say it. Sam, I'm sorry I ever said that. It was wrong of me and I've felt badly about it for so long. I should have apologized a long time ago but...I was scared and then you became famous..."

There was so much he wanted to say and he didn't even know where to begin. He'd practiced this conversation, but it hadn't gone like this. She hadn't capitulated right away and apologized. Funny, but it was slightly anti-climatic. In the last few days, he'd begun to forgive himself. Her approval was good, but it was his own that was important.

She took a visibly deep breath and set her hands flat on the table in front of her. "Please let me tell my story. I know that I said some awful things that last night. Things I can't take back, but I can say a million times how sorry I am. You didn't deserve any of it."

"I wasn't there for you," Sam protested. "I worked all the time when I should have been home."

"No, no, no." Trish shook her head, more tears escaping down her cheeks. She swiped at them but more took their place. Almost out of habit, Sam began to reach for her hand in comfort but then remembered that this wasn't the past. It wasn't his place to do that anymore and it would have made things even more awkward than they already were. They weren't a couple and he didn't love Trish. Sure, he cared about her and a part of him would always love her, but he wasn't *in love* with her. Those feelings had died long ago. "I need to tell you the truth about that day. I told Dan before we got married and now it's time for you to hear it, too."

The last sentence captured his attention. "Your husband knows about this?"

Sam wasn't sure how he felt about that but then he'd told Riley everything.

"He's my husband."

Trish didn't need to explain further. Before Riley he wouldn't have understood but he did now.

There was a long stretch of silence, but Sam couldn't tear his gaze away from his ex-wife. It was obvious she didn't want to discuss this. A wave of pity ran through him and he wanted to just make this easy for her. After all, he'd come for her...forgiveness? Absolution? Whatever it was, he didn't need to draw this out and make her life hell. That wasn't what he was trying to do here today. It was selfish enough just showing up but now she was crying and miserable.

"I just want your forgiveness, Trish. That's what I came for today. I wanted to say that I'm sorry that I wasn't there when you needed me. When the baby needed me. And I was hoping that you could say that you forgive me."

If anything, that made her cry even harder. He was

becoming more concerned when she scraped her knuckles across her eyes and snapped her teeth together with a click.

"I should be the one apologizing to you. You don't owe me anything. It was never your fault that I lost the baby."

CHAPTER
Forty-Four

SAM SHOULD HAVE FELT a huge weight fall from his shoulders. His own ex-wife had said it wasn't his fault. This was what he'd hoped for deep down inside, but the reality was he was pretty sure she was blaming herself instead. That didn't seem all that healthy either.

"Sometimes these things just happen," he said softly, remembering what Dr. Kate had told him. "They aren't anyone's fault."

Sniffling, Trish nodded. "That's what the doctor said. He said it wasn't anyone's fault and it was just nature's way of handling things. But I felt so guilty. That's why I lashed out at you when you showed up. I blamed you because I couldn't handle that it might have been something I did. I shouldn't have done it and I've felt so horrible about it all these years. When I said that I didn't want to see you again I didn't really mean it."

"I thought you meant it."

"I know." Abruptly, Trish stood and walked over the

roll of paper towels on the counter, yanking one off and blowing her nose. "And I understood why you wouldn't want to see me again. I was so awful that night. So cruel and mean. I was just so scared."

"About what?"

She dabbed at her red, swollen eyes and then wadded up the towel in her tightly curled fist.

"When you were gone, I didn't stay home. I went out and partied with my friends on the weekends."

That...was something Sam hadn't known. But he wasn't mad about it. They'd been so young so of course she'd wanted to go out with her friends.

"That's okay. You deserved to have fun, too."

"I went dancing that night and was out until about two in the morning. I didn't drink or anything, but I wanted to. I really wanted to, Sam." The tears slipped down her cheeks again. "I was so conflicted about becoming a mother. I wasn't sure I was ready. I still wanted to go out and have a good time, dance, drink, and watch the sun come up. What kind of mother would I even be? I'd already failed at the one thing I wanted more than anything and that was to be an actress. Maybe I'd be a terrible mom, too."

"You would have been a great mom," Sam protested. "You were good with kids."

She wiped at her cheeks with the now sodden towel. "I wasn't ready, and then I had a miscarriage. I thought...I thought that maybe I'd made it happen. That my brain had somehow made my body reject the baby and I felt so guilty. So when you arrived the next day...I blamed you."

"You blamed me."

Three words that had set him on this course for many years.

"It even worked for a little while." Trish came back to the table and slid into the chair. "I was able to keep my own crushing guilt at bay by convincing myself that you were the bad guy. It was all your fault. I already knew the truth. The doctor had told me that it was no one's fault but I stubbornly hung in there, wanting to paint you as the villain. You can take the girl out of drama class but you can't take the drama out of the girl. It was quite awhile later that I had to admit that I'd treated you terribly and owed you a huge apology. But of course, by then it was too late. You were a big star and I was sure you didn't want to hear from me. I'm so sorry, Sam. You cannot imagine how much. I've thought about this day for years. Wondering what I would say if I ever ran into you. I thought about calling your agent or publicist a few times and making an appointment to talk to you, but then I'd see an interview on television and you seemed so happy. You'd moved on and I would just pull you back. I couldn't do that to you."

He was a better actor than he'd given himself credit for if Trish had thought he had moved forward.

"Can you forgive me, Sam? Can you find it in your heart to do that? I know that it's a lot to ask and I wouldn't blame you if you said no."

There was no hesitation. He'd lived in a world of guilt all these years, trapped in a cage of his own making but Trish hadn't escaped unscathed. She'd lived with this as well, her own prison just as confining. It was time to set them both free, once and for all.

"Of course I forgive you. We both did and said things

we wished we hadn't. Neither of us were the best husband or wife. Maybe we married too young."

That gained him a watery smile from his ex-wife. "We didn't know shit about being married. Or compromising. Or how to be together forever. We just didn't know."

They hadn't, but he hoped he had more of a clue now.

"Are you happy, Trish? I mean, really happy? That's all I've ever wanted for you."

"I am." She nodded and her expression lightened. "I'll admit that every now and then when I watch the Oscars I think about what my acceptance speech would say, but then I see Dan and the kids and I wouldn't trade this for anything. Are you happy, Sam? Because I kind of get the feeling that maybe you weren't since you came here today and that hurts my heart."

He wasn't about to tell her how he'd taken her words that night and tucked them away so they could torture him off and on for fifteen years. She'd feel guilty and he wasn't enough of a sadist to do that to her all over again. He wasn't angry, although he knew some might argue that he should be. That he should hold a grudge. But he knew two women - Paula and Riley - who would tell him it was better to move on and forgive. They would never hold onto something like that, letting it fester for years. Hadn't Riley already proved that with her ex?

"I am happy." He wasn't sure what he should tell Trish, but he couldn't stop the pride in his tone. "I'm going to be a father, actually. In about seven months or a little less."

Her eyes widened and she clapped her hands over her mouth. "Oh my gosh, that's wonderful. Just wonderful.

Who is the lucky girl? Is it someone I might have seen in a movie?"

"Thank you, but Riley isn't an actress. She teaches kindergarten." He felt his face get warm. "I met her because Mom volunteers in her class helping children learn to read."

"So she has Paula's seal of approval," Trish laughed. "Even better. Is she nice? Is she...the one?"

Sam couldn't begin to explain how perfect and wonderful Riley was but just the thought of her had his heart pounding against his ribs. He missed her, and they'd barely been apart for an hour.

"She is. She came with me today and is waiting for me down the street at a coffee shop. She wanted to give us a chance to talk privately."

"She sounds like an understanding woman. And don't worry, I won't tell anyone about the baby. It's not public yet, is it? If it was, it would be on the cover of *People* magazine."

"We haven't decided when or how to make the announcement, but it won't be in *People*," Sam said firmly. "I'm thinking we'll just let the paps catch us in a baby store."

"No comment," Trish said, nodding in agreement. "Wise. Play it classy and quiet."

"I'm trying to keep a lower profile," he admitted with a grin. "I doubt you'll be seeing my photo in the tabloids anytime soon."

"A family man. I guess it had to happen at some point. This Riley is a lucky woman."

"I'm the lucky one," Sam replied immediately. "She's changed everything for me."

"Then I just have one more question." Trish took a sip of her coffee and wrinkled her nose. "Damn, cold. What are you still doing here? You probably shouldn't keep her waiting any longer."

Trish had always been the smarter of the two of them. Sam stood and she did too. Before he could say thank you she had launched herself at him, her arms going around his waist and holding tight. His own arms closed around her reflexively, returning the hug. There wasn't anything romantic about it. It was completely platonic and then it was over. She'd stepped back and dabbed at her eyes with the ball of paper towel.

"It was good to see you, Sam. You haven't changed a bit."

He knew what she meant. She was talking about his looks, but he didn't care about that. It was all just window dressing.

He'd changed. A whole hell of a lot. He was going to be a father. The best one he could possibly be. He was also going to be a husband. He just had to convince Riley to say yes, and he wouldn't give up until she did. Not even if it took a lifetime.

CHAPTER
Forty-Five

IT WAS LESS than an hour later when Sam confidently strode into the coffee shop where Riley was nursing a hot chocolate. A strange request on a warm day like today but they'd made it for her without complaint. She'd paged through her e-book but had trouble concentrating so she'd tried her social media, but even that seemed dull and uninteresting. Luckily he was here and she could find out what had happened.

"That didn't take long." She searched his face for a clue as to the outcome of the meeting with his ex but dammit, he was doing that actor thing again. She couldn't tell if he was happy or devastated. "Are you...finished?"

Sam nodded and held out his hand to help her up out of her chair. "We had a good talk. How about we get back to the city?"

A good talk. Okay, that sounded promising. Riley was an optimist at heart.

"What–?"

He shook his head, his gaze sweeping the little coffee shop. "Not here, babe. Let's wait until we get home."

She wanted to protest that she couldn't wait that long, but if he could wait almost twenty years for closure she could wait until they got back to the city. She didn't want to, but she'd do it.

They slid into the back seat of the rental and she couldn't stop herself asking one question.

"I know we're going to talk about this when we get home but...are you okay?"

Flashing his patented Hollywood smile, he pulled out his phone and began to tap out a text.

"I'm fine. It's all going to be fine."

A good talk. Fine.

Not exactly the most scintillating of descriptions, but she held tightly to them as they drove back to the city. The driver didn't even glance in their direction, all his attention on the road, but she understood why Sam wanted to keep quiet until they could be alone. Big ears were everywhere and what they said today could be front page in a tabloid tomorrow.

It was only when they were in the sanctity of their own home that he finally spoke.

"Trish and I talked. She's felt guilty all these years because of what she said that night. She apologized."

Riley sat down heavily onto the couch, falling back against the cushions. Was that it? All the angst that he'd held inside, all the self-doubt and blame, and it was gone? Poof! Because of one little conversation with his ex? Trish had apologized and all was right with the world.

I'm not ready to make nice yet.

"And what was her reason for blaming you? Or did she even give one?"

For some reason her query made Sam smile. "She did give one. A pretty good one, actually. How about I get you some ginger ale and tell you all about it?"

She hadn't even realized that she had her hand over her stomach. Her anger with Sam's ex had churned up the acid in her tummy, making her nauseous. A state she was becoming used to.

"I hope it's a decent explanation. She made you feel like a horrible person all these years."

Sam handed her a glass and then sat down next to her. "She's been feeling pretty shitty all this time, too. Once she explained it, I understood why she lashed out at me that night. It all made sense."

"It doesn't make it right," Riley muttered, taking a gulp of the ginger ale. "An apology doesn't give you back all the years in between."

Crooking a finger under her chin, he turned her face so she had to look up into his blue eyes. The tenderness in his expression and the love she saw there made her heart ache. She reached up and ran a finger down his face and over his jaw, enjoying the feel of the stubble under her fingertips.

"You're going to be the best mother ever. You're not only protective of our little one but you're protective of me." Leaning down, he lightly pressed his lips to hers and lingered until the kiss deepened. A shiver ran up Riley's spine as he pulled back only to quickly kiss her again, leaving them both smiling. "Let me explain and I think you'll understand too."

———

"So do you get why I accepted her apology?" Sam asked when he'd finished telling his story. "There was nothing to be gained at this point by resenting her or holding a grudge. We both did the best we could at the time but hell, we were basically kids. I don't think our lives turned out so bad under the circumstances."

That was true...but...

"You could have had a family much sooner," Riley pointed out. "You could have forgiven yourself a long time ago."

"Maybe." Sam seemed to consider her words. "First, a lot of that guilt was channeled into my career. I worked hard and was ambitious. If I hadn't had it, who knows where I'd be now? Everything happens for a reason, right? As for having a family sooner, I think that waiting for you was an excellent idea. I'm older, more mature, and ready to make compromises with my career. I can't imagine loving anyone else but you."

Her cheeks were red hot at the passion and desire in his gaze and her own body responded immediately, the room suddenly feeling much too warm.

"About those compromises..." There were still a few items they needed to get straight. "I don't think you should retire. You love acting and producing."

"I do, so that's why I'm not going to retire." Laughing, he dropped a kiss on her half-open lips. "You were right. I went overboard and wasn't thinking straight. I do, however, want to take some time off after the baby is born.

Maybe a year or so. Then we'll work it out together. I need to find some work-life balance that will make sense for our whole family. I wouldn't mind having a few more kids later."

"Let's take them one at a time," she protested but secretly the idea sounded kind of wonderful. A real family with Sam. "We can talk about that later after we have this one."

Grinning, he jumped up from the sofa and headed into the bedroom. "Whatever you say, honey. Just hold on one minute. I'll be right back."

Amused by Sam's departure, Riley relaxed for the first time that day. Maybe in several days. They'd both been on tenterhooks waiting for his meeting with Trish and now it was over and done. They had nothing better to do than go forward and live their lives. It was a relief and she hadn't realized just how stressed she was until it was gone.

Sam re-entered the living room holding a candle and a lighter. "Give me a minute to set the mood here."

He set the candle on the coffee table and lit it before helping her off of the sofa and leading her to the giant windows that overlooked the skyline of the city.

"It's the best romantic atmosphere I can put together on short notice, but this city has never let me down, Riley. I was here when I found out that I got the part in the first *Thunder* movie and I was also here when I realized that I loved you. So it only seems right that this city is witness to this."

"What are you–"

Falling to one knee, Sam dug out a small black velvet

box from his pants pocket. She hadn't even noticed it was there, but she was sure it hadn't been earlier.

Oh my stars. This is for real. He's on one knee. This is an honest-to-God marriage proposal. What am I going to say?

Her heart was beating a mile a minute and she could barely breathe. She had to lock her knees to keep from falling into a heap on the floor.

Idiot. Yes. I'm going to say yes. I'm not crazy.

"Riley," he began, his hand capturing hers and lifting it to his lips, brushing the knuckles. "You've made me happier than I ever thought I could be. You've stood by me and supported me. You've loved me and cared for me. Hell, you even love my mother. Would you do me the honor of becoming my wife and spending the rest of our lives together? I'm not asking because of the baby. I'm asking because I can't imagine a life without you. Let's be that team that we've talked about and build that family. I'll be the best husband I possibly can to you. I promise."

He was a man of his word. She already knew that. It wasn't going to be easy. There would be catty co-stars and ugly gossip. They'd have to learn to juggle schedules and make compromises. They'd fight and make up.

She wouldn't have it any other way.

"Yes." The word came out choked as she blinked back the tears. Happy ones. "Yes. I'll marry you, but I only have one request. Well...two, actually."

His smile was blinding and he rose to his feet, lifting her off of hers and swinging her around in a circle. "You name it. Anything you want."

"I'd like to get married before I show too much. Just because it will be easier to find a dress."

"Done," he stated, dipping his head so he could kiss and caress her neck. Her eyes almost rolled back into her head when he found that special spot that had her trembling in his arms. "What's the second?"

She had no earthly idea. Every thought had been driven out of her brain until only one remained. But it was darn good thought.

"Take me to bed."

She'd figure out the other thing later.

———

Somewhere between the living room and the bedroom Sam had managed to slip the engagement ring on Riley's hand. She lifted it up to take her first look and it took her breath away with its beauty and simplicity. An emerald cut diamond shone brightly, catching the light as she turned her hand this way and that. It was perfect.

"Do you like it?"

His tone sounded nervous but he didn't have any need to be. It was exactly what she would have chosen. Almost. She wouldn't have selected a diamond so large, but the style was on the mark.

"I love it." She held up her hand for his inspection. "I think they'll be able to see that rock from space, though."

Laughing, he brushed his lips over her knuckles. "I doubt that. It's not that big, actually. Five carats is about what Nate got for Paige and Max got for Carrie."

It looked freaking huge to her but she wasn't an expert in Hollywood engagements. The ring honestly didn't matter. She didn't need one. All she wanted was Sam.

"Well, I think it's gorgeous but I would have been happy with a simple wedding band."

"We can have that too," Sam promised, pressing her back onto the mattress. "Two gold wedding bands, one for you and one for me."

The ring was forgotten as his lips met hers. This time there was no frenzy, no hurry. With Paula out of the house for the day visiting friends, Riley and Sam had all the time in the world.

Touch. Taste. Explore.

Gentle fingers teased off her clothes, the fabric whispering against her skin as it slid to the floor. Hands glided over bare flesh, hot kisses were pressed against her abdomen, his tongue lapped at a pebbled nipple.

The room was filled with moans and sighs, the musky aroma of seduction heavy in the air. For a long time they were content to kiss, letting their hands and fingers catalog sensitive spots on their partner's body. Riley learned that Sam was slightly ticklish under his arms, and he learned that running his tongue along her lower back made her clutch the sheets with pleasure.

"Now, Sam," Riley breathed impatiently. Never in her life could she say that she'd craved a man's touch until now. She couldn't get close enough, wanting him on top of her, inside of her, his larger frame making her feel small and feminine.

His cock nudged at her entrance and she widened her legs to accommodate him, wrapping them around his waist as he pressed forward. His face was a mask of concentration but his eyes closed when he was in all the way. Her walls clenched, drawing a groan from deep in his chest.

His thrusts started out slow and lazy, his lips worrying a puckered nipple until her body was bowed off of the bed. Before long their movements became more focused, his strokes faster and harder. Her hips lifted to meet him over and over as the pressure built inside.

She ran her tongue over his salty skin, burying her head in the crook of his neck as her climax ran through her. It was heat and stars and fire and electricity all rolled into one amazing orgasm.

"Riley," Sam whispered when his own release hit. She watched his expression change from pain to pleasure and then to contentment. He collapsed on top of her but immediately rolled onto his side taking her with him.

Even then they couldn't seem to stop touching each other, their fingers busy stroking damp skin and whispering silly, romantic things. Sam talked about the future, telling her all the wonderful things they were going to do and she listened, enthralled at the mere idea of spending her life with him.

"I love you," she said huskily, pressing a kiss to his shoulder. It seemed so important that he know, but how could he not? It was so strong inside of her it had to show. Did she look different now? She felt different. Happier, more complete. They were becoming that partnership she'd always dreamed about. "So much."

"I love you too, honey. We're going to have so much fun. I promise you."

There would be fun, and fights, and love, and sex, and

a baby, and maybe more children. They'd travel, and work, and sleep and love some more. They'd live each day and some of it would be good and some of it bad. That's the way life worked. No one was promised smooth sailing.

As long as they had each other, they could handle the storm.

CHAPTER
Forty~Six

SIX WEEKS LATER...

The vows were spoken under a small flower-covered arch. All the guests had kicked off their shoes to enjoy the warm sand under their feet. It was a casual but slightly dressy occasion. No tuxedos but Sam had worn a suit along with his two best men, Max Hayes and Nate Mason.

Riley looked absolutely stunning in a simple white silk halter dress that pooled around her feet. It clung to all her perfect curves and they weren't bothering to hide the gentle swell of her stomach. The world knew they were having a baby. It had been on the cover of every tabloid around the world, and they'd announced it just the way they'd wanted to.

By not doing it at all. They'd simply been photographed buying baby furniture and clothes. They were going to live their lives under their own terms. The press could take notice or disappear. They didn't care one way or the other.

Tara and one of Riley's sisters had been her attendants, and both ladies were holding court near the bar, chatting up Tyler Gaylord and Kirby Glenn. The younger actor looked a little worse for wear after the bachelor party last night. He'd partied harder than all the other men put together.

Riley's family appeared to be having a good time at the wedding, and they were excited about the baby, although Sam had been pulled aside by her father and given a lecture about how he'd better never hurt their little girl. Sam had assured his new father-in-law that he loved Riley and wouldn't do anything to jeopardize their happiness, but he wasn't sure his in-laws were convinced. Time would have to prove that he was sincere.

Sam swept back a stray strand of hair from his beautiful wife's face, anchoring it behind her ear. There had been quite a breeze today despite the sunny and warm weather. But it had been the perfect day for a wedding.

The tang of salt in the air. The sound of the waves lapping against the sugar white sand. Hell, even the seagulls hadn't ruined their day. They'd rented out the restaurant from their first date for the reception, so the scavenger birds had to stay outside.

Riley nudged Sam's knee under the table. "Your mother looks very happy. I think she's told everyone in attendance today that she was the one who fixed us up."

Paula Collins did indeed look like the cat that had swallowed the canary, and she had for the last several weeks. When she'd returned home from her day with friends to the news that Sam had proposed and Riley had said yes, she had yet to stop smiling.

She'd smiled all through the preparations for their intimate beach wedding here in Florida.

She'd smiled through the ultrasound where she'd received her first look at her future grandchild.

She'd definitely smiled when Sam and Riley had announced they were going to buy a family-sized home near Paula's for when he was between movies.

She'd even smiled when his publicist announced Sam was taking a year off after the baby was born, but he'd assured her that he was planning to return to work. He and Riley were collaborating on a script idea that she'd come up with. A quirky little murder mystery. They might even be able to convince Nate's wife, Paige, to write it for them, although she had her hands full with their young twins. Currently, they were letting the babies have their first taste of wedding cake. It looked like more was on their faces than in their mouths.

"She did do a terrific job picking out my wife," Sam replied, dropping a kiss on Riley's nose, much to the delight of the guests who were giving them indulgent smiles. "But even if she hadn't pushed us together, I would have ended up with you. One look and I was a goner."

"I don't remember it that way."

He had clear memories of the first moment he'd seen her.

"I do. Why do you think I was trying to convince you to go out with me? Even if it was only pretend?"

"Because you're a nice man."

"I'm not that nice," he denied with a shake of his head. "I thought you were gorgeous."

"No, I thought *you* were gorgeous." She gave him a flirtatious giggle and peered at him from under her lashes. There was promise in that look. Sinful promise. He was a lucky man. "Even my students were taken with you."

That had been the sadder part of their year. Riley had decided not to return to teaching. She'd be having a baby in a few months and then they'd work on the movie. She could always change her mind later. Nothing was written in stone but he hoped she'd enjoy the film business. It would be good to work together as a team. It seemed to work for his friends.

"Are you happy?"

It was a silly question but he couldn't stop himself from asking it. There were still moments - albeit brief - when he had doubts about being able to do this. They were becoming fewer and farther between, but they were still there. They'd get through it together.

Riley slipped her hand into his, hidden by the tablecloth. The way they were gazing into each other's eyes it was as if everyone else had melted away and it was just the two of them. "I love you, Samuel Collins. I meant every word of the vows I said today, and I can't wait to spend the rest of my life with you."

"I love you, too."

The words didn't even begin to express all the emotion that Sam held inside. Riley had come into his life at the wrong moment but she'd managed to turn a confirmed bachelor into a family man. She hadn't even tried. She'd given him an out that day but he hadn't taken it.

He was a family man. Wife, children, love. He had it all. He'd never take it for granted.

I hope you enjoyed Sam and Riley's happily ever after! You don't want to miss Sierra's story - And the Winner Is!

About the Author

Olivia Jaymes is a wife, mother, lover of sexy romance, and caffeine addict. She lives with her husband and son in central Florida and spends her days with handsome alpha males and spunky heroines.

Visit Olivia Jaymes at
www.OliviaJaymes.com